Praise for Earl Murray

"Isabella Bird, an independent English woman of the nineteenth century, is fascinating. Earl Murray's fictional portrayal of the world traveler is enchanting. *In the Arms of the Sky* has to rank among the Montana author's best works. It is a must-read for anyone interested in the strong women of the Victorian Age."
> —*The Billings Gazette* on *In the Arms of the Sky*

"Murray's narrative style is polished. Fans of Western novels are likely to enjoy this one."
> —*Montana* magazine on *The River at Sundown*

"Murray skillfully weaves period detail and Native lore to create an engrossing tale featuring an uncommon heroine."
> —*Publishers Weekly* on *Spirit of the Moon*

"Murray gets better with every book."
> —*Rocky Mountain News*

"Murray is a gripping storyteller who knows the land and the people he writes about."
> —Elmer Kelton, multiple Spur Award winner and author of *The Buckskin Line*

"Today there are possibly a scant dozen writers of the Native American experience who really understand and feel its spirit. One who must be included on that short list is Earl Murray."
> —Don Coldsmith, author of *Ruin* and *The Spanish Bit*

"Earl Murray has a narrative gift that never flags."
> —*El Paso Herald-Post*

"There is nothing less than exquisite beauty in the power Murray wields to enfold the reader in the simple, yet explosive world of his very real characters."
> —Terry C. Johnston, award-winning author of *The Plainsmen*

By Earl Murray from Tom Doherty Associates

IN THE ARMS
OF THE
SKY

EARL MURRAY

A TOM DOHERTY ASSOCIATES BOOK

NEW YORK

This is a work of fiction. All the characters and events portrayed in this book are either products of the author's imagination or are used fictitiously.

IN THE ARMS OF THE SKY

Copyright © 1998 by Earl Murray

Maps by Victoria E. Murray

A Forge Book
Published by Tom Doherty Associates, LLC
175 Fifth Avenue
New York, NY 10010

Forge® is a registered trademark of Tom Doherty Associates, LLC.

ISBN: 0-812-55143-5
Library of Congress Catalog Card Number: 98-19414

First edition: September 1998
First mass market edition: January 2000

Printed in the United States of America

0 9 8 7 6 5 4 3 2 1

To my beloved wife, Victoria, with whom I have
climbed many steep mountains

ACKNOWLEDGMENTS

I owe a huge debt of gratitude and appreciation to those whose help and support made this novel possible:

—Eleanor Gehres and her staff in the Western History Department, Denver Public Library, for their open and gracious assistance in providing access to research materials.

—John Newman, in the archives of the Morgan Library, Colorado State University, for his able assistance and friendship; and Pat Van Deventer and Maureen Vincent, also in the Morgan Library archives, who worked with John in providing me with needed materials.

—Rheba Massey, librarian in the local history section, Fort Collins Public Library, for her help in locating research materials and reference sites.

—Michael Gorgan, Fort Collins museum, for his help with sites and businesses in early Fort Collins.

—My publisher, Tom Doherty, whose love for historical America has made this book possible.

—My editor, Dale L. Walker, whose encouragement and professional advice have benefitted me greatly.

—And last but certainly not least, many thanks to the lady who, during a ride on the shuttle from Denver International Airport to Fort Collins, pointed out the window to Longs Peak and said, "Do you know the story of Isabella Bird, the English lady who climbed that mountain and fell in love with an outlaw?"

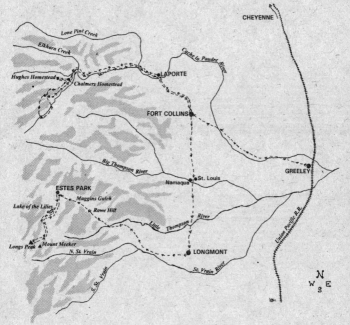

ISABELLA BIRD'S ROUTE TO ESTES PARK, 1873

CHEYENNE

Lone Pine Creek

Elkhorn Creek

Cache la Poudre River

Hughes Homestead

Chalmers Homestead

LAPORTE

FORT COLLINS

GREELEY

Big Thompson River

Namaqua   St. Louis

ESTES PARK

Muggins Gulch

Lake of the Lilies

Rowe Hill

Little Thompson   River

Longs Peak   Mount Meeker

N. St. Vrain

LONGMONT

S. St. Vrain

St. Vrain River

Union Pacific R.R.

N
W   E
S

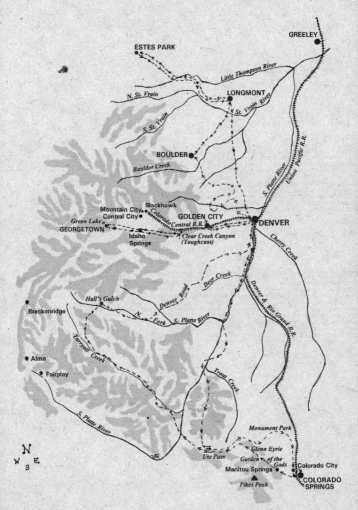

ISABELLA BIRD'S JOURNEY THROUGH
THE ROCKY MOUNTAINS, 1873

GREELEY

ESTES PARK

Little Thompson River

LONGMONT

N. St. Vrain

St. Vrain River

S. St. Vrain

BOULDER

Boulder Creek

Blackhawk

Mountain City
Central City

Colorado

GOLDEN CITY

S. Platte River

Union Pacific R.R.

Green Lake
GEORGETOWN

Central R.R.

Idaho
Springs

*Clear Creek Canyon
(Toughcuss)*

DENVER

Cherry Creek

Deer Creek

Hall's Gulch

Denver Road

Denver & Rio Grande R.R.

Breckenridge

N. Fork

S. Platte River

Tarryall Creek

Alma

Fairplay

Trout Creek

S. Platte River

Monument Park

Glenn Eyrie

Ute Pass

Garden of the
Gods

Colorado City

Manitou Springs

COLORADO
SPRINGS

Pikes Peak

N
W   E
S

INTRODUCTION

In September 1873, an Englishwoman named Isabella Bird climbed to the top of Longs Peak in Colorado for the pure excitement of reaching the summit. Assisting her were two young law students and an outlaw known regionally as "Rocky Mountain Jim," who quickly endeared himself to this unusual and enchanting woman.

Miss Bird was a minister's daughter and her early life had been restrained and quiet, the typical existence of the Victorian woman—yet she had been permitted to ride horseback whenever she pleased, a passion that remained with her throughout her life. In her journeys around the world, and in the United States, through some of the most demanding country our nation has to offer, she often traveled alone at a time when such daring was considered dangerous and unladylike.

Her deepest regret was not being able to take her younger sister along. Henrietta had never been well, and Miss Bird described her travels in a series of detailed letters to Henrietta that later became the basis for her book, *A Lady's Life in the Rocky Mountains,* first published in England during the last century. The book is the inspiration for this novel.

I became fascinated with this bold story of courage and determination. Isabella Bird, a woman whose life had been fraught with challenges both physical and mental, pursued and captured her dream of gaining freedom from the rigors of structured society, in the rugged wilderness of North America.

Her attraction to the outlaw Mountain Jim, a man of learning and deep feeling immersed in the turmoil of the frontier, went against all she had ever been told. Yet she saw something in this man no one had noticed before, and it changed her life forever.

Though many difficult journeys have taken place in the history of our great nation, there are none that overshadow this powerful journal of a woman's discovery of love and independence in one of the wildest regions of the early West.

Earl Murray
Fort Collins, Colorado
September 1998

Rescue the perishing, care for the dying,
    Snatch them in pity from sin and the grave.
Weep o'er the erring one, lift up the fallen,
    Tell them of Jesus, the mighty to save.
Rescue the perishing, care for the dying;
    Jesus is merciful, Jesus will save.

Traditional Hymn

ONE

THE ARRIVAL

ONE

Prairie Dogs and Rough-Cut Gentlemen

The surrounding plains were endless and verdure-less. The scanty grasses were long-ago turned into sun-dried hay by the fierce summer heats. There is neither tree nor bush, the sky is grey, the earth buff, the air blae and windy, and clouds of coarse granitic dust sweep across the prairie.

ISABELLA BIRD

September 1873

As the afternoon sun scorched the vast open plain, Isabella Lucy Bird peered out the window and wondered if she had made a grave mistake. She rode the train from Cheyenne, Wyoming Territory, south toward the Greeley Temperance Colony, a small farming community in northern Colorado Territory, hoping she might discover the beauty and wonder described to her by a friend back home in England.

So far that beauty had alluded her and instead she had been thrust into the unseemly underside of the raw frontier.

Early that morning in Cheyenne, a Wisconsin man, dying

of consumption, had crawled to her hotel room door and, coughing bloody phlegm, begged her to help his wife and infant son. She discovered the woman doubled over, dying of cholera, while the child wailed for nourishment.

Unable to find a feeding bottle or anyone who would help, she dipped a sponge in milk and water, pacifying the infant for a time. Later she found a young woman who agreed to take the baby for two dollars a day. So she gave the woman fifty dollars, packed her bags, and left early for the train station, desperate to get out of town.

Even as the train left she wondered if she shouldn't be headed back home and not deeper into this raw land.

She sat in the first passenger car, the only woman, queasy from the heat and the uneven ride, while the male passengers drank whiskey and fouled brass spitoons with chewing tobacco. They talked about her under their breath, wondering at the small but sturdy English lady, well dressed, with neatly combed dark hair and intelligent brown eyes, apparently unafraid of traveling alone.

Born at Boroughbridge Hall, Yorkshire, England, the eldest daughter of an evangelical minister in the Church of England, Isabella Bird had never married and now in her early forties did not believe she ever would. When not on her travels, her time was consumed in caring for her sister, Henrietta, three years younger, an invalid whom she adored.

The two had been inseparable as children. Belle and Hennie, as they called each other, had coped with many trials as their father had moved the family from parish to parish, where they never quite fit into the community. Both girls had received a basic education from their mother. In early womanhood, Belle began educating herself, as British women were forbidden from attending college, and soon began writing travel articles for magazines to supplement the family income.

Belle's travels had begun by a surgeon's order. In childhood she had been diagnosed with a fibroid tumor near her spine, causing her to suffer excruciating migraines and backaches. When she was eighteen the tumor was removed. The operation saved her life, but the physical problems remained.

The surgeon had suggested a "change of air" to renew her strength, a common prescription of the times.

So, with her father's blessing, Belle visited Nova Scotia, Prince Edward Island, Canada, and parts of the northeastern and midwestern United States, resulting in her book *The Englishwoman in America*, published in 1856.

It had been well received and the British public clamored for more of her views on faraway lands and people.

Her most recent travels had taken her to Australia, New Zealand, and Hawaii, before she arrived in San Francisco and then traveled eastward over the mountains. If she could do it, she would visit Estes Park and pacify her friend's great demand that she view the most spectacular scenery to be found anywhere.

But she still wondered if going back home to her sister wouldn't be more prudent. She had been close to Henrietta all her life and wished in the greatest way that her sister could be along on her travels.

After the death of their parents, she and Henrietta had taken up residence in a white cottage in Tobermory, on the island of Mull, where they lived off their inheritance and Belle's writing. While abroad she wrote voluminous letters home, each one a detailed account of the region and its people.

Only a week before, she had written of the Lake Tahoe area: "I have found a dream of beauty at which one might look all one's life and sigh. Not loveable, like Hawaii, but beautiful in its own way! A strictly North American beauty— snow-splotched mountains, huge pines, red-woods, sugar pines, silver spruce; crystalline atmosphere, waves of the richest color; and a pine-hung lake which mirrors all beauty on its surface . . ."

Since crossing the deserts east of the Sierras and the rugged, arid uplands of Utah, her views had changed. She had witnessed firsthand the remains of pioneer hardships; the bleached bones of oxen in the sand alongside the tracks and the broken-down cabins of those who had failed to strike it rich in the gold fields, their ragged children staring sullenly at the train as it passed.

Though she had seen similar conditions in Scotland, she was never prepared for suffering children and each tragedy tugged at her heart, further deepening her resentment of adults who would be so careless with their own flesh and blood.

The thought brought her attention to a boy sitting alone across the aisle from her, dressed in a ragged shirt and torn pants. He had been staring at her for some time.

When he noticed Belle looking at him, he asked, "Are you Miss Bird?"

"Yes, I am. How did you know?"

"I saw your picture in the paper. I can read pretty good for my age."

Belle knew that the press had been following her travels ever since her arrival in San Francisco. A lady alone, looking for adventure, made good copy. Newspaper articles had preceded her at every stop along the way.

"Would you mind if I sat with you?" the boy asked.

Belle thought a moment. "I suppose not."

The boy hurried across the isle and settled himself. He smiled.

"I'm Sam Edwards. My father owns a big ranch."

"Pleased to meet you, Sam." She turned back toward the window.

"Do you have kids, or grandkids?"

"No, I don't."

Sam thought about what he had said. "Maybe you're too young for grandkids."

"Maybe I am." She changed the subject. "What did you read about me in the paper?"

"It said that you travel all over the world and that you came here from some islands."

"The Sandwich Islands. Some people are calling them Hawaii."

"They say you climbed volcanos."

"I had some interesting times."

"What was the weather like there?"

"Warm and sunny. Lots of rain and lots of trees."

"You need a ship to get there, don't you?"

"Yes, a big one."

"I guess I ask too many questions."

"It's natural for a boy your age to be curious. But I've never known one to be traveling alone."

"I don't usually travel this way. In fact, I never have before. My father's going to be really mad when he picks me up in Denver."

The boy told how he had decided to see the country between Denver and Cheyenne. His father had been in the city on business and Sam had taken it upon himself to sneak down to the station and get on the train.

"The conductor thought I was with a family. Now he's mad at me, too. He wired my father from Cheyenne."

"Why would you do such a thing?"

"My father wouldn't let me go with him when he traveled, so I decided to go alone. I'll likely get a lickin' for it."

"Are you glad you took the chance?"

"No. There's nothing to see along here but flat ground and prairie dogs."

"That's a fact," Belle said.

Sam pointed out the window. "It is interesting to see those cowboys driving the cattle from Texas. They come through this way a lot."

Belle studied them, in their dusty suits riding dusty ponies, wearing wide-brimmed hats and knee-high boots with heavy spurs, armed with revolvers and repeating rifles, riding small broncos that turned on a dime.

"Do you suppose they're going to Cheyenne?" Sam asked.

"That would be my guess."

"Did you like Cheyenne?"

"No, did you?"

"No, but I wasn't a-scared of it none, either. There, they hang people who do wrong. They give them a warning by sending them a letter with a hangman's noose drawn on it. If they don't leave, they get the noose."

"I believe there are plenty in that city who need to get letters," Belle said.

"There are some bad outlaws around," Sam said. "We've got one out where I live. His name is Rocky Mountain Jim and he's done some mean things. So says my father."

"Why hasn't he been lynched?"

"Nobody wants to get near him. He'll shoot them."

Belle knew that sooner or later each outlaw would meet someone worse than himself or would die at the end of a rope. She had found that to be the code of the land. Her father had taught her to be God-fearing and to teach the same to others, when they would listen. She had no intention of ever getting near the people who needed the teaching most.

She had promised her father on his deathbed that she would carry on for him. "Take care of others and do not pursue selfish interests," he had told her. She felt that in some ways she had already betrayed him. Her travels had opened a new view of life, a view she loved and wished to continue pursuing.

She had experienced a great life change even before arriving in America. During the trip from New Zealand to San Francisco, a young man turned gravely ill and they were forced to dock at Honolulu. Overwhelmed by the beauty and grand climate, she stayed nearly a year.

In Hawaii she learned about living free and without the usual cares of polite society. The natives impressed her with their openness and honesty. They did many things for her, including risking their lives so that she might view the inside of a volcano.

As a result she grew to understand their concept of God, though she couldn't conform to their lax ways of life. Coming from a background of rigid structure to the most carefree existence imaginable proved too much too quickly.

A week after arriving in the States, she took on her role as the adventuresome lady of the mountains portrayed by the press. Near Truckee, California, she was thrown from her horse while riding above town, nearly falling on a grizzly bear that had rushed out from the brush. Her screams had spooked the bear and her horse as well, giving her plenty of time to view the scenery before a wagonload of teamsters arrived to help.

A young teamster who caught her horse told her, "These woods are full of bears, but you don't have to worry. They won't attack unless you aggravate them."

In Truckee she had heard a rumor about an outlaw who had traveled through town the day before with chopped-up human remains in a bag hanging from his saddle. A stable owner there had told her, "There's a bad breed of ruffians hereabouts, but the ugliest among them all won't touch you. There's nothing Western folk admire so much as pluck in a woman."

Belle wondered if Henrietta, in reading her letters, ever worried for her safety. From Cheyenne she had reported that in northern Colorado and southern Wyoming 120 ruffians were strung up and buried in a single fortnight.

"I would worry if I were your parent and knew you were in Cheyenne," she told Sam.

"We're way out of there now," he said.

"Perhaps it will change in time, when it becomes settled."

"So why did you come out here?" Sam asked.

She pointed toward the mountains. "I was told by my good friend that I had to go up there, where those two peaks touch the sky."

"That's where Rocky Mountain Jim lives, and that's where I live, right below them. Estes Park. Maybe I could take you."

"You'll have your hands full with your father," Belle said. "You'd better worry about that."

"I think I'll rest now," he said, leaning his head back against the seat.

Belle thought what her own father would have done to her if she had pulled such a prank at that age. Perhaps he would have smiled inwardly, for he had always realized how much she loved to see new places. But he would have disciplined her severely. She thought often that had he not been a minister, perhaps he could have expressed himself more.

Despite the role he was forced to play, she could not

complain about his interactions with her. When she was very young he would place her on the saddle in front of him and take her riding. She had never forgotten that and had grown up loving horses.

Her devotion to her father had remained even when two of his ministries had failed. Through the hard times he had remained steadfast to his family, and this had impressed her. In a time when the working world was changing, he had maintained that the Sabbath remain free of servile work. His parishioners had not agreed. Had he come to this land to preach, she thought, the results would have been no different.

She looked out the window. In the distance the mountains shimmered blue through the heat, a series of rugged ranges, one behind the other, topped by the two jagged peaks which stood out prominantly. Young Sam had told her that dangerous men lived there. Maybe it would be an interesting place to visit.

Frame houses and irrigated fields appeared, breaking the expanse of cactus and sagebrush. Belle continued to stare at the mountains.

Sam awakened and said, "You really want to get to the mountains, huh?"

"Can you tell me the names of those two peaks?"

"Sure. That one on the right is Longs Peak. It's the tallest. Next to it is Mount Meeker."

"It would be fun to stand up on top of the high one."

"That would be a hard climb."

At the station, a large group of bearded men dressed in gray and black stood waiting for the train.

Sam leaned over. "The people that live here don't like liquor."

"I can see that. Are you carrying any?"

The boy laughed. "No, are you?"

"No, and I never will. Don't you ever get started."

Sam said good-bye and Belle disembarked, wishing him

luck with his father, collected her bags, and asked directions to the nearest boardinghouse.

"The Greeley House is just a ways yonder, on Eighth Avenue," one of the men said. He removed his hat. "You're not carrying any liquor, are you, ma'am? Sorry, but I've got to know."

"Would you care to search my belongings?"

The man took a step back. Belle grabbed her bags and with two other passengers, a man and his wife, who carried their small child, plodded through the dust toward the Greeley House.

Shouting erupted behind them and Belle looked back to see the temperance men pouring whiskey from flasks and bottles into the dirt of the train station.

"Those men would have been smart to have stayed in their seats," the man said. "Or not even come at all."

"There can be no strong drink here," his wife said. "And if they choose to fight, they'll be bound and put back on the train."

They reached the Greeley House, and after taking an upstairs room, Belle gave it up to the man and his family, taking a small downstairs room.

It was just after five in the afternoon, the air hot and swarming with black flies. The coming of fall always brought the buzzing pests out in droves, as if they knew it was their last chance to propagate their kind before the frost settled.

Belle could not rest, so decided to help the landlady with her chores.

Angie Humphries, a short, stout woman in middle age, with red hair and ruddy cheeks, had introduced herself earlier and was thrilled to see Belle come into the kitchen.

"It's good to meet a fellow Brit," she said. "I can't say how much this means to me, you're agreeing to assist. I lost my help just this morning and don't know what I would have done without you."

"I prefer this to sitting in my room, warding off the flies," Belle said.

She might have thought better of speaking up, for the kitchen proved to be no less infested. Belle soon tired of swatting at them and set to work cutting meat and potatoes for the evening meal.

Angie had made bread that morning and began carving slices and placing them on plates for the three large tables that filled the center of the dining room. When she had finished she poured bacon fat from a coffee can into three different cast-iron skillets on the stove and filled them with steak and potatoes.

Belle helped her, turning the food in the skillet, wiping sweat from her forehead with a cleaning towel.

"I've heard that you're a world traveler," Angie said. "Does your government pay you?"

"No, I do it for recreation and interest solely."

Angie stared at her. "You travel just because you want to?"

"Everyone should have a chance to travel," Belle said. "It does the soul good to see other places, be they good or bad."

"Have you seen places worse than this?"

"Some. Not many. Why are you here?"

"I came from Liverpool to Denver with my husband. He found no gold but wanted to come up here and run a tavern. The temperance men destroyed his liquor supplies and he just gave up. His heart gave out last year, just before Thanksgiving."

"I'm sorry to hear that," Belle said. "You don't want to go back to Denver?"

"No, the city's too big now. I'll make a go of it here. It's hard, but the town's prospering and there's no ruffians to cause trouble."

"This is a settled place," Belle said. "I learned in Cheyenne that Horace Greeley, the founder of the New York *Tribune,* started this colony along with a number of others."

"Yes, there are settlers here from as far away as Pennsylvania and New York."

"Mr. Greeley has spent a great deal of time in this region, I understand. He's well known in Denver and has certainly succeeded here."

"Actually, Nathan Meeker, Mr. Greeley's agricultural editor at the *Tribune*, did more to start this town than Mr. Greeley himself." Angie said. "He traveled to Utah and saw how the Mormons and Indians irrigated their lands and brought the knowledge here, but he's far too modest a man to give a community his name."

Angie went on to explain that the settlers had put a lot of land under irrigation and a number of workers had come to the colony hoping to settle and marry.

But there was a grave shortage of eligible women and the men found themselves enduring a mundane life.

"They don't have a lot to say, the bachelors who board here," Angie said. "After breakfast they go into the fields and work all day, then come in to eat before going out to work until dark."

Belle watched them walk toward the boardinghouse from the fields, slapping dust from their pants and shirts, wiping sweat from their brows.

"I feel sorry for them," Belle said. "It appears to be a very hard existence."

"They work hard and for the most part, they're polite and devoid of violence," Angie said, "unlike the outlaws that come to Denver."

Belle mentioned Cheyenne. Angie had never visited there but had heard a great deal about the place.

"I met some ruffians while in that city," Belle said, "and I must say, they didn't leave a good impression."

"Wait until you visit the gold camps," Angie said. "You'll think those you met in Cheyenne to be perfect gentlemen."

TWO

The Road to Paradise

Except for the huge barrier to the right, the bound-
less prairies were everywhere, and it was like being
at sea without a compass. The wheels made neither
sound nor indentation as we drove over the short,
dry grass. In one place we passed the carcass of a
mule, and a number of vultures soared up from it, to
descend again immediately.

Isabella Bird

September 1873

Belle and Angie filled plates with steaming steak and
potatoes as twenty men filed in and placed their hats on
nails that lined the walls in the entranceway. Their
boots were caked with mud and their work clothes streaked
with sweat. Some of them washed outside in bowls and some
didn't. All of them took their seats with gaunt expressions,
rubbing dirt from their eyes with calloused hands.

As Belle watched them eat, she wondered why not a single one gave her so much as a glance. They appeared to care

little about what went on around them. When they had left, she helped Angie clear the table.

"There's four more who live here regular," Angie said. "They'll be here any time."

Belle served more food as the four men took seats at the table. Three of them took their dishes outside to eat, while the fourth man remained inside.

"This is Jess Sutton, from Vermont," Angie said. "He lives over near Fort Collins."

"Pleased to meet you, ma'am," he said to Belle. "I've read about you. So you plan to ride up into the mountains?"

"Yes, I do," Belle said. "The good Lord willing."

"You'll need Him, that's for sure."

"What brings you over here?" Belle asked.

"I come once a week for oats and hay, to feed my stock. I keep some horses over here, as I've got a few fields that I work."

"Would any of your horses be for sale?"

"I've got no fancy English racers, if that's what you're after."

Belle laughed. "I wouldn't expect to find anything of the kind in these parts. I just need something surefooted, a good mount that will do well along rocky trails."

"Around here there's nothing but Belgians or Clydesdales," he said. "I suspect you know they're for plowing fields, not riding. And there's the little bronco stock that come from the Indians and the Mexicans. Most of them are meaner than mules."

"Surely you can find me something."

"I have a little pinto that might work for you. Maybe you'd like to try him out in the morning."

"If it's all the same to you, I'd prefer to try him out this evening. I intend to be on my way toward the mountains by sunrise."

Sutton left to catch the horse while Belle helped Angie wash the dishes. After they had finished, the two women sat in rockers on a back porch that faced the mountains. The sun was falling and the night sky above the peaks had turned crimson.

"So you want to go up there, do you?" Angie said. "Whatever for?"

"Something up there calls to me. Do you know what I mean?"

"Can't say that I do."

"I suppose it's a wish to see the world from up there."

"It's dangerous," Angie said. "But I guess you're not afraid of anything. I read in the paper that you fight grizzly bears."

"I fear I'll never live that down," Belle said.

Sutton returned with the pinto. He tightened the cinch and held the reins out for Belle.

"I see you took me at my word," she said.

"Ride him and see what you think."

Belle rode sidesaddle until she was out of sight and then transferred one leg over the horn. Ladylike or not, she had to ride astride or her back would tighten up in no time.

The moon had risen and the night was filled with the chirping of crickets. In the distance coyotes howled. Dogs barked and strained against their leashes.

She rode out along the Cache la Poudre River, the lifeblood of the community, crossing ditches that brought water into the fields. She turned the horse from the bottom to an open, hilly area nearby.

She quickly discovered the pony to have tender feet.

"Too much walking in soft dirt," she said to the animal. "You won't do for a tough mountain ride, I'm afraid."

She tethered the pony back at the tavern, and at the door to her room met Angie, who carried a bottle of carbolic acid.

"You might want to put this around the bedposts," she said. "The bugs are quite bad, I'm afraid."

Belle struck a lantern and discovered "quite bad" to be an understatement. The floor was alive with beetles and earwigs and other insects, scuttling in and out of the walls. Upon checking the bed, she discovered the mattress to be infested as well.

She placed four chairs in a row and poured the carbolic acid along the legs. She took the top sheet from the bed and after shaking it vigorously outside, rolled herself up and got what sleep she could lying across the chairs.

Belle was up at first light, waiting for Sutton to come to breakfast. Perhaps he had another horse she might try.

The working men arrived at the tables for flapjacks and bacon, saying nothing, retiring to the fields after the meal. Angie apologized for the insect-infested accommodations.

"I wish I could have been more hospitable."

Sutton finally arrived and asked, "So, Miss Bird, how did you find the pony?"

"I'm sorry to say that he won't do. You must have guessed yourself that his feet are much too tender for rocky trails."

"Yes, I suppose you're right," he said. "But I can't imagine what other mount there is for you."

"You have no other riding stock here?"

"No. Sorry."

"I'll find another way over to the mountains."

"Might I suggest you travel with me? I'm going back with my wagon. It won't be nearly as fast as a horse, but it'll get you there."

"Thank you, I'll take you up on the offer," Belle said.

Sutton loaded her bags and they left at ten, the air still cool from the previous night. She wore a flowered print dress, strikingly red and yellow, that she had sewn for herself in Hawaii. She called it her riding dress and had split the skirt, making it easier to sit astraddle a horse.

Sutton studied the dress but declined to comment.

"Maybe you should get one for your wife," Belle suggested.

"I don't have a wife," Sutton said. "And if I did, I wouldn't let her wear something like that."

"Maybe that's why you don't have a wife."

They forded the Cache la Poudre River and followed a
trail that headed straight west. They were passed by a few
travelers on horseback and met a group of three wagons, settlers headed north toward the Overland Trail, which ran north
and south along the foothills below the mountains.

In the near distance, Belle once again saw a herd of cattle driven by heavily armed *vaqueros*.

"That's a rough life," Sutton said. "I worked a herd for
a while. That's how I got up here. But I'd never do it again.
Too much dust and boredom for me."

"So why do they need so many rifles?"

"There's some Indians who'll raid the herds, and some
ruffians who are looking for an easy mark. If you carry a rifle,
you're not considered an easy mark."

After a few more horsemen passed them they found
themselves alone, sharing the open grasslands with the count-
less prairie dogs.

"They are absolutely everywhere," Belle said. "It's as-
tounding."

"The cattle that come through here graze the grass down
to the ground," Sutton said. "Then these little varmints come
in and take over."

"They need no grass cover to survive?"

"You won't find prairie dogs in tall grass, ma'am. They
have to be able to see the coyotes sneaking up on them."

The morning waned and the cool air vanished. The sun
shone fiercely overhead and Belle opened a white umbrella
she had last used while touring New Zealand.

"We're nearly a mile high in elevation here," Sutton remarked. "Real close to the sun."

Belle motioned toward the mountains. "They're so beautiful, aren't they? The Alps, from the Lombard plains, are the
finest mountain panorama I ever saw, but not equal to this."

"Why do you want to go up there?"

"I want to see Estes Park and climb Longs Peak."

"Any particular reason?"

"To say that I did it. To have a story for my dear sister
when I return to her."

"Why not wait until spring? The weather up there is unpredictable this time of year."

"I don't have the time to stay. I can make it yet this fall."

"I assume you know winter weather."

"Yes, I've experienced severe weather before."

"You know," Sutton said, "besides snow that can cover a cabin completely over, there's all manner of wolves and wildcats up there, and grizzly bears."

"Yes, grizzly bears," she said. "Interesting creatures."

They forded the river again, allowing the horses time to drink. Belle noticed how the cottonwoods along the banks framed the mountains.

"That's a picture if there ever was one."

He laughed. "Everything's a picture, isn't it?"

"You take it all for granted, Mr. Sutton. I'm sorry for you."

Sutton started the team up again. They arrived at a cabin that fed meals to travelers and dined on steak and potatoes. Two young men ate at the table with them. They appeared embarrassed.

"I hope you'll forgive us, ma'am," one of them said. "My name is Bret Mason."

"Forgive you for what, Bret?" Belle asked.

He kept his head down. "I know we should be wearing dinner jackets."

"Oh, think nothing of it," Belle said. "I shouldn't think you would be that formal out here."

A young man sitting next to Bret Mason spoke up. "She's right, we don't need dinner jackets out here. Besides, we don't own any." He turned to Belle. "I'm Zack Fisher. That's quite an outfit you're wearing."

"I made it for myself in Hawaii."

Zack Fisher shook his head. "I've never seen so many flowers on one dress."

"That means he likes it," Bret said.

Belle smiled. "How kind of you both."

Sutton, sitting nearby with his plate of food, rolled his eyes.

"Let us at least pay for your meal," Zack said.

"That's not necessary."

"I'd like to," he insisted. "I've got a good roll of bills here. You see, we're headed to the polls. It's election day."

"What he means," Bret said, "is that we all got a good payment to vote for Jed Wilson to represent this district in the state senate."

"Payment?" Belle said.

"Yeah, Jack Cargill wouldn't pay near what Wilson does," Bret continued. "I don't know if Wilson can do us any good, but I said I'd vote for him when I took the money from that man who works for him, and I always keep my promises."

"What is this Wilson paying for?" Belle asked. "Is he part of the temperance movement out here?"

"Oh no, ma'am," Bret said. "He's on the other side of it. He wants to break up the Union Colony and stop any more temperance movements. He says a lot more people want to drink liquor and look for gold and that nobody should stop that if they want the territory to grow."

Belle turned to Zack. "How do you feel about it?"

"I like gold and liquor about as much as anything else, but I'm going to vote for Cargill."

"But Zack," Bret said, "Wilson paid you to vote for *him*."

"So?"

After the meal, the two men left their horses at the cabin and accompanied Belle and Sutton the rest of the way to Fort Collins. They dozed in the back of the wagon, oblivious to the jolting ride.

Belle gazed toward the mountains, which were obscured by shimmering heat waves. Her head and back ached terribly.

"It can get pretty hot out here, even in the fall," Sutton said. "We'll be in Fort Collins soon."

Fort Collins sweltered in the afternoon sun. Once a military post, the settlement had begun to grow rapidly. The main street of town was lined with businesses and hotels, many of them brick and multistoried.

Sutton told her that he would turn south toward his ranch and that she could travel on with him if she desired.

"I'm bound to have a horse that will suit you," he said.

"Thank you, but I can go no farther in this heat," she said.

He took her to the Agriculture House, a boardinghouse with a cabin attached to the back, which served as a dining hall.

Belle thanked him for bringing her, offering to pay him.

"Keep your money," Sutton said. "Just get down out of those mountains before winter sets in."

"I don't even know how to get into them."

Sutton thought a moment. "I've heard there's a settler part way up the canyon who takes in boarders. They'll know about him here."

Belle again thanked him and Sutton was on his way, his wagon creaking as he departed. Before picking up her bags, she breathed a long sigh, tired and in pain and distressed at the loss of view. Longs Peak and the other summits had disappeared behind the foothills. She would have to climb through them to see the lofty heights that had so caught her imagination.

But she took heart in the fact that someone along the Cache la Poudre might have a place for her to stay. From there she could determine how to make the journey up to Estes Park.

She found the Agriculture House to be much the same as the Greeley House, but without an Englishwoman to banter with. Instead, the landlady was curt and said little except what was owed for the room and when to arrive for supper.

Belle did discover an interesting woman who showed her the *Larimer County Express* and said, "I am glad you came this way instead of going directly to Longmont."

"Would that have been better?"

"Not as far as I'm concerned. My name is Elizabeth Stone

and I used to cook for the soldiers when the fort was active. Most people call me Auntie. When you're ready, I'll have tea with you."

Belle found her room alive with black flies but was so tired and worn down from the heat that she braved the bed and slept soundly until sundown. She stirred with the commotion of men coming in from the fields and found her way to the cabin and its eating tables.

Belle and Auntie Stone had tea while the men ate amidst the rattle of dishes and utensils. The workers looked no different than those in Greeley and were equally silent.

Auntie told her about the area and was fascinated to hear about Hawaii and other parts of the world.

"You are indeed a lucky woman to be able to travel like that. I envy you. Where are you going from here?"

"I'm trying to get to Estes Park," Belle said.

"You could go south and turn up the St. Vrain River. It's a fair distance."

"I've heard I can get across through the mountains west of here," Belle said.

"I suppose it's possible, and it would be shorter, but it would be a rough trip."

"Do you know anyone who boards travelers up there?"

"There's a man named Chalmers a ways up the canyon," Auntie Stone said. "He's a woodcutter, they say. Never met him so I can't comment on his character."

"If I can get up there," Belle said, "I can get across to Estes Park."

Auntie Stone excused herself and the room became quiet, except for the monotonous buzzing of insects. Though hungry, Belle cut her meal short. The meat was tough and flies floated in the melted butter.

No one seemed to know how she might secure a horse to ride up the Cache la Poudre Canyon but one of the men suggested she ride with his son, a young man named Willie who was seated at the end of the table.

"You can take her where she wants to go, can't you, Willie?"

Willie stared down at his plate.

"Well, can't you, Willie?"

"I 'spect I can, Pa."

"Be ready to take her at dawn then."

Belle was up and waiting before Willie arrived. The eastern horizon washed the plains in crimson, the light creeping up the slopes of the foothills.

The cool air invigorated her and a quick wash in the river refreshed her. Her stomach growling from hunger, she nevertheless declined the offer of breakfast, deciding to take her chances at the boardinghouse up in the canyon.

Willie pulled up in a buggy and sat still as stone while Belle threw her bags in and climbed to the passenger's seat. Two small horses pulled the buggy and Belle asked if one of them might be for sale.

"Pa won't sell none of these horses," Willie answered. "He told me to tell you as much. Besides, they ain't broke to ride."

No one at the boardinghouse paid any attention to her leaving and Belle was glad to be on her way.

A few miles upriver they passed through Laporte, a bustling settlement situated on the Overland Trail. The town had been established well before Fort Collins and a number of shops and dry goods stores carried items of every description for travelers headed to Oregon or California.

Willie answered Belle's questions about Laporte as best he could, then fell silent. Outside of town, they crossed an open flat toward the Cache la Poudre Canyon, seeing no other travelers. Nothing seemed to be moving but a few antelope in the distance.

Belle noticed they weren't following a road, but traveling across open grassland.

"Is this the right direction?"

"I don't know. I've never been up this way before."

Willie spent the next hour turning the buggy this way and that, wandering aimlessly across the bottom. Finally, they discovered a used wagon road that took them to where hay-cutters were at work in a meadow. Five frame houses were nestled against a nearby hillside.

One of the men pulled his horses to a stop and climbed down from his mowing machine.

"Excuse me," Belle said, "is your name Chalmers?"

"No, ma'am, he's way up the canyon."

"Could you tell me how to find him?"

"No, ma'am."

"Do you take in boarders?"

"I can't take no more on, ma'am," he said. "I've got reapers staying with me." He pointed to another of the men, who drove a mowing machine nearby. "I'd recommend Mr. Dalton there, but you see, he lost a child to snakebite last night and his missus won't let go of the boy so they can bury him."

"Very well," Belle said. "I'll leave you to your work. Thank you for your trouble."

Willie started the team and said, "I can find Chalmers."

"But you said you've never been this way before."

"No, but I've got instincts."

She sat silent in the buggy while Willie followed a little-used road through the foothills. She wondered why, if the road led to the Chalmers's place and he took in boarders, there weren't more signs of use.

The trail steepened and the hot, dry air became stifling. No wind blew and though clouds passed overhead, no rain fell. Animal skeletons appeared frequently and at one location, they passed a dead mule. The carcass was covered with vultures. The birds flapped noisily away as the buggy passed but returned immediately, fighting for position.

"Is this the right road, Willie?" Belle asked.

Willie stopped the buggy. "Maybe you'd like to walk from here."

Belle considered her options: She could insist they turn around and find someone who knew for certain where Chalmers lived, then find another, more courteous driver. But she wasn't certain there were any courteous drivers, or any more drivers at all, for that matter.

"Very well, Willie," she said. "Travel on."

Willie started the team again. "We just have to take this road and see where it goes to," he said.

Belle focused her thoughts on the red rock outcrops that broke through stands of pine and juniper. They passed a herd of deer browsing in a meadow, and on one hillside, mountain sheep were nibbling at shrubs that grew in dense profusion throughout the foothills. She was no botanist and knew better than to ask Willie what they were, so she contented herself with just viewing her surroundings.

They came to a fork in the road and without even as much as a question, Willie broke off toward a secluded gulch. Belle said nothing, holding herself in the buggy as it lurched over the rocky trail. Maybe he did know where he was going; he seemed prompt enough in taking the trail.

They soon arrived at a deep and rocky creek that proved impassable. There was no sign of any cabins or boarding-houses anywhere near, only shadows and heavy stands of pine.

Willie grumbled, worried that the horses were going to spook and run, and that he wouldn't be able to hold them.

"You want me to drive the team?" Belle asked.

Willie glared at her. "I can handle them."

"Then turn them around and let's get back to the main trail."

"You shouldn't get so angry with me," he said. "You don't know your way around here, either. That's not good for a woman."

Belle stared at him.

"I'm telling you this because I don't like to see a lady hurt. This is hard country. If you plan to stay here you'd better know where you're going and how to get there. Otherwise you'll die."

THREE

In the Lap of Luxury

I really don't know how I should get on. There was no table, no bed, no basin, no towel, no glass, no window, no fastening on the door. The roof was in holes, the logs were unchinked, and one end of the cabin was partially removed. Life was reduced to its simplest elements.

ISABELLA BIRD

September 1873

After reaching the main road, Willie turned uphill and said nothing for two full hours. Belle watched eagles soar overhead and listened intently to the bugling of a bull elk not far away. In the trees, blue jays squawked, their crested heads bobbing as they watched the buggy roll past their perches in the pines. Here and there a chickadee flitted, coming to rest long enough to sing its little *dee-dee-dee* song.

She enjoyed the scent of the mountains and the creatures she saw, but it was getting late in the afternoon and she dreaded the thought of spending the night with Willie. They had traveled for over nine hours and covered a considerable distance. It would be foolish to turn back now.

They crossed a low, pine-studded hill and a stream appeared below, cutting through a small valley.

"Look!" Belle said. "Wagon tracks!"

Willie said nothing. Soon they arrived at a log bridge where another stream joined the first one, splitting the valley into three parts. After much coaxing, the horses pulled Belle and Willie across.

There, along the stream amid a stand of aspens, stood a crude log cabin with a mud-plastered roof. Three large holes stood out prominently. Nearby, among scattered logs, Belle spotted a primitive sawmill.

A worn and tattered tent stood nearby, near a beaten immigrant wagon. A large fire pit had been dug and numerous pots and pans lay near blackened coals.

A hard-looking woman in a worn dress appeared at the cabin door. Willie got down from the buggy, and while they talked, Belle looked in vain for signs of a boardinghouse.

It was too late to despair over having traveled with Willie. Should she return to Fort Collins with him, she would risk losing valuable time.

If what Sutton had said the day before about early winters in the high country held true, she had no more time to waste.

Willie returned with a grim smile. "This is the Chalmers place all right, but there ain't no boarding for me or you, either."

Belle got down from the buggy and strode over to the woman, who stood with her hands on her hips, her hard, dark eyes showing no emotion. Her worn and hollow face was soiled, and as Belle approached, she ran a bony hand through strands of gray hair hidden under a large dusty sunbonnet.

"You're Mrs. Chalmers?" Belle asked.

"That I am. Etta Chalmers."

"So pleased to meet you. I'm Isabella Bird. Can't you put me up?"

"There ain't no room here. We sell milk and butter to

those who camp in the canyon but we ain't had no boarders but two asthmatic old ladies. You ain't asthmatic, are you?"

"No, I'm not."

Etta looked her over carefully. "But you are English. I can hear it in your voice."

"Yes."

"And you've got money to travel on?"

"I have money to pay you, of course."

"Maybe we can find some space, for five dollars a week. That is if you can make yourself agreeable."

"Agreeable?"

"We don't take nobody that ain't agreeable."

"I am an agreeable person and five dollars a week is certainly fair."

Upon hearing that, Willie headed for the buggy. He tossed Belle's bags out on the ground and stood waiting until she came up and paid him.

"Now that I know the way," Willie said, counting his money, "I could figure to come back up and get you when your stay is finished."

"Thank you, but no, Willie, I will no longer be needing your services."

Willie left and Belle carried her bags to the cabin where Etta waited to show her in.

The main room contained a stove and a table with benches, nothing else. Behind a canvas partition, Belle's quarters consisted of two chairs and two unplaned wooden shelves covered with sacks of straw to serve as a bed. One section of the wall had fallen away, to be used as a private entrance, according to Etta. A large hole existed in the roof in one corner and holes in the log walls served as windows.

"My mister—his name is Thomas—should be home directly." She handed Belle a cup of milk and a cut of dried beef. "If you'd stay out of the way, I'd be obliged."

The woman straightened her skirt and lifted her ragged hem as she ambled off to do chores. Belle took a seat on a wooden box. The milk was partially soured and the meat tough, but she had been without food all day and ate hungrily.

When she had finished, Belle stood outside the cabin and looked around. She knew Estes Park had to be toward the south, over rugged ridges and pine-clad slopes, along a far harder trail than she had already come.

Near dusk Thomas Chalmers appeared with a hired man who stared at Belle for a time, then walked toward the sawmill. She noticed children of various ages peering at her from behind trees or inside the cabin.

"This woman's got the money to be with us a spell," Etta told her husband. "Five dollars a week."

"She don't amount to much, size and all," Chalmers said.

"She said she's an agreeable sort, though."

Chalmers nodded. "Then she'll do."

A tall, gaunt man with one good eye, Chalmers had arrived from Illinois nine years before upon the suggestion of doctors who had declared him dying of consumption. In but two years he had regained his health, and he believed the ground he now walked upon to be the Promised Land.

He had filed on a hundred and sixty acres and immediately built a ramshackle sawmill. Their livestock consisted of two old Clydesdales, a good bronco mare, a mule, four skinny cows and an equal number of oxen, a few pigs, and a multitude of chickens.

Sharing the cabin with Thomas and Etta was a son of nearly twenty, named Harley, whose actions suggested that he lived in a different world, or wished to live in a different one; a girl of sixteen named Lorie, without a hint of manners; and two boys and a girl between the ages of eight and ten, each with a sour expression and little to say.

Across the river lived an older, married daughter, who came over to view the new arrival and whisper under her breath. Each of the children regarded Belle with suspicion.

The second night, Belle offered to help with dishes and Etta said with a smirk, "You'll make more work nor you'll do. Those hands of yours ain't no good. Never done nothing, I guess."

Lorie cracked a smile. It was the first expression nearing laughter Belle had witnessed from either of them.

Etta continued, saying to her daughter, "This woman says she'll wash up. Ha! Ha! Look at her arms and hands!"

Nothing Belle said seemed to bring her any closer to them. In fact, she seemed to be driving a wedge ever deeper. Were there a way out, she would take it. She looked up the road longingly for travelers, but none arrived. Too late in the season.

She spent her time knitting and washing her clothes, careful not to let Etta watch and judge her abilities. They were all critical of everything, yet each one of them had a hard time doing even the simplest of chores.

The sewing machine, long broken down, gathered dust near a corner of the cabin and to Belle's amazement, Etta had trouble threading a sewing needle, possibly owing to her failing eyesight.

Their own clothes had been washed and rewashed so many times the color had long faded. Everyone wore work boots, even the women, and never a matched pair. The entire family shared a single comb and there was not a washcloth to be found.

Etta busied herself with a small garden that had failed for lack of watering. Belle also noticed that Chalmers and his hired man arose early each morning but by the end of the day had accomplished little. The sawmill, due to continual breakdowns, rarely produced lumber, and when it was time to haul timber for cutting, the oxen were nowhere to be found, having crawled through poorly constructed fences. On the occasion the oxen were nearby, a harness broke or a wheel fell off the cart.

Chalmers never cursed but instead held his anger within, to the point that Belle wondered if he wouldn't soon burst open from pent-up fury.

At the end of each day, after a late meal, he would declare what was wrong with the world.

One evening, beside a fire of pine logs, he engaged Belle in a battle of wits, expressing himself as an authority on theology. He boasted that his ancestors were Scottish Covenenters and that he was a leader of a sect of Reformed Presbyterians. Belle knew them as "Psalmsingers" and realized why he and his wife, before even getting to know her, disliked her.

"You've done wrong and you should be ashamed," he said as they all sat and listened. "Almighty God will destroy you and all the Britishers of the world."

"What are you saying that we've done?"

"Oppression. You're guilty of it, same as your country-men."

"Oppression of whom?"

"Me and my family. I can see how you are toward us."

"I think you've got that backwards, Mr. Chalmers. I've tried my best to be friendly, but I can't get anywhere with you or your wife, let alone your children."

"I don't want my children knowing about England and all the hellish things that have been done in the name of that country."

"No one's country is free of wrongdoing," Belle said. "And not everyone in any country believes their government is always right."

"That might be true."

"So why pick on me?"

"Because you came up here, you and you're highfalutin ways. This is good, clean country here. Foreigners should leave it be."

Belle looked around the fire. Etta stared out from under her sunbonnet, though the sun had fallen hours before. The oldest son sat whittling a stick and Lorie stared at Belle in the same fashion as her mother. The three youngest had fallen asleep on the ground.

She dropped the conversation and from there on avoided religion or politics, subjects that made Chalmers's one eye grow large and his voice turn raspy with rage. That left little else to talk about, so she spent much of her time by herself.

Her lack of interaction with the Chalmerses increased her dispondency. She had no way of knowing what behavior to expect from them, except silence. Only a few habits remained constant.

Each night they slept under the trees, carrying sacks of straw out for their bedding. Belle followed their example the first evening but got little sleep. After that she retired in blankets on the floor of her room.

Every morning Etta would invade her room and start a fire, saying nothing. Belle would rise from bed and by seven be dressed and have her blankets folded and the floor swept. Chalmers would then enter with his family and wail a psalm in a high-pitched voice, followed by a chapter of biblical verse.

Chalmers would leave to go about his work and shortly thereafter Etta would soon arrive with beef and milk, or a bowl of gritty porridge, and leave it on a box by the door. Then she and the rest of the family would wander in all directions while Belle sat alone.

When sundown arrived the pattern was repeated. As they had no lamps or candles, she was forced to use a pine knot torch to find her way around after dark.

One night a fox entered at the open end of the cabin and rushed past her, brushing her face. The next morning she was met by a snake, whose head and three to four inches of its body protruded through a hole in the floor.

Belle wondered what she had gotten herself into. She had no way of knowing how to proceed with her plans and there seemed no means of escape from her situation.

The following evening she took pen and paper to a hillside and confided to her sister:

September 16, 1873

My Dear Henrietta,

Five days here and I am no nearer Estes Park. How the days pass I know not; I am weary of the limitations of this existence. This is "a life in which nothing happens." When the buggy disappeared, I felt as if I had cut the bridge behind me. I sat down and knitted for some time—my usual resource under discouraging circumstances.

She laid her pen down and watched four ravens flap overhead, cawing noisily. She continued with her letter, stating that she was forming a plan for getting deeper into the mountains and that she hoped her next correspondence would be more lively.

She had killed a rattlesnake that morning, taking its tail of eleven rattles, and was distressed at the number and different species of snakes that frequented the area and made her life miserable, causing her to jump at "the sound of a shaken leaf."

Along with the reptiles, insects in many forms crawled or flew through the air, their mission, as she put it, "stinging, humming, buzzing, striking, rasping, devouring!"

That night she avoided the fire, and the next night as well. The Chalmers family did not seem to miss her, which suited her fine. She decided that if she were to keep her sanity, she would need to find a way to get through the canyons to Estes Park, and soon.

Do you have a paper or know anyone who does?" Belle asked. It was the first Sunday morning she had spent with the Chalmerses and now, nearly noon, she was bored out of her mind.

Etta scowled at her. "That's a foolish notion. Who would have need for such a thing?"

"Don't you care what goes on outside of this valley?"

"No, I don't. This here's the place we belong. We don't need to know what wrong other folk are doing."

"How about an almanac then? Is there anything around here to read besides theological works?"

"We keep this house fit for proper learning," Etta said. "If it's not here, it's not fit to read."

Belle found a pile of worn volumes in the corner and selected *The Imitation of Christ.* She adjourned to the hills, following a trail along the creek that was covered with dry leaves. The grasses had all cured to a golden brown and as she walked, grasshoppers buzzed up from under her feet. Mosquitoes and biting flies filled the air near the water, so she walked out of the bottom and found a spot on a hillside under some pines, near a wagon road. A settler had built a wooden picnic table and Belle took refuge in the shade.

She would have made her way out into the hills far earlier but for Chalmers's long-winded oratory on the lessons of Job in the Old Testament. He had already given a long sermon just before breakfast and had continued after the meal. Belle had stayed, eager to "be agreeable."

Chalmers never allowed work of any kind on the Sabbath and told Belle she couldn't as much as wash a dress or mend a sock. Despite the many times she had told him that her father had been a clergyman, he never seemed to remember.

"I don't mind resting on the Sabbath," she told him. "After all, my father insisted on it."

Still, Chalmers continually meant to have the upper hand, saying often that if he had been her father he would never have allowed the "traveling bug" to enter her system.

As a result, she hadn't bothered to tell him or Etta much about herself. She certainly wouldn't tell them that she had published widely and would be publishing more when she returned to England.

She held back from telling them about her book. Certainly they were not aware of it and likely they had never heard of Dickens or Byron or Keats, or even Shakespeare.

Any mention of her works—or those of others whom she admired—would undoubtedly meet with ridicule, and she had already endured enough of that.

Nor did she wish to discuss her reasons for traveling to Estes Park and her desire to climb Longs Peak. They would certainly not understand her quest for enlightenment, which was said to come from time spent in lofty places.

As it stood, Chalmers was on the verge of throwing her out, believing that she would somehow taint his family and the "values" he had instilled in them. She wondered if he might not be jealous of her, as he had no education and knew little about travel of any kind.

After the second sermon Chalmers had picked up a copy of *Boston's Fourfold State* but had fallen asleep in the cabin, along with the rest of the family, and was now snoring loudly. That had given Belle her chance to escape.

Through it all she had tried to be charitable toward him and his preaching, but she couldn't help comparing him to her father, who had been equally as strong in his convictions but would never have subjugated his family. Her father had always wanted the best for everyone, though at times had been too forceful in displaying his beliefs.

In her childhood she had listened intently to her father's versions of biblical teaching, and though he had always been strict, he had also been fair. She could see nothing of fairness nor concern for others in Chalmers.

For that reason his preaching seemed as hollow as the cabin she had been confined to. Yet she realized now, in reading *The Imitation of Christ,* a volume with which she was thoroughly familiar, that she was being tested.

She opened the book arbitrarily to a series of passages:

The nobel love of Jesus impels one to do great things, and stirs one up to be always longing for what is more perfect.

Love desires to be aloft, and will not be kept back by anything low and mean.

Love desires to be free and estranged from all worldly affections, so that its inward sight might not be hindered; that it might not be entangled by any temporal prosperity, or by any adversity subdued.

Her journeys had always taught her something, usually about people and their similarities, though their customs and attitudes might be radically different. As a younger woman she had formed many opinions which had since gone by the wayside. She had discovered that her father's words to her from his deathbed had deep meaning: "No matter what you think of someone, know that within each lives a child of God," he had said. "There are forces which strive to keep that child from emerging, and those forces will anger you. But never fail to look into the farthest reaches of yourself and everyone you meet."

As time passed, seeing into others had become easier; but seeing into herself still remained complicated.

Her father had also told her that trust and faith would keep her going when all else failed.

"If you sincerely wish to please God," he told her, "always take the hardest road."

Her father's words now came back to her strongly. Since getting closer to the mountains, Belle realized that everything had become harder. Nothing about Cheyenne, or Greeley, or Fort Collins had brought her satisfaction, and she hadn't been able to understand the people or their behavior.

But how often had her father told her not to judge people either by their appearance or their mannerisms?

"Never be fooled," he often told her. "Even the most disgusting of beggars may be Jesus in disguise, testing you."

She closed the book and looked out over the mountains, their summits shimmering in the intense heat. She thought of Hawaii and the many hilltops she had climbed, the heights always cool after the daily showers.

This was a different land, beautiful and harsh, peopled with hardened souls who had ended the search for their dreams and now merely struggled for survival.

She wondered who would take her to Estes Park and thought about Rocky Mountain Jim and little Sam Edwards, the boy she had met on the train. Little Sam had seemed to know a great deal about the outlaw and said he knew the area well.

She tried to envision meeting this man, wondering if he was as wild as Sam had told her. She sat back as the birds flitted around her and a deer passed by on the trail. It would certainly be different from any previous experience, meeting a ruffian feared by many. She wondered what Thomas à Kempis would think of the idea.

FOUR

An Eye for an Eye

When I came to this area the grass was high and there were no wagon tracks. Now that's all changed and the only clear water left is in the high country, and that's hard-pressed, with a sluice in every gulch. I love Estes Park and I'll see to it this land stays pure, but there's a time soon coming when I'll have to use my guns to save her.

ROCKY MOUNTAIN JIM NUGENT

September

The mud stuck to the shovel as he dug, rain dripping from his wolfskin cap. He had picked a burial spot not far from the cabin, situated at the head of Gregory Gulch, one of the richest gold and silver areas in all of the territory.

Dressed in his signature beaver coat over a deerskin shirt and leggings, Jim Nugent, known to everyone as Rocky Mountain Jim, mourned the loss of his two friends. They had been dead since the night before and he wished he had come up the previous day, as he had planned.

He had come to Colorado twenty years earlier at the age of twenty-six and had survived the region's bloodiest years. Now the Indians, for the most part, had relinquished their lands, and the outlaws who had once stolen from the ranchers and stage stations had all been hanged or shot, except for a few who had gone into politics.

The name Rocky Mountain Jim Nugent was widely known along the Front Range, from Colorado Springs north to Laramie and Cheyenne, and into the high country on both sides of the Divide. A well-built man of six feet, he wore a Colt Dragoon, .44 caliber, tucked in a red sash at his waist, and sported a large Bowie knife sheathed at his side.

No one had ever seen him without his long, curly locks, reddish gold tinged with gray, or his dense mustache and imperial, and no one could mistake his stern countenance.

Five years before, a grizzly bear had blinded his right eye, and the torn skin of the brow had grown completely over the socket. Claw marks remained along his face and scalp and his left arm, bitten severely at the elbow, hung slightly twisted.

For ten years he had lived with his dog in a small cabin at the head of Muggins Gulch, the entrance to Estes Park, eking out a living by trapping and running cattle. Ring, a ninety-pound mix of collie and mastiff, lay quietly in the rain, watching his master finish his work.

"Who do you suppose did them in?" Jim said to the dog. "And why? They didn't have enough gold between them to buy a drink." He studied the sullen faces of his dead friends, who lay side by side in the same grave. "Or did they?"

Nugent had known the twin brothers, Tom and Tim Kirby, for nearly five years. Inseparable, they had provided him with many amusing hours. They had come into the country from Missouri and had settled along the upper reaches of the Big Thompson. Nearly sixty, the two had decided to stop wandering and make a permanent home in Estes Park.

"They should have stayed home and not come up here looking for gold," Nugent continued. "Look what it cost them."

Ring listened impassively, watching his master fill the graves.

Nugent had already fashioned two crosses from pine boughs tied with rawhide. "I'll bring two stones up for you before the snow flies," he said, pounding the crosses into the rocky ground.

He removed his wolfskin cap and began to sing two verses of a Scots-Irish ballad he had learned from his grandfather as a boy. The song happened to be a favorite of the Kirbys as well.

If I was a blackbird, could whistle and sing,
I'd follow the vessel my true love sails in.
And in the top riggin' I would there build my nest,
And flutter my wings o'er her lily white breast.

I offered to take her to Donnybrook Fair;
And to buy her fine ribbons to tie up her hair.
I offered to marry and to stay by her side,
But, alas, in the morning she sailed with the tide.

As he put his cap on, the rain began to lessen. "May the Good Lord give you a better time of it in the Land Beyond," he said.

When he got back to Estes Park he would write a sonnet about the Kirby brothers. He had written numerous poems and verses since coming into the territory. It helped him ease his pain regarding the past.

The past haunted him day and night and he had come to realize that no amount of writing could erase it from his memory. Still, he wrote.

He climbed onto Dunbar, his white mule, and started down the gulch. By midmorning, the rain had ended. From signs left by the horses, there had been three of them and besides whatever gold they had taken, they had ransacked the cabin and stolen a wagon the Kirby brothers had driven up to their claim.

Nugent knew he would have no trouble recognizing the wagon: The Kirby brothers had owned two Belgian draft horses, both a mottled gray, and their hoofprints showed clearly in the mud.

He followed the tracks from the cabin to a main road that led across the hills, linking with various mining camps. He met occasional miners with their pack-jacks, mules laden with gear and supplies, on their way up to diggings along the hillsides. It was a gold-rich area that had first attracted miners in 1859 and had boomed to greater proportions each year since. Large claims had been filed by men with money and now smelters poured dark smoke into the surrounding skies.

When gold fever had first struck, Mountain Jim had stampeded with the rest to find his fortune, but the area had never grown on him like Estes Park. No amount of money could buy peace of mind.

Over the years Mountain Jim had come to loathe Gregory Gulch. Past friends, trappers and soldiers alike, had found their way here, but had discovered no gold. Some had made it out alive, others hadn't.

He had ridden into the gulch the previous spring to try to talk the Kirbys out of their plans. They had been building their cabin and wouldn't listen.

"Come back to Estes Park," Jim had told them. "We need to sing more ballads together."

"We'll make our fortune," Tim had said, "and buy a gold-studded piano for you."

The Kirbys, with their sharp wit and contagious smiles, would be sorely missed.

He thought about them as he passed the cemetery on Bald Hill. Marble tombstones were mixed with flat board markers, the names and dates painted black or red, many of them hidden in dried bunchgrass, bleached by wind and cold.

Ordinarily he would have stopped to pay his respects to friends buried there, but today he had more pressing business.

A few miles farther he entered Central City with its clusters of brick and wooden buildings—hotels, saloons, brothels, opera houses, bakeries, livery stables, and dry goods stores—built on land almost too steep to stand on. All around, timbered slopes rose so high that the sun was but a fleeting promise during the fall and winter months.

He stopped momentarily at the Teller House, a Victorian hotel and eating establishment garnished with silver bricks for a sidewalk. It was so well known that visiting dignitaries to the region generally stayed at least one night.

Jim could tell that the wagon had stopped there, but had started down the gulch again. The killers had eaten a fancy meal on the Kirby brothers.

He followed the tracks through Mountain City to Black Hawk, named for a chief of the Sac and Fox Indians, and discovered the wagon and the Belgian horses outside the Toll Gate Saloon.

The imposing brick structure, open day and night, drew crowds of drinkers and gamblers and billiards players. There were rooms upstairs with sporting ladies waiting.

Nugent studied the back of the wagon. He saw no bags of gold, only flour and bacon, stolen from the cabin.

He dismounted and tied his mule to a hitching post, and pointed under the wagon. Ring lay down where he was told and made himself comfortable.

Mountain Jim walked into the Toll Gate and looked among the throngs of patrons, knowing that finding the three men he was looking for by ordinary means would be next to impossible.

He drew his pistol and fired into the ceiling.

"Who owns the wagon with the gray Belgians?"

Everyone scattered. The bartender reached for a shotgun.

"Put your hands on the bar," Jim said to him, leveling his pistol. "I want to know who drove the wagon with the Belgians into town."

The bartender, his hands trembling, said, "Aren't you Rocky Mountain Jim?"

"Yes. Answer my question."

"The wagon and horses belong to me."

"How do you have time to jump claims and run a saloon at the same time?"

"I bought the goods this afternoon from three men."

"Name them."

"The leader's name is Carlson. He's a big man, always wears a red flannel shirt. He rides with a man named Perkins, who's right jaw is shot off, and another man named Gibbs."

"Did you know that two men were killed for that wagon, and whatever gold they had?"

"I didn't ask."

"Did they drink in here?"

"Just a short time. They did buy the house a round."

Nugent studied him. "Where can I find them?"

"Over in Idaho Springs."

"You sure?"

"They live over there. I know that for a fact."

"What color horses are they riding?"

"Carlson rides a good-sized black gelding. Perkins and Gibbs both ride bays. None of them are branded."

Nugent put his pistol away. "I'll tell them you sent me."

As Mountain Jim rode his mule out of Gregory Gulch, he thought only of the three killers he sought. He had never met nor heard of them, but there were a lot of men coming and going through the mountains.

Ring ran back and forth along the trail, barking when a traveler appeared from the other direction. There was a party of three fancily dressed gamblers sitting in silver-tooled saddles on well-groomed horses, and a lady, wearing a satin gown and riding a donkey, with escorts. No one else caught his attention.

Into Russell Gulch and on down the twisting trail through Virginia Canyon, he kept his mind on what lay ahead. He had fought many times and had faced death often, but he had never backed away from a fight, no matter the odds.

He had grown up in Canada, the son of a British military officer. After leaving home he had joined the Hudson's Bay

Company and had fought numerous times in fueds over trapping grounds. Tired of fighting, he had married and settled
down to farm in Missouri. His greatest trial had come just a
year before his move to Colorado, something he had never
gotten over.

Nugent rode into Idaho Springs in early afternoon, checking the many horses lined along the street. He found the black
gelding and two bays hitched in front of a small saloon. He
dismounted and studied the horses. There were no brands,
and a large bag of gold nuggets was tied to the saddle on the
gelding.

It was not uncommon to see gold unattended in the
streets of mining camps. Men killed one another over minor
infractions, but left one another's possessions alone.

Inside the saloon Nugent was greeted by smoke and the
stench of stale whiskey but saw no one resembling the three
men named Carlson, Perkins, and Gibbs.

"They were here," the bartender said when asked.
"You'll likely find them at the bathhouse across the street."

Nugent left the saloon and untied the black gelding, leading it along with his mule across the street.

The bathhouse, attached to a small hotel, was nothing
more than a log enclosure surrounding three large potholes of
steaming sulfur water, open to the sky.

Nugent found the three lounging in the water, laughing
and joking, trading a whiskey bottle between them. They appeared naked except for their hats. Two women laughed and
splashed with them. Five other men and an equal number of
sporting girls occupied the other two pools.

Carlson, the big man, held a cigar between his teeth. Nugent addressed him.

"I see you're having a good time on my friends, the Kirby
brothers."

The three looked to one another. Carlson said, "We don't
know any Kirby brothers."

"They were just a couple of old-timers. Why did you
have to jump them?"

Jim noticed their pistols were lying with their clothes

along the edge of the enclosure and that all three men were eyeing them.

"The bartender over at the Toll Gate Saloon says he bought a wagon from you," Nugent said. "The same wagon you stole from the Kirby brothers. He said he'd testify to it."

"I told you, we didn't do it," Carlson spat.

The two women climbed out of the pool and, grabbing their garments, hurried past Nugent.

"Look what you've done," Carlson said.

"Sorry I bothered you," Nugent said. "I guess you won't mind if I take the gold you stole from them and give it to a good cause."

As Jim turned to leave, one of the men bolted from the water. He heard Carlson say, "Gibbs! Stay put!" Gibbs had picked up his pistol and cocked it when Jim drew and fired, sending two bullets into his chest.

Gibbs fell backwards into the enclosure, discharging his pistol into the ground. He bounced off the logs and fell forward to the edge of the pool, his blood pouring into the steaming water where Carlson and Perkins sat with their mouths open.

"You murdered him," Carlson said.

"Just defending myself," Jim said. "Any court would find as much."

The other five men, along with the women, left the enclosure. Carlson and Perkins began to tremble.

"I suppose you're going to shoot us, too," Carlson said.

"I should hang you," Nugent said. "But I've got nobody who saw you kill my friends. I'll content myself to leave with the gold."

Jim produced a pencil and a piece of paper from his pocket. On one side he had started to compose a verse about his home in Estes Park. He turned the paper over and wrote a bill of sale, declaring that he had exchanged a silver dollar for the bag of nuggets.

"Sign it," he told the two men.

They obliged and Nugent left, taking the gold and tying it to his saddle horn. He had a good three hours of riding ahead of him to Denver, where he would make good on his promise of contributing to a good cause.

Denver had come a long way from its early days as the Cherry Creek and Auraria gold camps. In fifteen years tents and log cabins had been supplanted by huge stone and brick structures, Victorian in architecture, that provided both comfort and entertainment to a clientele that included royalty from around the world.

Nugent rode down Blake Street, past the Tremont and the newly built Inter-Ocean Hotel, across the street from the famous American House. Where miners once contented themselves with pine chairs and tables, and beds of prairie grass, the American House boasted silk-upholstered walnut couches, plush-bottom chairs, and a stairway with curved spindle banisters and wine red threads.

In January of the previous year the American House had been the scene of a lavish ball held in honor of Russian Romanov Grand Duke Alexis. State and national dignitaries attended, including General Philip Sheridan, General George Armstrong Custer, Major George A. Forsyth, and Buffalo Bill Cody, all of whom had accompanied the duke on a large-scale hunt across the plains.

Mountain Jim had attended the ball briefly—not by invitation but by force of will and curiosity. He had dressed himself in coat and tails, for the first time in his life, and had entered by posturing himself as a coach driver looking for a senator in attendance.

Inside, he had danced with a senator's daughter twice before being asked by security to leave.

Having made it inside so he could say he had been a part of the occasion, Nugent had left without incident. It would be grand fodder for his narratives and poetry.

He had written often about Denver as he saw it, how it had grown from a few tents and log cabins to its present status as the "Queen City of the Plains." In the early days he had frequented the saloons and sporting houses but had tired of the monotony and now drank mainly by himself, soul-searching and longing for a better life, something he believed would never come to pass.

Nugent rode to a small Catholic church, apart from the stately buildings of the downtown area. After a large cathedral had been built elsewhere, the church had been left to occupation by three nuns, who had turned it into an orphanage.

Jim had come there occasionally to watch the children play. He climbed down from his mule, catching glimpses of kids running and playing ball in the back courtyard. The nuns had never allowed him in to tell stories as they were afraid he would scare everyone.

"I know you don't like me coming here," he told a nun who greeted him inside the church, "but I've brought you something."

When he handed her the gold, she asked, "Did you kill someone for it?"

"Do you want it or not?" Nugent said.

"Of course we do," another nun said, walking up behind the first. She took the bag. "Thank you very much."

The first nun glared at her. "We don't know where he got it."

"Judge not, lest ye be judged," the second nun said.

The first nun stormed away and Nugent said, "I just wanted to do a little good, that's all."

"Well, it's certainly appreciated, Mr. Nugent. We can buy a lot of food and new clothes for the children. Did you keep some for yourself?"

"A little," Jim said. "Just enough."

"I would ask you in for a meal, but I'm afraid it would cause trouble."

"I understand," Jim said.

The nun thanked him again and Nugent left the church. He climbed onto his mule and after a last look into the courtyard, where the children still played, he pulled a few nuggets from his pocket and inspected them. He had just enough for a bottle of good Irish whiskey. It might not make him forget entirely, but it would certainly help.

FIVE

Hardscrabble Valley

*One of the most painful things in the Western States
and Territories is the extinction of childhood. I have
never seen any children, only debased imitations of
men and women, cankered by greed and selfishness,
and asserting and gaining complete independence of
their parents at ten years old. The atmosphere in
which they are brought up is one of greed, godless-
ness, and frequency of profanity. Consequently these
sweet things seem like flowers in a desert.*

ISABELLA BIRD

September

A s the days passed, Belle continued to spend her
time alone, mending and knitting, writing to her
sister, and washing her clothes. She found following Thomas à Kempis's example too strenuous and hoped
to make gradual adjustments in her attitude toward the
Chalmers family.

It bothered her deeply, for she knew her father looked
down upon her, expecting her to work hard at improving her-

self. For now, she told herself, he would just have to understand; she needed time to develop patience enough for this task.

Her challenge lay not only in the Chalmerses themselves, but in everything they did or touched. One afternoon, after the children had left a gate open, she discovered a calf sucking on her favorite dress, second only to her Hawaiian riding dress, shredding the fabric to ribbons. She had no one to complain to, no one who would listen to her frustration. She could mention it only so many times in letters to her sister, and that wasn't like talking in person.

Finally tiring of the solitude, she began to take walks, venturing farther and farther up the valley, wondering how she might find her way past the high canyon walls to Estes Park. Though she had mentioned her intentions to Chalmers and Etta, they paid no attention to her.

In deciding to explore the valley, hoping to find someone who knew the way across the mountains, she soon became acquainted with many of the settlers in the area. They had all, to a family, come to improve their health. Though all were poor and still seeking the end of the rainbow, they greeted her cordially. None cared to grow closer to her than general conversation, though, and Belle found little in common with them, for many could neither read nor write.

The walks soon began to drain her strength and she realized that she had fallen victim to "mountain sickness," a temporary setback. She forgot her own misery and spent much of her time attending to a sick immigrant woman who had just given birth in a shanty nearby.

Helping the woman brought back her spirits and soon she was again active and looking forward to reaching Estes Park. Instead of retiring at sunset and lying awake, cringing at the night sounds, she found a tin cup and filled it with bacon fat, then placed a cut of rag into it to serve as a wick.

With her new-styled lamp, she remained up after dark, sewing a shell-patterned quilt for her sister. The light in the cabin aroused the Chalmerses' curiosity and they stared in wonder. By the second night they were peering in the doorway and by the third had decided to join her, staying up well past their normal bedtime.

The children, still wary, sat in the corner of the room and watched Belle's fingers move. The youngest girl inched forward just as her father opened the door.

He said nothing and the little girl scooted back to her place, her head down.

"Maybe they'd like to learn how to do this," Belle said.

"They don't need to learn that," he said, and left.

Despite the earlier interruption, Etta and Lorie moved forward to watch Belle. Etta kept getting closer and closer until finally, she had her nose almost in the quilt.

"I want to learn how your fingers move that way," Etta said.

"If you watch closely, I'll teach you," Belle said.

Etta and Lorie spent the next three days with Belle while she completed the quilt, which Lorie then snatched and took down the road to show off to other settlers. Belle was pressed into teaching a knitting class, attended by Etta in her bonnet, her married daughter, and another woman from the area.

Chalmers looked on but said nothing. He couldn't chastise the entire community. He remained mute toward Belle until late one morning when it was discovered that the mare had strayed away and couldn't be found. In her Hawaiian riding dress, Belle took a bridle and saddle and began to follow the pony's tracks.

Late in the afternoon, she returned astride the mare.

Chalmers came out of the cabin, his hands on his hips. "I never figured you for a horsewoman. You seem too proper."

Belle smiled and dismounted. "Being proper shouldn't stop a lady from riding. After all, how else would she get around in all this vast country?"

Chalmers studied her. "Women folk shouldn't be off riding. There's things to do at home."

"Mr. Chalmers, what others might want to call home is their own business, but my home is the outdoors." She tied the mare to the wheel of the rickety wagon and looked inside the cabin, where the rest of the family had gathered at the table to eat. "Am I late for supper?"

"Go on in," Chalmers said. "Just don't go giving any of your wild ideas to my women folk."

"Maybe you should allow them a little freedom of choice. You might be surprised how much more productive they could be."

Chalmers grumbled something and followed her inside. A Dutch oven filled with stew sat on the table. Belle had taught Etta how to cook a variety of dishes and stew had come to be her favorite.

"Looks good," Belle said, dishing herself a bowl.

Etta and the children were staring.

"Haven't you ever seen a woman ride a horse?" Belle asked.

Etta had come to like Belle, in spite of herself, and pointed to a piece of knitting in the corner.

"I should be done with that before long."

"You're doing very well, Etta. Your cooking and sewing are both going well."

"But there'll be no riding lessons," Chalmers said.

Etta turned to him. "I can ride well enough, thank you."

"Yeah, but you ain't going to learn to ride as good as this woman."

"Mr. Chalmers, my name is Miss Bird, if you please. Not 'this' woman."

"No matter your name, my missus ain't going to get too good a-horseback."

"Are you afraid she'll ride away and leave you?"

"That's none of your concern."

"Maybe you should insist Etta and the children all learn to ride well," Belle told Chalmers. "After all, what if you got hurt or fell ill? You'd need someone to find a doctor. Don't you agree?"

Chalmers said nothing. Etta spoke up. "She's right, you know. If you went and fell ill, we'd be in a fix."

"What's the matter with you, woman?" Chalmers said. "You've taken to her thinking, haven't you?"

"I just figure it makes sense, is all."

"You know what we'd do if I took ill, or any other of you. We'd let the Good Lord handle it. If we was meant to get better, we would. If we was meant to die, then I figure that would be for the best."

Everyone ate in silence for a time. The children looked back and forth from their father to their mother. They weren't certain what their father might do, his face being so red. But he hadn't struck their mother since Belle's arrival so they didn't fear that.

But if he grew sullen, there was no telling what he might do or where he might go. He had been known on such occasions to stay in his sawmill for days without eating. But it didn't seem likely he would do that, either; he hadn't been sullen since Belle's arrival.

The children grew restless with the quiet. They didn't dare ask to be excused. They were allowed to leave the table only after their father's command.

"Besides," Chalmers added, "if I was to take sick I wouldn't have far to go to a doctor. There's one over the high hill to the west."

"What?" Belle said.

"He's a thick-skulled Englishman, a polished sort, like you, and hard to tolerate."

Belle's eyes widened. "An Englishman you say? And a doctor to boot? What's his name?"

"How should I know? He's new to the area."

"Why on earth didn't you say something earlier?"

"You never asked," Chalmers said, and went back to eating.

Belle looked at Etta, who kept her head down, as did all the children.

"Does this doctor know the way to Estes Park?" Belle asked.

"No, or he would have gone up there himself."

"How do you know he hasn't?"

"Because I know, that's all." He studied Belle. "You know, I've a mind to take you to Estes Park myself. I know the way."

"And all this time you've never said a word?"

"I figured you needed to rest up before you took on a trip like that."

Belle decided it wasn't her rest but the five dollars a week that had appealed to Chalmers. Now he saw a way to earn more money and also be rid of her before she further influenced his wife and family.

"I'm fully rested," Belle said. "And I'd pay you a fair sum."

"I would probably need another hand to go with us," Chalmers said. "In them mountains, three's better than two."

"I agree," Belle said. "But what will you do about horses? The little mare is the only real mount you have."

"Leave that to me," Chalmers said. "I know where to get more horses." He looked to his wife. "You could come along, if you've a mind."

"You'd have me along?"

"It would be good for you for once to go for a frolic." He turned to Belle. "Wouldn't you say?"

"Yes, indeed."

"She would have to be paid the same as me."

"Agreed. When do we leave?"

"Day after tomorrow, after we pack some things."

"That sounds perfect." She watched Chalmers chew his food nervously. "You're certain you can get me there?"

"Why do you have to be so hardheaded?" Chalmers asked. "I could get there blindfolded. I swear, you're no different than them English over the hill."

Belle turned to Etta. "I'm going to visit them, right now. Would you care to come?"

Etta looked to Chalmers. "I don't figure it could hurt nothing."

Chalmers frowned. "Don't be too late."

Belle and Etta walked a short distance back down the valley and took an abrupt turn along a trail that traversed a steep slope. It was easy to see why she hadn't explored in this direction, as the way appeared difficult.

"The trees hide the trail," Etta said. She stopped for breath. "I don't know why you want to visit these folks. We about got you trained. They'll just spoil you again."

"They might have a map," Belle said. "It could help us find our way to Estes Park."

"Thomas said he knew the way. Can't you take him at his word?"

"He didn't seem too sure of himself."

"Sometimes I can't figure you at all," Etta said. "You cook and sew like you was born to it, then you go off riding horses like some man, like you was a trailblazer yourself or something. I've never seen the like of it."

They reached the end of the canyon where it broke into an open valley, allowing the river to spill out and begin a twisting course downslope. A short distance farther stood a log cabin with a second-floor addition that resembled a Swiss chalet.

Nearby stood a barn and small shed. A vegetable garden, irrigated with water from the river, lay between the house and the outbuildings. At the edge of the garden sat a man dressed in a striped garibaldi shirt and trousers, pulling husks from corncobs.

Belle looked out to where the sun shone like fire against the red rocks above the valley and saw a young woman herding milk cows in from pasture. Waiting to open the gate was a woman dressed in a clean print dress, holding a baby.

Belle and Etta walked toward the woman.

"I don't think we should have come," Etta said.

"Why not?"

"Because those folks ain't like us."

"Nonsense," Belle said.

They approached the lady and Belle said, "We've come for a visit. I hope we're not disturbing you."

"Oh, not at all!" the lady said. "It's good to hear the voice of another Englishwoman."

Belle introduced Etta and herself. Etta kept her head down, her sunbonnet covering her face.

"I'm Millie Hughes and that's my husband, Grant, finishing the corn. This is our daughter, Emilla."

"She's a beautiful child," Belle said.

"Thank you. We have four more. They should be along any time now. Have you both had your supper?"

"Yes, thank you," Belle said.

"Then we'll have some tea." She waved to her husband to come in from the field.

Etta grabbed Belle by the arm and whispered, "I don't trust nobody who drinks tea."

"It will be fine, just wait and see," Belle said.

Grant Hughes, a medical doctor, came in from husking corn while the young woman took the milk cows into the barn. The four children followed their father inside and sat down at the table.

After introductions, Belle said, "I should think you could build up a good practice in this area."

Dr. Hughes smiled courteously. "I think not. These people leave their fate entirely in God's hands, without the help of a physician. I've decided to take my chances raising produce. With all the people coming in, there's bound to be a market."

They entered the house via a log porch with support beams covered with cucumber vines. Inside, the room was filled with clematis and Virginia creeper, and white muslin curtains adorned the windows. A library of well-chosen books, including volumes by Kipling, Shakespeare, Wordsworth, Pope, and Byron, filled a shelf along one wall.

Belle felt she had discovered an oasis. "I should say that it would have been good to have known you before," she told them. "As it is, I plan to leave day after tomorrow and will likely not be back this way."

"Too bad," Millie said, brewing a pot of tea.

"I'd best get back home and tend to my chores," Etta said.

"Must you leave so soon?" Millie asked.

Etta kept her head down. "There's lots to be done and my mister gets to fretting if I'm gone."

"I'll be along shortly," Belle said.

Etta hurried from the cabin and lost herself in the dusk. Belle shook her head. "I can't seem to stay on the good side of that woman."

"She's of the same variety that inhabits most of the valley," Millie said. "They're hard-pressed to trust anyone but their own kind."

She handed Belle a cup of tea, then placed a cup of her own on a lampstand and sat down in a rocker with the baby.

Dr. Hughes, taking a seat and lighting his pipe, said, "We came here for the dry climate, just like everyone else, but you seem fit in all regards."

"I've come to reach Estes Park and to climb Longs Peak," Belle said. "I've been traveling some in the States, and before that, Hawaii."

"My, you have been getting around," Millie said. "Do you plan to settle in Denver then?"

"No, I'll go back to England before the winter. But I must complete my journey to the top of the peak first. Otherwise, I would wish to visit you a few more times."

"A pity you can't," Dr. Hughes said. "But for our Swiss maid and our family, we have no one to converse with."

"That's the truth," Millie said. "We haven't seen an educated lady for over two years."

They discussed England and the large number of immigrants who had come to the United States to settle, many in the West. They told her that had she come to them earlier, they might have been able to arrange for transportation to Longmont, south of Fort Collins, where an easier route to Estes Park originated.

"Your best bet is to follow the St. Vrain River," Dr. Hughes said. "Going across from here will be tricky at best."

"Mr. Chalmers says he knows a trail over the mountains," Belle said.

Dr. Hughes puffed on his pipe. "Perhaps."

"What Grant is saying is that we don't know Mr. Chalmers all that well but he doesn't appear to be a mountain man," Millie said.

"I would have to agree," Belle said. "I can't say how well he knows the country."

"Maybe you should find your way to Longmont," Millie suggested, getting more tea.

"Let's not interfere, Millie," Dr. Hughes said. "If Mr. Chalmers says he knows the way, then Miss Bird should take him at his word."

They talked a while longer about politics and the area, and how change would soon be coming to the region.

"Denver is getting larger all the time," Millie said. "Perhaps you should consider settling there."

"I don't know that I'll ever settle anywhere," Belle said. "I have much of the world left to see."

"I must say, we've never met anyone like you," Millie said.

"Why would you want to travel all the time?" the doctor asked.

"I was born a curious sort," Belle said. "Perhaps I'm looking for something I have yet to find."

"Or someone," Millie said with a smile.

"I'm very content with life as it is," Belle said.

Millie smiled. "Certainly."

Belle set her cup down. "I'll be getting on back to the Chalmers place. I thank you so much for the hospitality."

"But you can't walk back in the dark," Dr. Hughes said.

"It's not that far."

"No, it's not," Dr. Hughes said, "but the trail is difficult in the dark. You must borrow a horse."

"I couldn't trouble you."

"It's no trouble," the doctor said. "We insist."

Belle walked to the barn with Dr. Hughes. Elsa, the Swiss maid, had just finished milking the cows and was cranking a separator. Milk poured from one spout into a bucket and cream from another into a second bucket.

After Dr. Hughes introduced Belle, he said, "I'm letting Miss Bird borrow Dan, so she might ride him back over to the Chalmers place."

Elsa, a stout, blond woman just over twenty, smiled and said, "Would she like me to accompany her?"

"I can find my way, thank you," Belle said.

"Fine," Elsa said. "I'll go over in the morning and get him."

Dr. Hughes saddled the horse and Belle said, "You've been so kind, both you and your wife. I should hope to see you again someday."

"Yes, we won't say good-bye. One never knows what can happen."

The Chalmers cabin stood dark in the rising moon. As often as Belle had offered to show them, neither Etta nor Chalmers wanted anything to do with burning a lamp or candle. They had contented themselves for so long with torches burned only in necessity that they seemed unconscious of life by any other light.

When she arrived in camp, Belle discovered the entire family sleeping under the trees. They all awoke, watching her closely.

"Where'd you get that horse?" Chalmers asked.

"Dr. Hughes was kind enough to lend him to me."

"We ain't got enough grass around here for another horse."

"The maid will be over to pick him up in the morning."

Etta stood next to Chalmers. "Those English talked just like savages," she said. "I couldn't understand a word they said."

"They are a perfectly decent couple," Belle said. "If you had stayed longer, you would have learned as much."

"I ain't got the time to just sit and talk," Etta said.

Belle entered the cabin and lit the lamp. Chalmers followed close behind, his one eye narrowed into a slit.

"What is it now?" Belle asked.

"I want to know what you talked about with those English."

"Their name is Hughes, Dr. and Mrs. Hughes."

"Whoever they are, I want to know what was said."

Etta had come in with the rest of the family and they were all staring.

"We discussed books and travel," Belle said. "Do you want details?"

"That don't interest me."

"I didn't think so." Belle began packing her clothes and rounding up her other belongings.

"What are you doing?" Chalmers asked.

"I've decided to leave for Estes Park immediately," she said. "Can you still take me?"

"I got us a mule and two horses," he said. "We can't take that mare, you know. She's jittery."

"If you would work with her often enough, you could have her broke to ride in no time," Belle said.

"Well, there ain't no time for that now."

Etta sent the children back to bed. They filed out of the cabin and she said to her husband, "I don't think I'd ought to go."

"Yeah, you're going," Chalmers said. "This woman's paying you to work with me."

"But what will become of the place? The hired man can't watch everything."

"Things will take care of themselves."

"I don't figure they will," Etta said. "The oxen and the pigs will run off for sure, and the hens will meet their fate with no one to shut them in for the night."

"Get one of the girls to look after them."

Etta shook her head. "Ain't a one of them will remember to do it. You know that."

Belle, barely able to hide her smile, wanted to tell Chalmers that Etta was right. She wanted to say that the oldest son and the hired man were conspiring to leave the sawmill and go hunting and fishing, and that it was true, the livestock would all wander away and never be seen again. And worst of all, the skunks would raid the henhouse.

"I still don't think I ought to go," Etta said.

"I would like to have you," Belle said. "After all, what's a trip without a lot of talk. You don't get that with men, you know."

Etta managed a smile. "I reckon that's right."

"So we're set," Chalmers said. "You two women get your work done. Come tomorrow night, we'll be sleeping at the foot of Longs Peak."

SIX

A Tough Trail for Horses

This is indeed far removed. It seems farther away from you than any place I have been to yet, except the frozen top of the volcano at Mauna Loa. It is so little profaned by man that if one were compelled to live here in solitude one might truly say of the bears, deer, and elk which abound, "Their tameness is shocking to me."

ISABELLA BIRD

September

They left at dawn and Belle felt uneasy from the start. Chalmers's clothes were torn and on one foot he wore a high boot with his pant leg tucked in and on the other an old brogan, from which his toes protruded.

He rode a pack mule, whose tail hair had all been shaved, except for a tassle at the end. From the saddle horn hung Belle's canvas bag, two lariats, a frying pan, and a battered canteen, and behind he had tied on four leaky flour bags.

Etta, always in her sunbonnet, was mounted on a respectable little mare, dark brown in color, that she called Cora. She wore an old print skirt with an short, frayed gown over it, and a print apron over that. From the badly worn saddle hung a saucepan and a bundle of clothes.

Belle, in her Hawaiian riding dress, had tied the cover of her umbrella to a hat she had found, and had tied a kerchief across her face to ward off the intense heat of the sun.

The journey would certainly test her. She had been given the worst of the riding stock, an old, iron gray gelding, nearly blind, with but a few front teeth left behind a droopy lip.

She sat in an old McLellan cavalry saddle. Chalmers had stuffed two heavy quilts underneath as cushions, leaving the saddle at an awkward angle. The bridle reins consisted of a rotten leather strap on one side and a piece of frayed rope on the other.

They rode up the narrow valley, past rock and trees, breaking into an open park four hours later. From there Belle viewed mountain ranges north, south, and due west as far as the eye could see. Including Longs Peak, she counted twenty-two peaks that she judged to be higher than ten thousand feet above sea level. The greatest number of these lay within the Snowy Range, the main divide.

She marveled at the many small valleys, richly grassed, teeming with elk and deer, and conifers of many varieties that gave the slopes a deep green color, broken in places by brilliant red rock.

She looked back and viewed the plains, stretching like an endless brown ocean toward the east. Though intriguing, it was the mountains that captivated her, with their endless meadows and steep rock walls that fell for hundreds of feet into small, foaming creeks.

Within a day's ride lay North Park, an area rich in gold but held stubbornly by Indians known to scalp and mutilate miners who ventured into their lands. Chalmers knew nothing of the place, except that the "ungodly" lived there, those who would surely "perish in hellfire."

Belle kept her eyes on Longs Peak, its snowcapped summit glistening in the afternoon light. As the sun continued to fall, casting purple shadows against the peak, she remembered Willie, who had brought her from Fort Collins in the buggy, having no idea where he was going, and wondered if Chalmers had taken the right trail, or like Willie, just hoped he could find the way.

"Land's sakes, Thomas!" Etta said often. "How long's it going to be before we get there?"

"Be still woman and just ride," he would tell her. "You just follow me and we'll get there just fine."

Near midday they discovered a deserted cabin and Chalmers used a piece of wire to pick the lock.

"Are you sure this is a good idea?" Belle said.

"Can't see nothing wrong with it."

"But you don't own this property."

"Whoever owns it should be up here taking care of it."

Inside, Chalmers rummaged through empty food tins on the table and threw a half-filled bottle of whiskey against the log wall.

Belle watched the bottle shatter, the whiskey splattering everywhere.

"Maybe we should go," she said.

"Don't fret. We need to rest a spell," Chalmers said. "We'll have some bacon and coffee and be on our way."

Etta built a fire in the cookstove and wiped dust off three dishes laying on the table.

"I'll eat from my own tin," Belle said.

She brewed herself some tea and drank slowly while Etta and Chalmers slurped coffee and tore off mouthfuls of half-cooked bacon. Belle let hers cook until crisp and made herself some biscuits to go with the meat.

After the meal, she walked out of the cabin, followed by Chalmers and Etta, and looked across the vastness.

"The Big Thompson River must be somewhere out there."

"I know that!" Chalmers said.

"What I'm saying," Belle continued, "is that if we don't

know where it is yet, we'll never get to it and across by nightfall."

"We'll get to Estes Park," Chalmers said. "You stay here with Etta and I'll find the river."

He mounted the mule and left. Belle and Etta sat in silence for a while, listening to birds chatter in the trees. A magpie flew into the cabin, bold as you please, and began pecking at the empty plates.

Etta got up and paced, looking into the distance for her husband, who had vanished among the trees and rock.

"You don't really know what to do if he's not around, do you?" Belle said.

Etta frowned. "I know what to do."

"I'm simply asking you why you believe he should govern your every move."

"He don't. I tell *him* what to do."

"I haven't seen that yet."

Chalmers returned and with a wave of his hand bid Belle and Etta to follow him. He led them across a ridge above the cabin and into a steep ravine filled with deadfall timber. They dismounted and walked, slipping on the slick surface of shelf rock that stuck out from the hillside.

Belle's horse fell, rolling twice and breaking a strap loose on the saddle. She jumped to one side, stumbled, and fell to the ground.

Etta hurried to her. "You hurt?"

Belle brushed herself off. "No, I'm fine."

"Thomas, you going to get us out of here anytime soon?" Etta said.

"I told you to be quiet," he said. "Leave me be to find the way."

"You'd better find the way soon."

Chalmers stared at his wife. "You sassing me?"

"Call it what you want. Just get us out of this damnable canyon."

His eyes widened but he said nothing. He led them on farther, slipping and tripping along the trail. His surefooted mule waited for him to get up each time he fell, standing with its ears back, obviously annoyed.

Then Etta insisted on taking the lead. Her pony fell and the mule tumbled over on top. The two animals began squealing and fighting. Before Belle could separate them, they had bitten each other fiercely.

"There must be a better trail than this," Belle said.

"There ain't no good trails through these mountains," Chalmers said. "But we'll make it."

Chalmers retook the lead, struggling over more fallen timber and under huge shelves of overhanging rock. The air became chilly and the shadows deepened. Belle imagined the rock shelves above them giving way at any second, flattening them instantly. Certainly no one would ever find their remains.

As the shadows grew longer it became increasingly difficult to see. Chalmers led them to a thick grove of chokecherry bushes, where the trail abruptly ended.

They peered over a five-hundred-foot cliff into the darkness below.

"This is it, Thomas?" Etta said. "We come all this way and now we have to jump over that cliff to get out of here?"

"I don't need your whining," he said. "How many times do I have to tell you?"

"Well, you ain't a fit guide."

"I don't need to hear that, Etta."

Chalmers had never experienced his wife in such a state and didn't know how to handle it. He slapped his hat against his leg and stared at her.

"Listen, arguing won't help," Belle said. "We need a plan."

Chalmers turned and stomped away. He stared into the bushes just off the trail and moved closer to something he saw on the ground.

"I think we'd best turn around now and skedaddle," he said. "Some bear left a fresh pile here, and I mean a *big* pile."

"That's good, Thomas!" Etta said. "You brought us down here to be et by bears!"

Belle turned her tired horse around and looked to the top of the gulch. The trail back up, long and steep, would be treacherous in the dark. But they couldn't camp in a grove of chokecherries owned by grizzlies.

She thought about her experience near Truckee, when the bear had bounded out of the brush in front of her. That had happened in the daylight and she had been lucky. This country was steeper and should a grizzly appear, the mule and the horses would likely tumble off the trail in fright, spilling her and the Chalmerses into the canyon below.

As they started back up, she realized a bear was nearby, for her horse snorted frequently and turned to look behind. All three of the animals fell often and Etta whined at her husband. As they reached an opening in the trees, they stopped to rest and Belle observed a huge dark shape standing no more than thirty yards away on the steep slope below.

The mule and the horses became almost frantic.

Etta gasped. "Oh, dear God!"

"Quiet," Belle said.

They held the animals as steady as possible as the bulky shadow, its nose in the air, rose onto its hind legs. Belle believed she was viewing the largest creature she had ever seen.

The grizzly suddenly lost its balance and slid downslope, its legs spread apart. It piled into a tree and, grunting loudly, righted itself and disappeared into the brush.

"Thank God for loose rock," Belle said.

Etta turned to her husband. "Thomas, could you keep us free of bears from now on?"

Chalmers said nothing. They continued on, walking and leading their mounts behind them, negotiating their way up the steep trail through the darkness. The closer they got to the top, the steeper the trail became. Belle stepped on a cactus, embedding a spine in her foot. She tripped and fell many times, struggling to stay away from her scrambling horse's hooves. Broken branches stabbed at her like dull knives, tearing her dress. Blood oozed from cuts along her arms and back.

Etta complained constantly, falling often as well. Chalmers remained quiet except to groan when he tripped or the mule stepped on his foot.

They finally reached the top and Belle sat down to pull the cactus spine from her heel.

"You have that doctor take a look," Etta said, "and send the bill to Thomas."

Belle patted the old horse, its sides heaving, its head drooping. "We're past the hard part," Belle said. "No more steep trails like that."

Chalmers looked in every direction, obviously disoriented, then started his mule down a nearby trail.

"You're going the wrong way," Belle said.

"How do you know?"

"You're headed downhill." She pointed. "The cabin is that way, upslope a ways."

Chalmers wanted to argue, but realized she was right. They climbed to where a ridge ran east and west but couldn't find the cabin in the dark.

After locating a suitable place to camp, they gathered wood for a fire. Most of the provisions had been lost in the canyon, but a little flour and bacon remained.

A violent wind arose and attempts to start a fire failed. Exhausted, Belle decided that she could wait until sunup to cook.

Chalmers found a clump of evergreens and threw his bedroll down.

"What about the stock?" Belle said. "Aren't you going to hobble them?"

"Don't fret, they'll be fine."

The wind worsened and became filled with snow. Seeing was impossible and the stock disappeared from view.

Belle took shelter in an aspen grove. Etta was shouting at Chalmers to find the mule and the horses, but the storm muffled her voice.

With snow flying and Etta yelling, Belle made her bed in the grass and, using her saddle as a pillow, wrapped herself in quilts. She knew that come morning her back would be so stiff she might not be able to move. Despite that and her sore foot, together with the pain of numerous cuts and bruises, she closed her eyes and while Etta and her husband continued to argue nearby, fell into a sound sleep.

Belle sat in the early morning light, writing a letter to her sister, to be mailed God only knew when. She looked up and watched a huge bull elk, supporting a large rack of antlers with fully eight points on each side, stroll out in front of her. Its heavy coat of hair glistened with frost. After staring at her momentarily, it turned and trotted away, its feet and legs raking the frosty grass.

Nearby, two blue jays pecked the snowy ground. She watched one of them inspect a pile of chokecherry seeds and recalled how she had awakened earlier to find that an entire bush only yards from where she had made her bed had been stripped by bears while she had slept. Their tracks were still fresh.

She wondered how anyone could survive here year round, calling it the "Great Lone Land" in her letter to Henrietta. Her breath rose in thin clouds as she wrote. Seven o'-clock and the sun had not yet risen high enough to warm the air. She sat in complete stillness while from far off came the distant roaring of the Big Thompson River as it hurtled through the canyon.

She blew warm breath into her ink well often and decided finally to finish the letter at a warmer time. She placed her pen and paper back in her bag and searched the mountainsides for Etta and Thomas Chalmers, but could see no one. They were out looking for the stock, gone since the night before. She had warned him they would stray and he hadn't listened. She knew Chalmers didn't have any picket pins and that he should have at least fashioned hobbles to keep them from wandering off.

Belle had awakened at dawn, aching from cold and her cuts and bruises. The hole in her foot from the cactus spine had swelled shut and the area around it had turned a mottled blue. In addition, her back hurt terribly, making it difficult to even get up from her blankets.

It troubled her more that the horses and the mule were gone.

Upon their leaving camp that morning, Etta had told Belle, "He's the most ignorant, careless, good-for-nothing man I ever saw."

"I see you've decided to speak up," Belle said.

She nodded. "I finally realize what a blowhard I married."

"Perhaps, but he means well."

Belle had surprised herself, saying something charitable toward Chalmers. She was so tired and ached so terribly that all she wanted to do was return to the broken-down cabin near the sawmill.

She wondered now if she had made a mistake in getting Etta to stand up for herself. The two of them still hadn't returned with the stock and if they got to arguing, there was no telling what they might do to each other.

A strong breeze developed at midmorning, carrying the sting of snow and ice off the summits. The snow melted, leaving the ground slippery and drying fast. There had been few storms that summer and fall, and the ground absorbed the moisture quickly.

Though she had eaten some snow earlier, she had drunk no water since the previous afternoon, before the mule had fallen with their only canteen. She wished now that she had thought to somehow collect some snow, for if they didn't find a stream sometime during the day, they would become very thirsty.

She built a fire and continued her letter, describing the glorious beauty surrounding her. The cool air had restored her energy and despite her aches and pains, she felt refreshed.

She described the deep, vast canyons lying in purple gloom, and upland valleys surrounded by pines artistically placed, threaded through by the cherry-fringed beds of dry streams, all below pinnacles of bold gray rock that pierced the blue sky overhead.

Never had she been alone in such impressive country, strong in itself, unforgiving and treacherous, yet so fulfilling to the soul. She told her sister: "The Rocky Mountains realize— nay, exceed—the dream of my childhood."

She thought again of Estes Park, hidden from view yet beckoning to her as strong as anything she had ever felt in her life. She considered the possibility that she might never reach this glorious place but wouldn't allow herself to dwell on it. She would find her way and learn what there was about it that called to her so strongly.

Chalmers and Etta arrived at nine-thirty. He rode the mule and Etta one of the horses, leading Belle's old gelding behind.

Chalmers climbed down from the mule, his face twisted in rage.

"Can't trust him to lead the horses, or lead the way, either." Etta said.

"I'll show the both of you," he said. "I'll find the trail, you wait and see."

He walked away, breaking limbs off trees and slamming them into the trunks. After a few minutes he climbed on the mule and started off. Belle and Etta followed in silence while he led them through gulch after gulch, trying to make good on his word as a guide.

Belle had to tell him often that he was headed the wrong direction and that if he did find a trail, it wouldn't lead to Estes Park. He became so aggravated that he took off on his own, returning an hour later with news that he had finally discovered the way.

It was a main trail used by hunters, as drag marks from pulling a fallen elk through the timber were evident. Again Belle had to point out that they were headed the wrong way.

"We're going northeast, not southwest," she said. "And

we're supposed to be ascending, not descending, toward the park."

Chalmers took off again and they traveled another two hours. After passing through an aspen thicket the trail disappeared and they broke over an open ridge. Just above them and not far away was Storm Peak, at eleven thousand feet in elevation.

"We can't be anywhere near Estes Park," Belle said.

Etta jumped down off her horse and fell to her knees. She pounded her fists against the ground.

"Thomas, you're no doubt the worst guide there ever was!"

He scratched his head. "Well, maybe I don't know where I am, at that."

She glared at him. "I'm not having much of a frolic, I'm telling you."

"We'll get this figured out." Chalmers took a deep breath and looked out over the country.

Etta got up and stood in front of her husband's mule. "Tell me, which direction is Estes Park?" Watching him look all around, she added, "You don't know, do you?"

"Let's eat," Belle said. "We'll be ready for a fresh start then."

"He needs something to set him straight," Etta said.

They sat for a while, chewing dried bread, with no sound but the birds and the whisper of a cool breeze that blew across the ridge. Belle found it difficult to bring saliva to her mouth and the bread almost gagged her. She knew she needed nourishment but she wanted water more.

Chalmers chewed loudly. He got up and looked out in all directions.

"You ready to lead us in another circle?" Etta asked him.

"I'll lead the way," Belle said. "I've had some experience at following trails."

"Sounds right good to me," Etta said. "And it sounds good to you too, don't it, Thomas?"

He said nothing, but kept looking around.

"It's easy to get lost in all this country," Belle said. "It could happen to anyone."

"You're too easy on him," Etta said.

Belle stretched her aching back. "We're all tired."

Chalmers momentarily studied his wife's narrowed eyes. "Let's get moving," he said.

Belle led the way and discovered a well-used trail that she knew led toward the valley bottom. She remembered looking down the canyon the previous day and seeing travelers far below.

The trail cut across a rocky hillside and there was no choice but to cross on the loose, fractured stone or go back up and try to descend somewhere else. The mule and the horses were near exhaustion and could never make another trip back up and then down another gulch.

They started across the rocky slope, the footing treacherous for the suffering animals. Behind, Chalmers was silent and Etta was alternately praying and crying.

The mule proved to have the best coordination and constantly pushed into the back end of Belle's gelding.

"Keep your mule back," she told Chalmers. "He's going to knock my horse off balance."

"He's scart crazy," Chalmers said. "I can't hold him."

With the next bump, Belle's horse slipped. She felt herself falling over his neck but held onto the mane with both hands. The old horse recovered, snorted, and kept going.

Belle's breath caught in her throat as her mount stumbled again. Just below, a dropoff fell at least four hundred feet into a jagged slope of rock and trees. But the gelding again regained his footing.

They rejoiced on the other side but their celebration was premature as the main girth on the mule's saddle gave way and Chalmers slid over the animal's head. He landed on his feet but stumbled and fell into the flour sack, which burst and spread all over the trail.

"Damn all of England!" he said. "The curse of the Lord be Britain's misfortune!"

He salvaged a portion of the flour and threw the saddle back on the mule, pulling the latigo until the animal grunted for air.

Farther on, the girth on Etta's saddle gave way and she rolled over her horse's head, landing heavily on the trail.

She looked up at Chalmers. "You're the one saddled this critter, so it would go to figure that it wouldn't be right."

Chalmers turned to Belle. "If it weren't for you, Etta and me wouldn't be in this fix."

"Had I realized that you didn't know the way to Estes Park," she said, "I wouldn't be in this fix either."

Chalmers threw the saddle back on Etta's horse and began fumbling with the straps, cursing England.

While Chalmers ranted and raved, Belle cut a piece of rope from one of the lariats and tied the saddle back on Etta's horse. They rode on without incident, discovering that the trail broke out into a large meadow. They gathered wood and built a fire, frying bacon in the pan.

"I still can't figure a woman who'd cross an ocean to climb mountains," Chalmers said.

"You had your reasons for leaving home," Belle said. "I've got mine."

They finished their meal and, after a two-hour search, discovered a spring, where animals of all sizes and shapes had drunk. What remained was a small basin of muddy froth.

After letting the horses and the mule drink, Belle said, "Anyone for some tea?"

Chalmers and Etta stared at her.

"We'll strain the water through a flour sack," she said, "and then boil it."

Chalmers and Etta drank tea for the first time in their life, enjoying it. Etta smacked her lips and held out her cup for more.

"Maybe you'll take to drinking tea regularly now," Belle said.

They sat for a while, catching their breath and regaining strength. Belle made a mudpack for her swollen foot and held it in place, hoping it would draw out the inflammation caused by the cactus spine.

"You figure this is all worth it?" Etta asked her.

"To gain something grand," Belle said, "you have to make some sacrifices."

"I guess it depends on what you see as grand," Etta said.

Belle smiled. "You must have thought this to be an adventure, since you decided to come along."

Belle checked the straps on her saddle and mounted the old gelding. They began the remainder of the journey back to the Chalmers camp, determined to keep a steady pace and not become discouraged.

The sunset blazed red over the mountains and a hard frost set in, making life miserable for all of them. They rubbed their aching limbs for hours as the night passed. Etta fell often but didn't complain once, as the end was nearly in sight.

Chalmers kept up his harangue against England and all religions besides his own. Belle and Etta had both tuned him out long ago and kept their thoughts trained on the trail.

When they finally arrived at the Chalmers place, they headed directly for the creek. The horses and the mule broke into a trot. Belle knelt down and swallowed handfuls of cold water. Etta joined her, crying for joy, lowering her face into the current as her kids assembled from the cabin and stood watching nearby.

After drinking his fill, Chalmers sat and stared at the sky. He led his family over to the trees and they all rolled up in their blankets.

With the Chalmers family sound asleep, Belle washed herself in the cold water, rubbing herself dry with a clean blanket from the cabin. She built a fire in the cookstove and peered out at the stars through the holes in the roof. The moon rose and the mountains became a long jagged line against the backdrop of sky. She lay down in her blankets and dreamed of a view of the world from the top of Longs Peak.

SEVEN

When the Work's All Done in the Fall

These are our halcyon hours, when we forget the deeds of the morrow, and that men still buy, sell, cheat, and strive for gold, and that we are in the Rocky Mountains, and that it is near midnight. But morning comes hot and tiresome, and the never-ending work is oppressive.

ISABELLA BIRD

September

Belle awakened before dawn and climbed a hill in the darkness. The mudpack had drawn most of the inflammation from her foot and the swelling had subsided, but the pain lingered.

She sat and watched while pink and scarlet broke into the eastern sky, washing the plains below in gold. Birds erupted into song from every tree. When the sun finally topped the horizon, she turned and gazed upon Longs Peak, aflame in purple and crimson.

She stared for some time, wondering about the feeling of

standing atop the summit, looking out over the world. She had come so far, yet the peak seemed a lifetime away.

Descending to the cabin, there seemed no chance that she could accomplish her desire. Finding her way to Denver and onto a train seemed her only choice.

Chalmers finished breakfast quickly and left the cabin. Etta spoke only of catching up on her work. In their absence, the children had allowed the pigs and the oxen to wander away and the garden to deteriorate.

Chalmers had mentioned before leaving the table that he would "string everyone out to dry" if the stock wasn't all gathered by nightfall. The children all ate quickly and vanished.

While washing the breakfast dishes together, Belle tried to make conversation, but Etta held herself distant.

"Are you so quiet because of our not reaching Estes Park?" Belle asked.

"I'd like to have seen you climb that mountain," she replied. "I don't feel good about our letting you down."

"We tried and we failed," Belle said. "That's nothing to be ashamed of."

Etta blinked back a tear. "We figure you'll be moving on now."

"Yes, I've decided to go back to Fort Collins and on to Longmont. If I can't make arrangements to get to Estes Park from there, I'll likely go to Denver and catch a train."

She looked up to see Chalmers approaching with Cora, the little mare. He handed her the reins.

"She's yours, if you've a mind to have her."

"Mine?" Belle said.

"Not for free!" he said quickly. "But we figured it was only fair that we sell her to you cheap."

"But won't you be needing her?"

"I don't ride all that much," Etta said, "and Thomas don't neither. But mostly we figured that since you want to get to Estes Park so bad, you ought to have a horse."

"How much to you want for her?"

"Twenty dollars is fair," Chalmers said.

"I'll give you twenty-five. She's a good little horse."

"She ain't that good, but we'll take it."

Belle paid him and he studied the money like it was the most he had ever seen at one time. He rolled it up and stuck it in his pocket, staring at the mare.

"I reckon she'll do good by you," he said.

Belle packed her belongings and by midmorning was ready to leave. The younger children sat watching under a nearby tree. Carlie was nowhere to be seen.

"She's likely showing her friends a new quilt she made," Etta said. "Being as you showed her how and all."

"Tell her I enjoyed knowing her," Belle said.

Chalmers came out in front of the sawmill and waved, then went back inside.

"He ain't much on good-byes," Etta said. "Especially if he's taken to someone, and that's rare."

Belle tied her bags to the back of the saddle and checked the cinch. Etta took her by the arm and spun her around.

"I ain't much at good-byes, neither," she said, hugging Belle clumsily. "But I figure if I'd had a sister, you'd be her."

Belle held her, feeling awkward. "You take care of yourself, Etta. Just remember there's a world outside of here, in case you're ever interested."

Etta lowered her head and brushed away a tear. "I'll likely be here forever."

"Forever is a long time."

Belle climbed into the saddle. The horse shifted to one side and then the other.

"She's a bit high-strung," Etta said. "But she'll be fine when you work her some."

"I'll ride over and see Dr. Hughes and his family. Maybe they know of someone who can take me to Estes Park."

Etta waved a last good-bye and said, "Don't forget us now, you hear?"

"I won't, Etta," Belle said. "Take care."

❖ ❖ ❖

Belle rode to the Hughes place and Elsa, the maid, who was holding the baby, waved from the door toward the garden.

She found Millie hoeing frantically, seemingly lost among the tangle of squash and pumpkin vines and towering stalks of corn.

At seeing her, Millie jumped up and shouted, "You've come back! I thought you'd left for good."

"I had intended to," Belle said, dismounting. "It seems that Mr. Chalmers is not the guide he wishes to be."

"Ah, I see. You seem to have injured your foot."

"I stepped on a cactus in some nameless gulch."

"Poor soul! You haven't had a good time of it, have you?"

"It's been a challenge." She saw that Millie had filled a number of sacks with onions and had stacked them near the scales.

"We're getting ready to take a load to Longmont in a few days. Would you care for a spot of tea?"

"That would suit me nicely, thank you."

Inside, she relaxed in a chair and settled into conversation with Millie. Elsa, who had been taking care of the baby, excused herself and adjourned to the barn to work.

Dr. Hughes had left that morning to deliver a baby somewhere in the valley. The demand for his services was growing and Millie was concerned he would have to devote himself to his practice full time.

"I wish he would consider that we've work to do here," she said. "But I shan't stop him. It's who he is and though the people have nothing to give us, he insists on caring for them."

"I assume from the conversation we had before that he hopes to reform their attitudes toward medical care."

"Oh, yes, but he'll not get far, not with these people. Perhaps in time he'll see that."

"It is a far different place here," Belle said. "I suppose that Denver is much more civilized."

"That depends on what part of Denver you're talking about. All kinds of people travel there. They come from everywhere and have all kinds of attitudes. Those with money will prevail and the town will eventually be settled."

"Have you met anyone who is a true and honest guide, who could take me across to Estes Park?"

"There's no one here with that capability, I'm certain. I have heard of a man who lives in Estes Park who knows this country well. But they say he's an outlaw."

"An outlaw?"

"They call him Rocky Mountain Jim. I heard he traveled through here once and everyone locked their doors."

"I've heard of him. He sounds like a bad sort."

"Some say that he's not all bad, except when he drinks. And he's a true guide, not like the imposters around here."

"It's a moot point, I suppose," Belle said. "After all, the man isn't here to take me."

"You should be counting your lucky stars," Millie said.

Belle thanked Millie for the tea and rose from her seat.

"Leaving so soon? We've hardly had a chance to talk."

"I must be on my way if I'm to reach Fort Collins before nightfall."

"You've really got that mountain on your mind."

"I'm afraid I can't think of much else. Please tell your good husband farewell for me."

Belle climbed on the mare, anxious to depart. She turned to see the doctor approaching, calling to her.

The little mare began to buck, turning and twisting and crow-hopping around the yard. Belle held on tightly, gasping for breath.

Millie looked on in wonder. She had once heard of a rodeo but never expected to see one in her own front yard.

The doctor watched helplessly as Belle's horse continued to buck. Nearing a fallen tree, Belle kicked the mare on one side in an effort to turn her but only made matters worse. The horse bucked even harder and the cinch came loose.

Belle toppled off backwards with the saddle, landing on the fallen tree and taking a parting kick in the knee as the mare bucked away.

"Oh, good Lord!" Millie said, running to Belle's side.

Dr. Hughes made his way to where Belle lay on her back,

holding her badly bruised left arm. He checked her eyes and felt for broken bones. There were none, and after determining that she had suffered no serious head injuries, he helped her sit up.

"I need to look at your back," he said.

A broken tree branch had ripped through Belle's dress, from the left shoulder to the right hip, scratching her badly.

"It's a nasty scrape," Dr. Hughes said. "But I don't believe it's all that deep."

"A fine time for this to happen," Belle said.

"You won't be leaving today, I'm afraid," the doctor said. "You'll need some time to mend."

He and Millie helped Belle inside and upstairs to their straw bed. It was the only comfortable sleeping accommodation in the house.

She spent the next day and part of another on her back. The following day she rose and walked gingerly. Millie fitted a rocker with a pillow and Belle took the time to mend her riding dress, even as the doctor dressed her wound.

"My back will heal easier than this cloth," she said.

Still too weak and sore to travel, she decided to stay on for a time. Despite her protests, the Hughes insisted she keep the bed. Millie slept upstairs in the same room, on the floor with her baby, rolled in blankets, while the child cried through the better part of each frosty night. Dr. Hughes slept on the floor of the living room, exhausted from each day's work.

"His is not of the temperament for such toil," Belle told Millie one afternoon after Hughes had come in from the field for the third time and sat in a chair gasping for breath.

"He has to keep up with the crops or we can't harvest them," Millie said.

"For land sakes, why not give up the crops and move to a city where he can practice medicine?" Belle said.

"I'm afraid he would take no more payment for his work there than he does for his crops out here."

Belle understood what she meant the following day when she caught a neighbor woman raiding the garden for melons.

She walked out to ask the woman what she was doing, anger growing with each step.

"I need these melons," the woman said.

"The doctor and his wife are in another field working," Belle told the woman. "You can return for the melons when they get back."

The woman, dressed reasonably well, laughed. "I'll just take these melons now," she said, loading them in the back of a wagon.

"When do you intend to pay for them?"

"When I get good and ready."

Belle, not used to confrontations, nevertheless refused to back down. She found herself growing even angrier

"You put those melons back," she told the woman.

The woman stared at her. "What did you say?"

"You heard me."

The woman sized Belle up. "You ain't big enough to talk that way."

"If you don't do as I say, you'll learn just how big I am."

"They've never run me off. They let me take what I want all the time."

"They're nicer than I am. How do you expect them to make a living?"

"I guess it don't matter to me one way or another."

"It will from now on. Now unload those melons or you'll wish you'd never been born."

The woman did as she was told and drove away in the wagon, staring back at Belle. When the Hughes arrived, nothing was said. The woman never returned.

Belle wrote her sister that the story of her hosts was a story of misfortune and demonstrated who should *not* journey to Colorado. As Dr. Hughes and Millie, both under thirty-five, had come from upper-class backgrounds and higher education, it seemed hard for Belle to understand that they could suffer the fate they had at the hands of their neighbors.

Belle felt sorry for the family and their constant struggle. Millie could never keep up with her work, trying to care for a family of seven, plus feed Elsa, the maid. Often she had little time to fix a proper meal and the children ate what they were given without complaining.

They grew to love Belle and played around her much of the time, prying for stories about her travels and saying thank you with their eyes when she cooked for them.

Though she had never been around children for any length of time, Belle found herself drawn to the Hughes family. They were all well behaved and courteous, never rude or impudent. They were in fact a rarity in the region.

In the evenings all the day's hardships seemed forgotten as Belle, along with Millie and Elsa, sat mending shirts and socks, taking time out to read segments from Rudyard Kipling or from James Fenimore Cooper's *Leatherstocking Tales.*

Upon discovering Cooper's caustic critique of American civilization, *The American Democrat,* Belle spent two evenings devouring its contents and commented, "I find Mr. Cooper's observations to be entirely accurate. Perhaps he would have come down harder had he ventured farther in this direction."

Millie smiled. "If you choose to continue your travels through this region you may discover the reason *why* he never ventured out here."

As she grew stronger, Belle became anxious to leave for England and home. She felt fit for travel: Her back pain had subsided and her injured arm had improved considerably. There seemed no reason to linger, as her dream of reaching Estes Park and climbing Longs Peak seemed impossible now, with winter ever closer and no one to guide her.

Dr. Hughes was preparing to take his produce to market and Belle saw the opportunity to locate a stage stop that would take her to a train station. It would be good to return home and see her sister again.

She helped the Hugheses harvest the garden. They picked three hundred pounds of tomatoes and nearly two tons of squash and pumpkins, with a couple of squash plants that weighed well over a hundred pounds. It would take four loads to get it all to town.

"I suppose you'll be leaving when Grant takes the first load of produce to Longmont," Millie said.

"I believe so. I will leave my pony with you as payment. You've both been so very kind."

"Then I guess it's time to let you in on a secret. I'm expecting another child and if it's a girl, we'll name her after you."

"Congratulations!" Belle said. "I'm honored."

The next day Belle insisted that Elsa take the children to Fort Collins to the county fair. After they had left she saw to it that Millie and the doctor took a long nap, undisturbed, upstairs, while she did the cleaning and washing. Her bad arm had kept her from working as much as she had wished to, but a new clothes wringer installed on the side of the washtub now enabled her to get the clothes finished quickly.

As she placed the last shirt on the line to dry, a man in a wagon approached and asked if the crossing was passable.

"You'll have no problem," Belle said. "How's the road to Denver?"

"It's filled with travelers, tourists coming in from everywhere. Winter's coming on up above and the surveying parties are getting out while the roads are still open."

"The trains to the East," Belle said. "Do they run regularly?"

"Like clockwork. You'd be going back there?"

"As soon as I can make my way."

The man studied her. "I would guess you're too frail for this life."

Belle pointed to Longs Peak. "I came to climb that mountain, but nobody knows the way. Do you?"

"No, ma'am. I'm no mountain climber."

"Good luck to you then," Belle said.

"And the same to you, ma'am."

She watched the driver take his team across the creek and walked to the top of a hill. She watched the sun filter through thin, windswept clouds knowing that soon those clouds would be heavier and darker and filled with snow, and Longs Peak would be huge and white, and she would never be able to tell her sister how it felt to stand on the summit and touch the sky.

Belle sat in the wagon for over eight hours before Longmont appeared on the horizon. Hughes had borrowed two horses from a neighbor that had never worked together before and they fought each other most of the way.

In addition, the tack was in disrepair. There were no blinders for either horse, both harnesses were cracking for lack of oil, and parts of both reins had been fashioned from rope and twine.

"It's the best he had," the doctor said.

"If either horse sneezes," Belle said, "everything will fall apart."

Since he had never been to Longmont, Hughes knew nothing about getting there. He lost his way three times, taking wrong turns and ending up circling back each time to look for the main road. They choked on alkali dust while crossing open plains dotted with sage and greasewood and across the bottoms they slopped their way through irrigation ditches and undid the wire from fences to make passage across hay meadows.

At midday they stopped to rest at the Little Thompson River, now reduced to a series of mudholes. No rain had fallen for over two months and all the watercourses were drying up.

While Hughes repaired a broken harness, Belle fell asleep under a cottonwood.

"We've got to push on," he said, awakening her.

"Come back and get me when you've discovered Longmont," Belle said. "I can't take another minute in that wagon."

"Have faith. We're almost there."

"My faith has already been sorely tested, so I guess I'll test it some more."

At midafternoon they approached a series of brown houses built erratically against fields of wheat and barley stubble, the crops having been harvested the previous month.

The trail now followed the twisting flow of Irrigation Ditch Number Two, from which the crops had derived their water. The project had been developed to allow farmers to irrigate crops that would normally not grow under the scant rainfall that fell on the plains. The doctor commented that the farmers would be getting anxious soon, as there was no water in the ditch to irrigate the ground for the planting of winter wheat.

"They won't have a crop next year," he said, "unless they get moisture from the ditch or the sky, one or the other."

They followed a well-used wagon road to where it widened into a street. Frame houses and shops lined both sides, with hitching posts and wagons and a lot of horses and mules standing lazily in the sun, switching flies.

"This is the Chicago Colony of Longmont," Hughes said.

Belle studied the scene. "Chicago would sue, should they be informed."

They reached the St. Vrain Hotel, a two-story structure glaring white in the afternoon sun. Hughes helped with her bags and inside Belle met the landlord, Cort Rainey.

"I can't help the heat," he said, "but I'll give you all the water and towels you want. And a flyswatter."

"I'll make do," Belle said, and walked outside with the doctor.

"I don't know how to thank you," she told him. "You and Millie have been so gracious."

"If I had no family responsibilities and knew the way, I would guide you to Estes Park."

Belle shook his hand. "I'm certain you would. Take good care of your family. I'll be writing you from time to time."

The doctor left and Belle settled into a room on the first floor of the St. Vrain, which was slightly more comfortable than anything on the scorching second story. When she came back to the desk to inquire about meals, Cort Rainey asked her about her plans.

"We've all read about you in the papers," he said. "It seems you're quite a traveler and adventurer."

"I've had the good fortune to move about," she said. "But I fear I shall miss seeing Estes Park, for I have no guide to take me there."

"It's a bit late in the season for travelers," he said. "And a bit dangerous now. You see, there's a land war starting up there."

"I hadn't heard that."

"It seems a British nobleman is seeking to acquire much of Estes Park as his own. The locals, especially one, are literally up in arms. Perhaps you've heard of Rocky Mountain Jim."

"I've heard his name mentioned a number of times. They say he's a ruffian."

"I know the man. Treat him well and he's a gentleman. Get on his bad side and you'd better move out or use your pistols."

"You say he's at odds with a British nobleman?"

"One Lord Dunraven, who wants to make a game preserve of Estes Park."

"Then it's not a simple feud," Belle said, "but something much more serious."

"I'm afraid so. There could be shooting. It would be a risky place to visit."

She returned to her room and a maid quickly arrived with a pitcher of water and a bowl. Belle washed her face and fought black flies until Kay Rainey, a stout lady with deep blue eyes and red hair piled atop her head, knocked on her door to announce the evening meal.

The dining room was a step up from Greeley and Fort Collins, but the plank tables were equally as crude and the wooden benches just as uncomfortable. The town's working single men arrived for their meal and ate in the same silence that Belle had witnessed in the previous two towns.

While waiting for them to finish, she drank tea and relaxed for the first time in two weeks.

"I'm glad you like it," Kay Rainey said. "We bring it

back from Denver when we go. We can find anything we'd ever want there."

"It will be interesting to visit that city," Belle said. "But I won't be staying long, as I need to be getting back to England."

Kay Rainey refilled their cups. "Cort told me that you so wanted to reach Estes Park. I'm so sorry your luck hasn't been good."

"Perhaps another time."

"I feel that Estes Park is among the most beautiful places in Colorado. It's a shame that you will miss it."

Belle fought tears. During dinner she said little, thinking about her dream. After the meal she sat in her room, looking out at the mountains.

Cort Rainey knocked on the door and announced to Belle that two young men had just arrived who were traveling to Estes Park the next day.

"You're in luck," he said. "They have agreed to take you with them."

"When can we leave?" Belle asked.

"Tomorrow. Get a good rest tonight. It's a thirty-mile ride up there through mountains and canyons. When you get there, you will have earned the view."

EIGHT

Where Wise Men Fear to Tread

There comes a day in every man's life when he must decide what road he will take. As for me there can be no choice but to face the coming storm. I will face it alone if I must, but I will stand firm until I can stand no longer.

ROCKY MOUNTAIN JIM NUGENT

September

By the light of a kerosene lantern Jim Nugent and his neighbor, Griffith Evans, sat at a table in Nugent's cabin, a bottle of whiskey between them. Ring lay at Jim's feet, growling occasionally, as the men had been arguing all night, passing the bottle back and forth.

Evans, the same age as Nugent, short and small of frame, sat staring at Mountain Jim, drumming his fingers on the table. Evans lived with his family in Estes Park, a short ways distant, in a cabin that he used as a hunting lodge, where he took hunters into the mountains for a fee, something he wanted to do full time. He saw the cattle business in the mountains as a thing of the past.

"I can't believe what I'm hearing," Nugent was saying. "You've sold your half of the ranch to Lord Dunraven and now you want me to sell my place, too?"

"You would get paid a good price."

"I make plenty as it is."

"Who are you trying to kid?"

Nugent glared. "I make all I need. You understand?"

"When will you come to your senses, Jim? Your best bet is to throw in with us, and you know it."

"I know nothing of the kind."

"Just think of it, you can guide his hunts. He'll pay you more than you've ever seen before."

"I don't want his money."

"You should sell, Jim. It's good advice."

"And what if I don't?"

"Then Dunraven will force you to sell."

"He can't own this whole area. He'll learn that."

"He's a very powerful man, Jim."

The Right Honorable Wyndam H. Thomas, earl of Dunraven and earl of Mount, had concluded that the whole of Estes Park might someday belong to him so that he might establish a game preserve and profit by issuing hunting permits to prominent people of his choosing.

Lord Dunraven had first visited the region in 1869, during a hunting trip in the Rocky Mountains, encouraged by General Philip Sheridan, whom he had met in Chicago. The general had even written the commander at Fort McPherson, Kansas, directing him to allow scouts from that post to accompany Dunraven.

A return trip in 1872 solidified his notion that the region was ripe for plucking. He picked a location for a lodge and began his plan to take over Estes Park.

As a war correspondent for a London newspaper during the Franco-Prussian War and with Stanley during his famous trip to Africa in 1871 looking for Livingstone, Dunraven had developed a taste for adventure. After hunting in the Rockies and the Yellowstone River region with William F. Cody, who eventually became Buffalo Bill, he had decided that big game hunting was something he could market.

Dunraven neither feared nor cared about the few established families, as he believed none of them would be foolish enough to confront him. He had already brought his own settlers into the area to homestead so that when the surveying reached completion, he could buy them out.

Griffith Evans had already made an arrangement with Dunraven to sell his half of the ranch. He believed that his co-owner, a man named Edwards, would be forced to sell his half as well. Then, when the time was right, Evans would be in partnership with the British lord in a lucrative business.

"I'm telling you, Jim, Lord Dunraven will give you more than a fair price," Evans said. "Don't be a fool."

"You're the fool, Evans. And so is he if he tries to force anything."

Evans drummed the table again. "You can't just shoot everyone who displeases you, like you did that poor man in Idaho Springs."

"What do you know about that?"

"Everyone knows it."

"Does everyone know he and two others killed the Kirby brothers for their gold?"

Evans smiled. "The Kirby brothers had no gold."

Nugent studied him. "Are you saying the Kirby brothers were killed for some other reason?"

"I just said they had no gold. Everyone knows their claim was poor and that they were coming back up here."

"Let me get this straight. They were coming back up here and, like me, weren't about to sell their holdings to Dunraven, either. So Dunraven hired those three to see that they didn't make it back up here. Am I right?"

"You can't go accusing people of things like that."

"You as much as told me that's what happened."

"I didn't tell you anything. I came here to talk sense into you. I failed."

"You did at that. Don't ever again ask me to sell."

Evans rose from the table. Ring growled.

"I suppose you'd have him chew me up," Evans said.

"He knows bad meat when he smells it."

Outside, the rim of the sun edged over the treeline. Evans walked to the door.

"How much longer do you think you can hold out, Jim? With your boozing you're liable to cause more trouble than you can handle."

"You've changed, Griff. You'd ought to know better than to sell out for English gold."

Evans glared. "Someday you're going to say something you'll get shot for."

Nugent stood up and rested his hand on the butt of his revolver. "You going to be the one to shoot me?"

"You'd kill a man with a family, wouldn't you?"

"You'll be doing the same, if you stick with Dunraven. He'll drive the settlers out of here and they'll starve."

Evans left and Jim sat back down. He drank from the bottle and stared down at Ring.

"What are we going to do, old pardner?"

Ring stared up.

"Evans and Dunraven are set to ruin this beautiful place. They've got no right."

Nugent rose from the table and strolled outside, drinking casually, as he had been all night, while he watched the early morning sunlight stream down into the middle of Estes Park. Bottle in hand, he walked to a nearby log corral and caught his mule, saddled and bridled him, and led him out. He tied the mule to a corral pole and finished the bottle.

Ring, sitting at Jim's side, looked up and whined.

"No, Ring, you've got to stay here. Go over and lay down."

He pointed to a spot against the side of the cabin where a pile of skins lay. Ring made his way slowly to the bed and plopped down with his head between his paws.

Nugent climbed into the saddle and rode past the cabin. He stopped to address Ring.

"You keep a watch here while I'm gone. No telling who might try and ride through here."

Dunraven Lodge, a prominent structure of two stories on nearly two acres, rested in a meadow above Fish Creek, near its junction with the St. Vrain River. It stood for all to see as a model of power and wealth.

Lord Dunraven sat at breakfast, discussing the day with two associates, when a wide-eyed maid interrupted.

"There's a rough-looking man arriving, sir. I believe it must be Rocky Mountain Jim!"

"Who?"

"The man Griffith Evans told you about. The outlaw."

The men at the table looked alarmed.

"Please, settle yourselves down," Dunraven said. "I'll have this handled in no time."

Tall and slim, with thinning dark hair and piercing dark eyes, Lord Dunraven made an imposing presence. He wore only the finest suits tailored in the fashions of the day and was rarely seen without his derby hat.

He strode out onto his porch and stared coldly at the man sitting on the mule in his yard.

Jim Nugent leaned forward in the saddle.

"A good morning to you," he said.

"State your business," Dunraven said.

"You know why I'm here."

"I don't even know who you are."

"Yes, you do. I came here to tell you to leave. Your scheme won't be tolerated."

"Sir, you are drunk."

"That might be so but I am also right."

"You will leave my property now or I will have you extricated."

"Extricate all you want but you'll play hell getting me to leave."

"What exactly is it that you want, Mr. Nugent?"

"Send the squatters you paid to come up here back to Denver, then pack up and do the same."

"I have every right to be here, as much right as you."

"You *had* every right to be here until you connived with Griff Evans to take over. Living here is no sin. Hunting here is no sin. But working to take all the land and keep it for private hunting is against the law."

"There is no such law!"

"It's an unwritten law, and I'm the enforcer."

"If that's the case, then you'd just as well shoot me now, for I do not plan to leave."

"Find yourself a gun."

"I only fight gentlemen. Now if you will excuse me, I have matters to attend to."

Dunraven turned and walked back into the lodge. The maids and guests, who had been peering through the windows, disappeared from sight.

"Dunraven!" Nugent called out. "Maybe you won't fight but I'll bet some of those squatters you brought up here will."

Dunraven reappeared. "Murder is a capital crime, sir!"

Nugent smiled. "I'll make certain they take the first shot."

He rode away and left Dunraven fuming. A mile upriver he turned up a gulch and approached a newly built cabin where two men sat playing checkers. Upon seeing him one of them, skinny and scar-faced, reached for a rifle.

"Don't," the other one said. "He'll kill us."

"You figure to just sit here and let him shoot us?"

"You know who he is."

Nugent reined his mule in and said, "I'll tell the both of you just once, leave here and don't ever return."

One of them said, "Will you kill us if we don't?"

Jim pulled his pistol and shot a checker from the middle of the board. Both men jumped back from the stump.

"I'll just shoot all your checkers and you won't have anything to do."

The scar-faced one looked at the rifle.

"You'd best forget about that," Jim said. "Time to leave."

The men got up and began walking, looking back nervously as Nugent followed them on his horse. They passed Dunraven Lodge and the lord watched from his balcony.

"Do you know how powerful he is?" the little one asked.

"Maybe where he comes from he's powerful," Jim said. "Up here I'm the boss."

Farther down the trail the scar-faced one asked, "Do you expect us to walk all the way back to Denver?"

"Hell is a lot shorter. Which do you pick?"

The two men walked away, looking back occasionally, until they were out of sight. Jim rode up to his cabin, where Ring lay obediently on the skins, waiting for him to give the command to come.

After he had dismounted, Ring bounded over, tail wagging furiously.

"I hope you kept the varmits away while I was gone," Jim said. "There's a lot of them coming in and we've got a lot of work to do."

Griff Evans rode his horse to the front of Jim Nugent's cabin. Ring came to his feet and growled.

Nugent came out, chewing on a piece of beef jerky.

"Did you come to share another bottle?" he asked.

"I won't be doing that ever again."

"So why are you here?"

"I heard you threatened Dunraven."

"I asked him to leave. Nicely."

"You're way out of line."

"I hope you didn't come over here just to argue with me."

"No, I came to warn you," Evans said. "I don't want you on my property ever again."

"I've never done anything to you."

"I won't take the chance that you will, or hurt my children, either."

Nugent stiffened. "You've got no call saying something like that."

"Your crazy ways scare everybody," Evans said. "Just mind what I say. Don't ever come over again."

"Then maybe I should extend you the same courtesy."

"You can't block the trail in and out of Estes Park."

"Just watch me."

"Are you saying that if I tried to come through with my wife and kids, you'd stop us?"

"Yes, if you're fool enough to test me."

"You've a dark mind, Jim Nugent."

"There's dark times a-coming, Griff, if Dunraven stays in these parts."

Evans turned his horse. "You remember what I said. Stay away from my ranch."

He rode toward Dunraven Lodge, thinking about the future of Estes Park and what a name he would make for himself as a guide and outfitter in the mountains. There would be hunters from all over the British Isles, taking their stories back and looking upon him as a man who knew his trade.

He had brought his cattle to Estes Park ten years before and had started hunting immediately. Elk and deer roamed the area in vast numbers, with many trophy heads for the taking. It was the best place to hunt of any in the region. Only Jim Nugent stood in the way of making his dream come true.

He reined in his horse at Dunraven Lodge. It was the first time he had been there, and seeing a structure of that magnitude in the middle of nowhere made him stare.

Lord Dunraven came out to the porch.

"Did you talk to Nugent?"

"Yes, but he won't budge."

"You said you could talk him into it."

Evans climbed down from his horse. "I said I would *try.*"

"We must get this problem solved very soon," Dunraven said.

Inside, a maid brought tea. The guests were out touring the region with a guide and the remainder of the help had decided to move down to Longmont until the Mountain Jim matter was resolved.

Evans held his teacup and walked around the lodge. It was filled with bear, elk, and deer skins, and mounted heads of deer and antelope on the walls.

He studied a photograph of Dunraven and William F. Cody hanging below one trophy. The two men were posed over a fallen bull buffalo.

"Where was this taken?" Evans asked.

"On the Yellowstone. We made many kills that week."

"You take a photographer with you on your hunts?"

"Always."

"There'll come a day soon when you and I can kneel beside a big bull elk," Evans said.

Dunraven grunted. "Yes, perhaps, but we have more pressing matters immediately at hand." He called for the maid and she brought more tea. "What do you propose we do to stop Nugent?"

"It will take some careful planning."

"Tell me again," Dunraven said, "why can't we bring the law from Fort Collins up here?"

"What law? There's a circuit judge but no marshal."

"Then how about Denver?"

"He hasn't killed anybody in front of a witness."

"Do we have to wait for that?"

"If we want a conviction."

Dunraven clenched a fist. "This has to cease. My settlers are all leaving and I can't keep dredging new ones up, just so this barbarian can run them off as well."

"If you get enough of them, they'll stay."

"Just the presence of this outlaw has driven even my help away, and news travels fast. I won't be able to get anyone to come up here, no matter the pay."

"Maybe you should offer them more."

"What I give them is far more than they've seen in their entire wretched lives. We have to find a way to deal with Nugent." Dunraven got up and paced the floor. "Those men who took care of the Kirby brothers want revenge for losing their friend. That may be the answer."

"You told me they were afraid of him."

"That means only that they'll be careful in how they make their plans."

"I don't think you can depend on them, not after they saw Nugent shoot their friend."

"But that's exactly why we *can* depend on them. They want to get their gold back from that outlaw, as well as kill him."

"I didn't see any gold at his cabin and I didn't hear him talk about any."

Dunraven finished his tea. "It doesn't matter. Contact them and double the amount that was paid for the Kirby brothers. They will surely agree to that."

"And what if they don't?"

"Then surely you can find someone."

"I suppose so. Where can I find you?"

"Don't worry about finding me for a time. I have other matters that need attention. Just get the job done and we'll proceed with our plans."

NINE

No Cause for Alarm

His face was smooth shaven except for a dense mustache and imperial. Tawny hair, in thin, uncared for curls fell from under his hunter's cap and over his collar. One eye was entirely gone, and the loss made one side of the face repulsive, while the other might have been modeled in marble. "Desperado" was written in large letters all over him. I almost repented of having sought his acquaintance.

ISABELLA BIRD

September

Sylvester Downer and Platte Rodgers, two rawboned young men heading to Estes Park on vacation, led Belle along the trail that followed the North St. Vrain River. Both would return to law school in Denver that fall and thought the time off might well be spent relaxing in grand mountain scenery.

The fact that Estes Park could become a battleground did not escape them. Stories abounded of Mountain Jim Nugent, and the fact that he lived at the entrance to Estes Park gave them cause for concern. He had been known to turn back parties he didn't want in the park. But they believed there could be no reason Nugent would stop two young men escorting a refined English lady.

The two wanted to get to Estes Park in a hurry, and having a female companion was the last thing they had expected.

Neither wanted to spend any more time with Miss Isabella Bird than necessary. Rodgers had decided from the beginning that she did not fit his womanly ideals as he had never seen a woman ride "cowboy style," as he termed it, in a Hawaiian riding dress that looked to him more like colorful bloomers.

"I thought she might be nearer our own age," he had whispered to Downer at the start of the trip. "Maybe we should have asked to look at her first."

Still, the day went well and after an early start, the three were riding together without concern. The landlord at Longmont had referred to the pair as "seemingly innocent" and Belle had yet to see them in any other light.

She could see immediately that Rodgers could be obnoxious and temperamental, more so than Downer, who tried to moderate his friend's impulsive and often indiscreet remarks.

Belle surprised them from the beginning, however, and they could say nothing to criticize her ability on horseback. She displayed more agility than either of them.

She had bought a new horse from the livery man, one that proved stout and surefooted, filling her with enthusiasm. He never bucked once and allowed her to mount him from either side, even following her from behind without being led when she spent time afoot.

She had at first believed the day's start would be a repeat of her terrible fall at the Hugheses. The gash in her back, though healed, remained tender and her arm very sore, but the longer she rode, the more confidence she gained.

The horse reminded her of the mounts she had ridden in Hawaii. She believed this one had been raised on kindness, without the use of whip or lash, trained to voice instead of spur commands.

Equally refreshing was the change of climate. She had long since tired of the incessant heat, ending each day with a terrific headache and often nauseated as well.

The trail into the mountains proved delightful. Though the sun shone brightly through a clear sky, cool air slid down from the peaks ahead, invigorating her.

They reached the Big Thompson River and entered the mouth of a huge canyon of the same name, crossing and recrossing the river often as it wound its way higher and higher into the mountains. Neither Downer or Rodgers had a firm grasp of the best trails to take but when they became confused, homesteaders stacking hay directed them back on course.

"We agreed to take you with us," Rodgers said while he looked for a trail, "as a favor to the landlord."

"It's a good thing you agreed to help me find my way," Belle said. "Otherwise, who else would offer encouragement when you get lost?"

Her experience at traveling kept her from becoming either demoralized or excited when the boys' frustration peaked. "Have a little patience," she told them. "As long as we're going up, we can't be far off course."

"There's too many mountains out here," Rodgers said, "and too many Indians."

"You mean too many *stories* about Indians," Downer said. "They've been driven out."

"Yeah, but you hear about renegades coming back."

"We don't have to worry about our scalps," Belle said. "The landlord at the St. Vrain said we would likely have more troubles with bears than Indians."

While Downer and Rodgers worried about what lay just off the trail, Belle marveled at the scenery. So different from down below, so much more fair in texture, with endless variety, a great change from the brown and burning plains.

She wrote this to her sister, adding that the cottonwood

trees were green and bright and the aspens were in the height of their glory, their golden leaves shimmering in the cool breeze, and that "the wild grape vines trailed their lemon-colored foliage along the ground and the Virginia creeper hung its crimson sprays here and there, lightening up green and gold into glory."

She had found the world of her dreams and was now on a trail of discovery.

During the morning and early afternoon they crossed and recrossed the river several times, passing through dense stands of trees laden with vines and choked beneath with wild roses and gooseberry.

Overhead, high walls of granitic rock formed grand castles "patched and splashed," she wrote Henrietta, "with carmine, vermillion, greens of all tints, blue, yellow, orange, violet, deep crimson, coloring that no artist would dare to represent, and of which, in sober prose, I scarcely could tell."

Downer and Rodgers, who had other scenic matters on their minds, began to complain when Belle would stop to admire a particular view or a richly colored shrub or vine. They had heard that the settlers' daughters in Estes Park had not seen a young man for some time.

"We've not got all day," Downer said. He had become the spokesman for the two. "This canyon is not a good place to be after dark."

"I can't find anything wrong with it," Belle said.

"Do you see the berries scattered through here?"

"Yes, they're quite beautiful."

"Beautiful, but food for bears."

"I promise I won't take their berries."

"How would they know that?" Rodgers asked.

"Don't you read the papers, Platte?" Downer said, with a grin. "She *fights* grizzly bears."

"An exaggeration," Belle said. "But I have met up with a few in my day."

"What happened?" Rodgers asked.

"One in Nevada turned tail and ran," she said. "But most

of them stay and talk and we become good friends. If you've got a bear for a friend, you don't have to be afraid of anyone."

"Then we're safe," Rodgers said.

Farther on, he broke out in song:

> *Oh, my darling, oh, my darling,*
> *Oh, my darling, Clemantine.*
> *You are lost and gone forever,*
> *Dreadful sorry, Clemantine.*

"Is there a reason you're singing that song?" Downer asked.

"It takes my mind off my worries."

"Worries?"

"Bears, Downer. I'm still worried about bears."

Downer laughed. "After that song, there's likely not a single bear within ten miles of here."

They passed over Rowe Hill and down into the Little Thompson, where they stopped to water the horses. The late afternoon sun glistened on the water.

Belle dismounted to stretch her legs.

"This is indeed a paradise. I can understand why that mountain man would want to keep it safe."

"The real trick is to stay safe from Rocky Mountain Jim," Downer said.

"They say you've got to get by him to enter the park," Rodgers added.

"I hear he's a gentleman," Belle said.

"I, for one, am not going to take any chances with him," Rodgers said. "I'll wait here while you two go meet him."

"Do you expect me to come back for you?" Downer asked.

"Yes, if you're still alive."

Belle said to Rodgers, "I understand you are studying law."

"Yes."

"How do you expect to handle problems in court? You can't wait behind and hope the judge sees it your way."

"I'm not worried about any judge shooting me."

"What makes you think Mountain Jim will?" Belle asked.

"They said in Longmont that if he's drunk, he's apt to do anything."

Belle mounted her horse. "Perhaps it's all exaggeration."

"She's right," Downer said. "You can't stay behind."

"I'm still not going to take the chance," Rodgers said. "You go ahead and maybe I'll catch up."

Downer climbed on his buckskin. "Suit yourself, but I'll laugh if we get past Mountain Jim and you get eaten by a bear."

In less than an hour Belle and Sylvester Downer reached Muggins Gulch, a long and narrow passage of grassland bordered by stately pines on either side. Downer had been fretting about his partner and didn't notice the old cabin until Belle pointed it out to him.

"That's got to be the place," she said.

Smoke rolled up from a rock fireplace. The roof, barely visible, was covered with animal skins—wolf, lynx, fox, badger, wolverine, and beaver. In a nearby tree hung a butchered deer.

From a pile of furs near the door came a large dog, who stood growling, hackles standing.

A trapper dressed in skins appeared at the door. One side of his face had been badly scarred.

"That's him, by God!" Downer whispered.

The dog continued to growl, inching toward Belle and Downer.

"Ring, get back here!" the man yelled.

Downer stood up in the saddle as if to show that he was all grown up, but said nothing.

Belle heard a trace of a Scots-Irish accent. She studied the man, wondering if Rodgers wasn't right in avoiding this place. His scarred face made him appear malevolent. His clothes were held together by a red sash at his waist, from which protruded a knife and a large revolver.

"Sorry to disturb you, sir," Belle said. "We're just passing through."

The trapper smiled and tipped his cap.

"My name is Jim Nugent. Is there anything I can get you, ma'am?"

"A cup of water would be nice, thank you."

He dipped water from a barrel beside the cabin and filled a battered tin cup. Belle introduced herself and thanked him.

"My pleasure," he said, helping her down from her horse. "What brings you up this way?"

"I came to see Estes Park. I understand its the most beautiful spot in this region."

"It is and you don't have far to go."

"That's good to hear. It's been a long day."

Nugent turned to Downer. "Why don't you get down and relax?"

Downer remained mounted at a distance. "I'm just fine, thank you."

"He must want to get a jump in case I come after him," Jim said with a laugh.

"I believe you're right." Belle held the back side of her hand out to the dog and he licked her. "This is a very nice animal."

"He seldom takes to strangers, but he likes you."

Belle scratched Ring's ear and pointed to the cabin. "What kind of animal skin do you have staked out on the logs?"

Nugent strolled over and returned with the skin. "This is a beaver." He laid the pelt over Belle's saddle horn. "It's yours, for good luck."

"It's gorgeous. I'm very grateful to have it, and I can use some luck. I was bucked off a horse a while back and haven't fully recovered."

"I saw that you favor one arm. You might have noticed that I had some bad luck of my own."

He described how a grizzly had jumped from a thicket and attacked him, defending her two cubs. He fired his revolver into her, making her all the more enraged. He lifted his left arm.

"She bit into me here at the elbow. I could hear the bones crunch. I kept shooting her but she wouldn't go down. She got on top of me and bit me on the head. One tooth got my right eye. My last shot finally killed her."

"How in the world did you survive?"

"I lay unconscious for a while. Then I came awake and crawled out from under her and made it to my mule. I rode all the way to Grand Lake, where two settlers saw me. They thought I'd been scalped by Indians, but they found me a doctor and he stitched me up."

"There must be some reason you're still among the living," Belle said.

Jim agreed and began to discuss his concern regarding the attempt by Lord Dunraven to secure the surrounding area as a hunting preserve.

"You can't have been here for very long and not heard about it."

"Oh, yes, I've certainly heard."

"I don't know how much longer I've got in this life but if there's one thing I want to do before I go, it's to stop Dunraven from ruining this place."

"Some have said it may end up a shooting war," Belle said.

"It will if he doesn't leave. I won't let him bring all kinds of people in here just to take up squatter's rights for him."

"How do the others here feel?"

"There's only one I know of on his side."

"Then the majority should rule."

"No, Dunraven's a powerful man with a lot of money. He'll buy his way in if I don't stop him."

"Why should you do it alone? Why not call a community meeting?"

"No one would come. Everyone's afraid of me."

She felt the softness of the beaver pelt he had given her. "I don't know that I've ever received a gift so lovely."

"I'm certain you've received many gifts. A lady of your gentle nature must surely be married to a lucky man."

"Actually, no. I travel by myself and hire guides when I must." She motioned to Downer. He rode over and she introduced them. "This young man, and one other, were kind enough to help me find this place."

"The other one, would he happen to be sitting his horse in the pines over there?"

Platte Rodgers had been certain of his hiding place. He rode forward sheepishly.

"Do you have a good reason for hiding?" Jim asked.

"I didn't know if we were welcome," Rodgers said.

"I don't worry about those who ride straight in. It's those who stay to the shadows who concern me." He extended his hand toward his cabin. "Won't you all share supper with me?"

"I wish we could," Belle said. "But I must get on to Estes Park before nightfall. I'm planning to climb Longs Peak and I want to begin before the weather changes."

Nugent smiled. "Well, you've got your work cut out for you."

She climbed on her horse. "I know it won't be easy. But I've come this far and I simply must chance it."

Rodgers and Downer began riding, eager to leave Muggins Gulch and Mountain Jim's cabin. Belle gave Ring one last pat and climbed on her horse.

"Thank you for the water and the good conversation," she said.

"You're entirely welcome." He removed his cap again. "I hope you will allow me the pleasure of calling on you."

"I'd like that," Belle said. "I don't as of yet know where I'll be staying. But I'm certain you will find me."

TEN

A Piece of Paradise

We saw at last Estes Park in the glory of the setting sun, an irregular basin lighted by the bright waters of the rushing Thompson, guarded by sentinal mountains of fantastic shape and monstrous size, with Longs Peak rising above them all. The rushing river was blood red, Longs Peak was aflame. Never, nowhere, have I seen anything to equal the view into Estes Park.

ISABELLA BIRD

September

At the end of the gulch they crossed a ridge, nine thousand feet above sea level. Fifteen hundred feet below, bathed in the light of the setting sun, lay the valley Belle had dreamed of seeing for so long.

Rodgers had ridden ahead and had already started down. Downer, who had remained behind with Belle, said, "There it is, pretty as you please."

At first words wouldn't come to her. "I've never beheld such a beautiful sight," she said.

They descended to the valley floor and Belle kicked her horse into a full run, whooping and shouting for joy as she rode over the grassland. When the horse became winded, she reined in and waited for Downer.

"I can't remember when I've felt so happy," she said.

Rodgers sat his horse atop a small hill, waving to them. When they reached him he pointed to a small lake just ahead.

At the water's edge sat a large log cabin, well kept, with a flat roof layered with spruce branches and hay and sealed with mud. Nestled behind were smaller cabins. Two corrals and a shed served to hold cattle and horses, and nearby two men on horseback herded twelve Brown Swiss milch cows toward a log dairy barn.

Belle and the two boys rode in and were greeted by a small man with a cheerful smile.

"If you're looking for supper, you're just in time."

Belle dismounted and shook his hand, introducing herself. "We'll take you up on that."

"My name is Griff Evans. I hail from the slate quarries near Llanberis. From your manner of speech I trust that you might know the place."

"I do, indeed. My original home was in Yorkshire."

"Ah, a lady of the Isles," Evans said. "Let me show you the main cabin."

Rodgers and Downer watered the horses while Belle followed Evans inside. The main room was large, with a massive stone fireplace and glass windows that looked out in two directions. On the boarded floor stood a large round table, two rocking chairs, and a large couch upholstered with carpet.

Off one end of the main room was a bedroom, and off the other was a kitchen and a small dining room.

"We call it the Queen Anne Mansion," Evans said. "The main room was the first cabin built in these parts, by Joel Estes himself, the first white man in these parts. We're right proud of the place."

She noticed the large logs were not chinked but were covered in many places with animal skins and rugs. The remaining space on the walls was decorated with elk and deer antlers, and all forms of Indian artifacts—bows and arrows, lances, war clubs, and finely beaded medicine pouches. In the corners, rifles were stacked military style.

Seven men lounged in the chairs and on the floor, smoking pipes and telling stories while one man who appeared ill lay on the couch. A middle-aged woman took a seat at the table and began a letter.

"I would like a place to board, but it appears you're full," Belle said.

"I have a single cabin off by itself. It's small, but clean. Let me show it to you."

Evans led her out of the lodge and along a path that circled the lake.

"Mirror Lake is what they call it. Prettiest spot in the park, I'd say. But then I'm biased."

She watched the fading sunlight sparkle off the water. "I'm so glad to have found this place."

"You gave me a start when you rode in," Evans said. "I must confess that when I first saw you I thought you were Jim dressed like a woman."

He laughed and Belle asked him if Mountain Jim often dressed like a woman.

"I heard a story about a time when he wanted to avenge a friend's death," Evans said. "They say he dressed up in a black gown and waited for the man he was after in a whore house in Colorado Springs."

"Did he get his man?"

"He always gets his man. That's why you don't want him against you."

"So you know him quite well?"

"We came to this valley about the same time. Sometimes we see eye to eye, sometimes we don't."

"When I spoke with him he seemed quite pleasant."

"He must be out of whiskey. When he's sober, he is a perfect gentleman."

Belle's cabin stood at the edge of the lake, against a grove of quaking aspens. A window near the door faced the water and the towering peaks behind it, now drenched in purple light.

She took in the scene with wonder and listened while a loon called from the opposite shore. Chickadees flitted among the trees and small swallows swooped and darted over the surface of the water.

Evans opened the door and lit a lantern. Inside, a small pine table covered with a blue checkered cloth and three chairs sat near the window that faced the lake. A stone chimney stood on one side of the room while a door in the opposite wall opened into a small bedroom.

On a pine bedframe lay a hay mattress covered with a blue checkered bedspread. A chair at the door held a tin basin, and a shelf and a few pegs hung from the wall.

"The door has no lock," Evans said. "In fact, I doubt if you'll get it to close all the way. It's swelled from moisture."

"That won't bother me. How much?"

"Eight dollars a week. That includes the use of any of the horses. Breakfast at seven every day but you can eat anytime. The kitchen is always open."

"I'll take it."

"You can stay here as long as you'd like. There's another cabin back along the trail for the two young men, if they've a mind to take it."

"I should think they would. They can't do better."

"Very good. Bring your horse over and get yourself settled. Supper will be on soon."

Evans left and Belle sat in the rocker, enjoying the last moments of twilight. The swallows were still active, diving up and down and around, making small cries as the darkness settled in.

With the last light touching the top of Longs Peak, she rose from the rocker and started off the porch, where she met Rodgers and Downer leading their horses. Downer had her horse as well and handed her the reins.

"Mr. Evans says he's got a place for us up the trail." He pointed. "A little cabin not far back."

"Good," Belle said. "Hobble your horses and we'll go to supper."

Everyone gathered in the main cabin. A steer had been freshly butchered and the evening meal consisted of tenderloin, potatoes and gravy, and garden vegetables. Genevieve Evans had baked fresh bread that morning and she served it with homemade butter.

Belle helped her set the table and bring the food from the kitchen.

"My friends call me Genny," she told Belle. "I trust we'll be friends from now on."

"I have no doubt we will," Belle said. "I haven't been so happy and comfortable in a long time."

"You can stay as long as you like. In fact, I overheard Griff telling someone that he'd like to put you to work herding cattle, if you'd like to try it."

"I would indeed like to, after I climb Longs Peak."

"I don't want to discourage you, but it's so late in the year that I'm afraid you won't find a guide."

"I see no problem with the weather."

"The weather can change at any time now. A snowstorm can come that will trap us here for the season. In fact, we're trying to get the cattle down from the slopes before we go to Denver."

Belle was puzzled. Evans had just told her she could stay as long as she liked but Genny was talking about leaving.

"You don't live here year-round?" Belle asked.

"Oh, no, the weather's too much for us. I'll take the children to school in Denver and Griff will come back up until the hunting season is passed."

Belle had already noticed that the boarders were not of the working class she had seen down below. These were men with money who had come to hunt and relax.

"We're hoping in time to devote all our efforts to taking sportsmen out for game," Genny continued. "Raising livestock up here is a tough go."

"You need a lot of land for hunting, don't you?"

"Griff is working with a man from the British Isles, hoping to secure enough land to make the plan plausible."

"Lord Dunraven?"

"Yes, do you know him?"

"I've only heard of him. It's all the talk down below, this trouble that's started up here."

"There's only one man causing trouble and that's Jim Nugent."

"I understand that most of the settlers are worried about your plan," Belle said.

"If they could see the benefit in it for them, they would be pleased. But all they know is hard work, beating yourself to the bone. I, for one, don't want to live that way any longer."

A woman came into the kitchen through the back door, carrying two pails of fresh milk.

"This is Ellie Edwards," Genny said. "Her husband, Lem, is Griff's partner in the ranch."

Ellie nodded politely and began pouring the milk into a separator.

Belle had yet to meet Lemuel Edwards, Griff Evans's partner. They had three children, all boys eight and under. The two youngest trooped into the kitchen and seated themselves at a rough table.

They were followed by Genny's four young children, three girls ages seven, six and five, and a boy of four, who crowded onto chairs at the same table, the smaller ones seating themselves on the laps of the older ones.

Genny's oldest daughter, Molly, seventeen and very pretty, joined the women, curtsying when introduced to Belle.

Lemuel Edwards then walked into the kitchen, a tall, lanky man in his middle thirties, with dark, thinning hair and a long, somber face. He had been one of the men herding the milch cows in from pasture.

He inspected his two sons, who sat stiff as boards.

"Where's Samuel?"

Neither of them spoke.

"I asked you two a question."

One of them pointed. "Here he comes."

Sam Edwards entered the room, head down, and sat down next to his brothers.

"Samuel, why are you late for supper?" his father asked.

"I was feeding my dog."

"Your dog can wait. Do you understand, young man?"

"I'm sorry."

"You won't let it happen again, will you?"

"No, sir."

Lemuel Edwards addressed all his children. "I want no talking while you eat. Is that understood?"

The boys remained stiff, careful not to make eye contact.

"And when you're finished, it's straight to bed."

Ellie had been standing behind him. When he turned, she said, "Lemuel, this is Miss Bird, the traveling lady."

Sam turned quickly, his eyes big, but turned and lowered his head when his father noticed him.

Edwards studied Belle. "I'm pleased to meet you, though I don't agree with your ways."

"I'm sorry you feel that way."

"What I mean is, I don't understand a woman who travels and does not stay at home."

"Not all women stay at home, Mr. Edwards."

He nodded, unconvinced, and left the kitchen. Ellie began talking about fresh cream and how just a little added to flour with the milk and yeast yielded the tastiest bread and biscuits.

"It's hard to imagine anything better," she said. "Unless, of course, its pie dough with a hint of cream, and more fresh cream to cover the berry pie when its brought from the oven."

Ellie continued to separate the milk, talking all the while as if everyone were listening intently. Belle and Genny dished up huge platters of steak and potatoes.

"Ellie spends too much time in the kitchen," Genny said, ladling gravy into a large bowl. "Griff and Lem work together, but they seldom agree. It's astonishing that they've been able to make a go of it as well as they have."

"Maybe it's the law of opposites," Belle said.

The men ate first, saying little. Rodgers and Downer sat

among them, taking advantage of the abundant food. The women stood back, drinking tea and waiting to serve someone if needed.

In the kitchen the children gobbled their food, some of them sharing a single plate. When Belle came in for more gravy, Sam Edwards stared at her and finally said, "Do you remember me?"

"I certainly do."

"Tell my brothers and the Evans kids how you ride horses all over the world."

"I like to travel," Belle said. "And I love horses, but I haven't exactly been all over the world."

"Would you tell us some stories about where you've been?"

Ellie said, "Sam, you should eat, not talk."

"But I met her on the train."

"You heard me. You don't want your father to hear, do you?"

He frowned and filled his mouth with potatoes.

"I'm sorry," Ellie said. "He talks a lot."

"I'm sure he means no harm," Belle said.

"He's been talking about you ever since he got home. Do you have any children?"

"No, I've never married," Belle said.

"Perhaps you'll meet a gentleman during your stay here."

"Well, I'm not really looking for a gentleman. I'm looking for scenery and I've certainly found that."

After small pieces of apple cobbler, the children hurried to their rooms, all except Sam. He began talking to Belle and had to be escorted from the kitchen by his mother.

The men adjourned to the main room to resume their stories. Rodgers and Downer settled in to listen, keeping their eyes open for Molly.

Belle took a seat with the women. Molly joined them, smiling sheepishly.

"She's wondering if you don't get afraid riding through the wilderness all by yourself," Genny said.

"I'm never alone," Belle said. "I always have my horse to

talk to and the forest is filled with birds and other creatures. Besides, the Almighty is always with me."

"Amen," Ellie said.

Genny said grace over the food, thanking God for bringing Belle to their table, and they ate with little conversation. The men's laughter drifted into the room, along with the smoke of nearly a dozen pipes.

After the meal Belle helped with the dishes and paused in the living room briefly, listening while the men sang a chorus of "D'ye ken John Peel?"

Evans sang loudest, holding his glass of brandy high. He noticed Belle and excused himself from the group.

"Are you ready to retire?"

"Yes, but Mr. Rodgers and Mr. Downer will escort me."

"I don't believe they've had enough just yet. They seem quite enthralled with it all."

"Indeed, they do. I'll just wait until they're ready."

"Nonsense. I'll take you."

He grabbed a lantern and Belle followed him up the trail. The grass, crisp with frost, crunched under her feet.

"My what a beautiful evening," she said. "And the air is so pure. I almost feel lightheaded."

"It will take some getting used to."

Owls hooted in the trees and from the distance came a long howl.

"Wolves," Evans said. "They prowl the passes and often come down into the park looking for elk or crippled livestock."

At the cabin Belle viewed the North Star, shining like a lamp in the sky. The surface of the lake was alive with trout jumping in the moonlight.

Inside, Evans lit a candle. "I understand Ellie has already asked if you might be interested in driving cattle with us."

"I would like to, after I climb the peak."

"How will you get up there?"

"I'm hoping to find a guide."

"There's one who could take you but I'd advise you stay clear of him."

"Mr. Nugent?"

"Yes, please heed my warning."

She walked to the door and looked out over the lake.

"I do not see him as the ruffian they say he is."

"Believe me, he's an outlaw."

Belle turned and studied Evans. "Is it because you two don't agree on the future of Estes Park?"

"Begging your pardon, Miss Bird, but you shouldn't involve yourself in these troubles."

"I'm afraid it's too late for that."

"I want to be friends, Miss Bird."

"As do I, Mr. Evans. I believe you to be a man of strong principles, whether others see them as right or wrong. I only hope that you can understand my position as well."

"I shall strive to do that, Miss Bird. Enjoy your stay."

After he left, Belle stood outside the cabin and watched the trout jump. All her life she had expressed her viewpoints on controversial issues, having learned to do so from her father and her relatives on his side of the family. Her cousin, William Wilberforce, had led the fight to abolish slavery in England and her aunts, living at Taplow Hill, had refused sugar in their tea to protest slavery in that industry.

In Scotland, she had joined a committee of Edinburgh women determined to help the Highland farmers. Wealthy landowners were changing over from crops to grazing sheep, displacing the farmers and leaving them and their families to starve.

Belle had written contacts in Canada and soon shiploads of Highland families were crossing the ocean, eager to begin a new life.

With the farmers on their way, Belle had taken up a new cause. The poor in Edinburgh were being forced out by developers tearing down the old neighborhoods to make room for upper- and middle-class housing. The city's Old Town overflowed with the sick and starving.

She had written a series of articles, entitled *Notes on Edinburgh,* detailing the hellish living conditions she observed, describing naked and starving children. She had even petitioned the town council for washrooms and running water, but her pleas went unheard.

Land issues in a remote part of Colorado seemed to pale by comparison, yet she could feel the same frustration. She had begun to feel very strongly about the concept of preserving this wilderness. She knew that hunting clubs in England had depleted large populations of game and it bothered her to think of that happening in Estes Park.

She returned to the cabin and sat down at the table with the lantern and some paper. She thought about writing to Henrietta concerning the problems in Estes Park, but decided against it. Her sister had often heard her viewpoints on political matters and had long since tired of them.

So Belle confined her letters to describing the magnificent scenery and commenting on the people she met.

She arranged her bed and snuggled in. The cabin was quiet and she soon began to drift off to sleep, only to be awakened by a scratching under her bed. She lay petrified, unable to get up and check on the disturbance, for her candle had burned out.

The scratching persisted but it seemed to be of no threat and she quickly gave in to exhaustion, falling into the deepest and most satisfying sleep she had enjoyed in a very long time.

ELEVEN

Mountain Splendor

So in this glorious upper world, with the mountain pines behind and the clear lake in front, in the "blue hollow at the foot of Longs Peak," at a height of 7,500 feet, where the hoar frost crisps the grass every night of the year, I have found far more than I ever dared to hope for.

ISABELLA BIRD

September

Belle awakened early, scarcely believing that her hair hadn't whitened from her experience the previous night. She eased out of her blankets and checked under the bed. Nothing but dust balls and a few mouse droppings, something to be taken care of later with a broom.

The morning felt fresh and the open sky shone deep blue overhead. The lake was covered with ducks and Canada geese, swimming leisurely, preening their feathers. The swallows were again darting and diving over the surface of the water and not far away, a mule deer drank from the shallows, his head crowned with a rack of large antlers.

She arrived at the lodge in time to help prepare breakfast. The women talked about their work for the day and their work for the next day, worrying about adequate time to harvest their garden.

"Winter will be here and we won't have all the spuds and onions in," Genny was saying. "There's not enough time in the days, with the sun going down earlier and earlier."

The men came in for breakfast and Belle mentioned that a strange noise under her cabin had nearly driven her mad.

Evans, nursing a hangover, cracked a little smile. "Was it a loud scratching noise?"

"Yes, and very loud," Belle said.

Edwards, forking through his breakfast, frowned.

"I hope you didn't investigate."

"I would have, had my candle still burned."

"Thank the good Lord," Genny said, "that your candle burned out."

Belle looked at them. "My goodness, my bed's not big enough to harbor a bear beneath it."

Evans laughed. "No, it's worse. You've met the skunk."

"The skunk?"

"We haven't named him yet but he's becoming quite a pet."

"I'd rather he wasn't there," Belle said.

"Do you know how to get rid of a skunk when he doesn't want to leave?" Evans asked.

"I see your point."

"He won't bother you if you don't go poking at him," Evans said. "Live and let live is the order of the day."

After breakfast Belle walked back to her cabin. On her way she met Rodgers and Downer, mounted on their horses.

"We're going to check out the valley," Downer said. "Would you care to accompany us?"

Belle realized Downer was being polite.

"Thank you," she said, "but I must decline. Why don't you ask Molly Evans?"

"Her mother's watching her like a hawk."

Belle smiled. "Good luck elsewhere."

The two rode off and Belle entered the cabin and settled into a chair at the table. She had just begun a letter to Henrietta when Sam Edwards burst in with a yellow lab mix that stood as tall as the boy's chest.

"This is my dog, Plunk," he said. "Sorry, I should have knocked."

Plunk sniffed Belle's hand and allowed her to scratch his ear, his tail wagging.

"He says he likes you."

"He's a very nice dog."

"I wanted to talk to you last night but I couldn't. My father's still mad at me for going on the train."

"Does your father know you're here now?"

"I just wanted to hear a quick story. I'll even sing you a song first, to make it even."

Sam broke into his own personal version of a popular tune, changing lines liberally whenever the need arose:

> John Brown's body lies a-smoldering in the grave
> John Brown's body lies older in the grave
> John Brown's body lies a soldier in the grave
> His soil goes marching on.

"Now," Sam said. "Tell me a story about Rocky Mountain Jim. You met him yesterday, didn't you?"

"I don't know that much about him."

"Didn't he tell you how he shot men in Denver and how he fought Indians along the Overland Trail?"

"Do you think he's all that bad?"

"I don't know. I want to meet him sometime. My father says he's bad, but he says Lord Dunraven is good, and I don't believe him. He was here once. He didn't even look at me. Do you know him?"

"I've never met the man."

"Mother says he can make life real good for us. I don't think it's us who he wants to make life good for. Maybe just himself."

Genny Evans began shouting from her doorway. "Sam! Where are you?"

"Uh-oh," Sam said. "I didn't tell her where I was going. Could you walk back with me? She won't be as mad then."

Sam put his hand in Belle's as they walked toward the lodge, with Plunk right behind. Genny stood waiting, her hands on her hips, covered with flour.

"Samuel Jeramiah Evans, where have you been?"

"You can blame me," Belle said. "I thought it would be nice to hear him sing."

"You took him all the way to your cabin?"

"I think we met partway, didn't we, Sam?"

Sam knew enough to keep his mouth shut.

"I just worry about him is all," Genny said. "You know, with outlaws in the area."

"I was safe," Sam said.

"You know the rules, young man. I'll let it go this time. Don't let it happen again."

Sam ran off with Plunk to join the other children playing stick horse, riding around the lodge on broom and mop handles, using twine and cord as bridles.

"He's so difficult to handle," Genny said. "If his father knew half the stunts he's pulled . . ."

"I'm sure he'll grow up to be a wonderful man," Belle said.

Genny went back to baking and Belle returned to her cabin to write her letter. She couldn't concentrate and walked outside to watch the swallows swoop over the lake's surface.

She thought about little Sam, wondering why he had taken a liking to her. She didn't know what to say to him. He was obviously a very good boy and better behaved than most.

She went back into the cabin and struggled with the letter before lying down on her bed. The warm sun shone in and the sounds of a slight breeze rustling the leaves outside put her quickly to sleep.

❖ ❖ ❖

She awakened in midafternoon and took a walk along the lake shore, discovering more of the ranch. On the banks of Fish Creek, a stream that flowed from the lake, she found a small dairy made of logs, with a waterwheel used for churning butter. Nearby stood a shed for housing wagons and a corral for livestock.

A hired man lived in a room off the dairy, there primarily to care for sick cows and calves.

Belle had noticed him the night before, receiving bread and meat from Genny at the back door and leaving before the guests sat down to eat.

"I hope I'm not bothering you," she said.

He turned from pail-feeding an orphaned calf.

"You won't bother me none. In fact, I'm glad to have the company."

He stared at her and smiled. Most of his teeth were missing, his face was unshaven, and his hair was long and unkempt beneath a soiled felt hat.

"You needn't be afraid of me," he said.

"I'm not."

"Good, then you can help me hold this calf."

He showed her how to press the calf against the long wall of the shed with her left knee, and with her right knee and leg, block its hind feet. Belle showed him that she already knew the trick.

"You've spent time with animals," he said.

"Horses, mainly. I'm Isabella Bird, up here to sightsee."

"I know who you are. Everybody does. My name is Beasley and I hail from Virginia."

Belle knew better than to inquire as to how and why he had come to Colorado. She had learned that in the American West such questions were never asked.

She held the calf tightly while Beasley forced its nose into the pail of milk, pressing his finger between the lips and teeth. The calf began sucking on his finger, gulping in milk at the same time.

"He'll be drinking on his own in no time," he said.

"I see you have a few more in the corral."

"There's more work than I can get done. I hear you want to climb Longs Peak."

"That has been a dream of mine since I arrived in Colorado."

"Don't dally, if you're serious."

"I'm very serious, but Mrs. Evans told me the weather wouldn't cooperate."

"Maybe she wants you to stay around here and help her husband with the cattle. He's always short on hands."

"He's already approached me on that himself. Maybe after I climb the peak. Do you know the way up?"

"Oh, no, ma'am. I'm no climber. There's one in particular who could guide you, but I don't know if I'd trust him. Maybe there's one other I could ask for you."

The calf finished feeding and Belle released it.

"How soon could you ask?"

"Give me a day or two. I have to get these calves to drinking on their own or they'll die."

"I understand. I've noticed this is a big operation. Mr. Evans and Mr. Edwards must do very well."

"There's nigh on to a thousand head of cattle scattered hereabouts, a lot of them longhorns from Texas. And there's fifty head of horses. They could do a lot better if they'd get me some help. But I don't see that happening."

"I understand they want to give it all up, to make Estes Park an exclusive hunting camp."

"If you want my opinion, it's a lot of foolishness. That Dunraven character is taking Griff Evans for a ride."

Beasley went on to say everyone knew that Dunraven was bringing men from Denver to settle on land not yet claimed. After the land had been surveyed the following spring and they had proven up, he would purchase their interest in the property. Using this method he would soon acquire the deed to much of Estes Park.

"The main thing going for us is the government land up here," Beasley said. "Dunraven can't get that for his own. But he'll take everything else unless he's stopped."

"A pity," Belle said. "Mr. Evans seems like a nice sort of fellow."

"He's carefree, that's for certain, not like Lem Edwards, who's so tight he squeaks."

"Who does Mr. Edwards side with?"

"I don't think he really knows how serious this all is. If he does, he won't let on."

"What will happen when he realizes what's going on?"

"He'll do whatever Evans wants. He don't approve of Griff's ways but he won't argue. As for Griff, I don't think he's using his head. You don't intend to tell him that, I hope."

"Of course not. But knowing English aristocracy as I do, it will be hard to persuade this Lord Dunraven to abandon his plan."

"There'll be somebody who'll persuade him," Beasley said, "and he's riding up the trail right now."

Jim Nugent, mounted on a striking Arab mare, dismounted and tipped his cap. He had covered his bad eye with a rawhide patch and had combed his long hair.

"I was just headed to Black Canyon to check my traps. I thought I'd pay a visit." He looked at Beasley. "I hope I'm not interrupting anything."

Beasley stared at the revolver in Nugent's belt. "You certainly are not. We were just talking about Lord Dunraven."

"Are there any more of his squatters in the valley?"

"I haven't seen a one," Beasley said. "But I haven't been out for a spell."

"Let me know if you see any." He turned to Belle. "Might I escort you on a walk around the lake?"

"That would be pleasant."

They bid Beasley a good day and walked back toward the cabins, Jim leading the mare behind him.

"How do you like it up here?" he asked.

"This is the most beautiful country in the world."

"I'm glad you think so, too. I don't ever want to see it change."

"You have to allow for some change, Jim."

"I'm talking about bad change. I think you know what I mean."

"Yes, I've heard all about Lord Dunraven. To hear it, one would think he was organizing an army to conquer this area."

"Not an army, just a bunch of two-bit squatters he pulled out of the saloons in Denver."

"I hear you tried to shoot two of them."

"No, but I ruined their checker game."

"What would you do if they came back?"

"They won't."

"Others will take their place. Then what?"

"It's too nice of a day to discuss such things. Let's forget about Dunraven and you can tell me about your stay so far."

"We would only be talking about another skunk."

He laughed. "Are you telling me that you don't like Griff Evans?"

"No, Mr. Evans isn't all that bad. There's a real skunk under my cabin."

"I would sooner deal with the real thing than Dunraven and Griff Evans."

They crossed behind the lodge and took the trail to Belle's cabin. Molly and the children were out digging potatoes. The kids all went dashing to the lodge except Sam. He came running with his dog.

"I'm glad to meet you, Mr. Mountain Jim." He held out his hand.

Nugent laughed and shook with the boy. "That's a good dog you've got."

"His name is Plunk. The reason he's smelling your pants is because he knows you have a dog, too."

"Yes, his name is Ring. Maybe you can meet him sometime."

Sam turned to Belle. "Will you tell me a story now, Miss Bird?"

"I'll tell you one tonight, Sam. Now run along."

Sam walked away disappointed.

"Why didn't you tell him a story?" Jim asked. "He's a likable kid."

"I just don't think I'm that good at it."

"You don't know how to tell stories to kids? Or aren't you comfortable around them?"

Belle began stroking the mare's neck. "She's a beauty."

"You know, kids can teach you things if you'll let them."

"Is she a good mountain horse?"

He realized Belle wanted to change the subject. "The best," he said. "As surefooted as you could ask for."

"I'm hoping to find a good horse among those that Mr. Evans owns. The gelding I rode here on has turned up lame."

"He has a lot of good horses."

"One that can take me to Longs Peak?"

"We'll go out and find one."

They circled the north end of the lake on foot, closing in on a small herd of horses that had come to drink. Belle pointed to a stout roan mare.

"I like her."

Jim mounted his Arab and uncoiled a rope. A shout from the water's edge stopped him.

"Nugent, what are you doing?"

Griff Evans rode up and demanded again to know why Jim was in his horse pasture with a rope in his hands.

"I'm catching a mare for Miss Bird," he said. "Didn't you say she could have her pick of the herd?"

"I'll catch the horse for her."

"I don't understand the problem," Belle said.

"Mr. Nugent and I had a prior discussion. He's not allowed on my ranch." He turned to Jim. "The lady's presence does not give you the right to catch my horses."

"I just wanted to help her."

"I was hoping to have a horse for a trip up to Longs Peak," Belle said. "I intend to go, one way or the other."

Evans studied her and took a deep breath. "The weather is good now and may continue to cooperate."

"I shall go whether or not it cooperates," Belle said.

"Who's going to guide you?"

"I don't know yet."

Evans glanced at Nugent. "Even if you don't reach the top," he said, "it will be worth the journey just to see the view from the timberline."

"I believe I'll make it all the way up," Belle said.

Evans then announced that he was leaving for Denver in the morning on business and would likely be gone most of the week.

"And, Mr. Nugent," he added, "I will count on your absence from this land from now on."

Jim turned to Belle. "Will you excuse us for a moment, please?" He jumped on his horse and motioned for Evans to follow him.

When they had ridden a distance away, Nugent said, "I intend to see that Miss Bird gets to the top of that mountain. And that means that I'll have to come back here to get her."

"You'll have to make other arrangements."

"Didn't you tell me that I could never do a decent thing for anyone? That I would never be able to make a good account of myself?"

"I did say that."

"Well, this is one time in my life that I can do good by someone. There's no one else who can get her up there."

Evans thought a moment. "I suppose you're right. But she won't stand for your drinking."

"I don't intend to drink."

"And there's the two students. They'll want to go."

"I anticipated that."

They rode back to where Belle waited. Evans said, "Mr. Nugent has agreed to guide you up on the mountain. Will that be satisfactory?"

Belle smiled. "That will be excellent."

"I could lend you a pair of my hunting boots, if you'd like," he told Belle. "I don't believe yours are equal to the task. Enjoy your climb."

When Evans had left, Jim smiled and said, "Let's catch that mare for you."

TWO

❖

THE CLIMB

TWELVE

Traveling Toward the Clouds

There were dark pines against a lemon sky, grey peaks reddening and etherealizing, gorges of deep and infinite blue, floods of golden glory pouring through canyons of enormous depth, an atmosphere of absolute purity, an occasional foreground of cottonwood and aspen flaunting in red and gold to intensify the blue gloom of the pines, the trickle and murmur of streams fringed with icicles, the strange sough of gusts moving among the pine tops—sights and sounds not of the lower earth, but of the solitary, beast-haunted, frozen upper altitudes.

ISABELLA BIRD

September

After three days of preparation, Mountain Jim led the way toward Longs Peak. Ring, excited about going along, ran back and forth, barking.

Equipped with fresh bread tied in bundles and beef packed in tins, along with tea, sugar, and butter, the party would be well fed. Rodgers and Downer, eager to make time, broke into the lead often and were finally told by Nugent that they would take orders from him or turn back.

In her Hawaiian dress, with three blankets and a quilt tied on behind her saddle, Belle felt ready to face any weather. She felt comfortable in Evans's boots, though she had to wear three pairs of socks to make them snug.

Jim wore knee-high boots and deerhide trousers belted by the red scarf that held his knife and revolver, a leather shirt, and three waistcoats, one over the other. In place of his wolf-skin caps he wore a large hat that shielded his entire face.

"There's plenty of sun up there," he said, "and the wind can cut you like a knife."

He had tied a beaver skin to the seat of his saddle, complete with paws that hung down and flopped when the Arab mare trotted. A canteen and an ax hung from the saddle horn and he held a Springfield rifle across the saddle in front of him.

Ring remained near Jim's horse, looking up at his master often. Finally, the mountain man allowed him to go ahead a short distance and the dog loped off, coming back shortly as if to say that the way ahead was safe.

After crossing the frost-cured bottom of Estes Park, they took a steep trail along a gorge and emerged into a grassy valley where they found the Lake of the Lilies. Here they stopped to rest and water the horses, allowing them to graze in the deep grass.

"We'll let them graze as often as they want down here," Jim said. "Once we get up in the rocks, there won't be a lot of feed."

As they sat at the water's edge, Belle marveled at the beauty, which she considered magical, sleeping in silence. She stared at the dark pines, mirrored motionless in the lake, and myriads of great white lily cups and dark green leaves resting gently on the sunlit surface.

Rodgers walked over to where she and Jim sat. Ring, who lay next to them in the grass, raised his head and growled.

"Don't come up behind him so quick," Jim said.

"I don't know why we're waiting here," Rodgers said. "We'd be better off to get going."

"I told you, the horses need plenty of feed before we get to climbing those high rocks."

"Haven't they eaten enough?"

"You go on ahead, if you're so anxious. We'll catch up. But if your horse weakens and you lag behind, I'll leave you for the bears. And that's a promise."

Downer came over and took Rodgers by the arm, pulling him aside.

"Don't you know enough to shut your mouth?"

"I just can't understand lollygagging around."

"Maybe you should ask if you can lead the way."

"Oh, sure. He'd feed me to that dog for breakfast."

The two of them walked away and Belle, who was still staring out over the lake, said, "If it were possible, I'd want to be buried here."

"I suppose that could be arranged."

"I didn't mean right now."

"No," he said with a laugh, "when you're old and gray."

"I'm getting closer and closer."

"Well, you look good to me."

"You just want to keep my spirits up."

"I meant it. You're a very attractive lady. Maybe it's your eyes when you see a mother duck leading her young through the water, or your smile when the wind blows through the pine trees. You're the first woman I've ever met who loves this land as much as I do."

They resumed their journey, ascending into a deep pine forest where the light was scarce and the shadows long. The floor lay soft underfoot, layered with mulch and pine needles. From moist pockets sprouted delicate lady-slipper lilies, and the beautiful three-petaled trilliums.

At the edge of a meadow where more sunlight prevailed, Belle dismounted and knelt beside a patch of wood lilies, their striped red petals brilliant in the moist dew of the forest.

"The God of our fathers certainly lives here," Belle said.

They broke from the forest onto a rocky trail where she

stopped to look back. To the east, below the expanse of ever-
green slopes and purple gorges, rolled the endless Great Plains,
clothed in the shades of autumn, appearing, as she told her sister, as a "baked, brown expanse transfigured into the likeness
of a sunset sea rolling infinitely in waves of misty gold."

The traveling became difficult. The trail grew ever steeper
and choked with dead trees, whose sharp and broken limbs
tore at the riders and their supplies. With little room to pass,
they were forced to fight their way forward single file and
stop often to rest.

Belle took her turn with the ax, knocking sharp limbs
aside and chopping through deadfall timber. Her horse,
breathing heavily from the climb, often leaned against trees
for support and, reluctant to move, had to be severely prod-
ded to continue.

Once, while everyone sat down to gather strength, Belle
could hear her breath rattling in her lungs. Jim, nearby, was
rasping, almost gagging.

"What is it, Mr. Nugent?" Belle said.

"Don't worry yourself," he said.

"Do you need assistance?"

"No," he said sharply.

With a pained look on his face, he took a few deep
breaths, then got up quickly and lost himself in the dead trees,
Ring following closely behind.

Rodgers and Downer stared at Belle. They could all hear
him coughing and vomiting.

"Is he going to die?" Rodgers said.

"You're always worried about something," Downer said.
"Why don't you just relax?"

"He'll be fine. Won't he, Miss Bird?" Rodgers asked.

"I believe he will," Belle said. "Let's not be alarmed."

Nugent returned and sat down. Belle could see traces of
blood at the corners of his mouth.

An eerie stillness settled in, broken only by dead branches
creaking in the wind and Ring's occasional whining.

"He's worried about you," Belle said. "As am I."

"It's nothing, just a chest cold is all."

"My heaviest colds have never been that bad."

"I would appreciate it if you'd stop fretting about me."

"I apologize," she said, and turned her attention to the forest. "This is an ancient place and very awe-inspiring."

"It's as old as time up here," Jim said.

"Here no lumberer's ax has ever rung."

"Nor ever will."

"How much farther?" Rodgers asked.

"We'll camp up ahead," Jim said, rising to his feet, "and ascend tomorrow, rain or shine."

They resumed their journey, passing out of the dead trees and through a belt of live timber, deformed and twisted, barren of either branches or needles on the windward side. A crisp breeze stung Belle's face and she imagined what an icy winter blast could do to anything unprotected in this hostile world.

Past the stunted trees lay only rock—an open, barren, broad-topped ridge that fell off on the southwest side to a secluded meadow. An ice-clogged stream twisted its way through spruce and dense clumps of grass and blue gentians.

Belle gazed upon the slope above. "The trees seem exquisitely arranged," she said. "their slim spires trained perfectly toward heaven."

"It's something truly special," Jim said.

The beauty escaped Rodgers and Downer. They had come for adventure and were interested only in the upcoming climb.

"That's where we'll be tomorrow," Rodgers said, pointing up and ahead.

Just ahead and nearly three thousand feet above them towered Longs Peak, its crest bald and pure white, reflecting the setting sun.

Belle helped Jim unsaddle and picket the horses while Rodgers and Downer collected firewood. Overhead the afterglow of evening gave way to a half moon that hung in the distance.

"Is that snow always there?" Belle asked, pointing to a glacier on the northeast side of the peak.

"Yes," he said. "All that leaves is what the terrible winds blow away."

"It looks quite peaceful up there tonight," Belle said.

Rodgers and Downer settled in, each with a tin of meat.

"Let's get our beds ready before we eat," Nugent said.

The pair groaned and headed into the trees. Jim showed Belle where she would sleep, beneath a crude arbor created by an artist who had attempted to climb Longs Peak the year before.

"He didn't make it up," Jim said. "The winds drove him back down and he left a lot of equipment up there. You can have the shelter he built."

She arranged her bed, inverting her saddle for a pillow and spreading her blankets over freshly cut boughs. After rearranging the pine matting several times, she felt comfortable and returned to where Jim had built a huge fire. Rodgers and Downer were lounging in their beds, watching the flames dance.

They opened four of the beef tins and cut the meat into strips. They skewered the strips on peeled branches and roasted them over the fire. Belle used the empty tins to boil tea and soon they were all eating with their fingers and drinking from the warm cans.

Ring begged for tidbits and Jim fed him, then handed Belle a strip of meat.

"He'll love you forever."

Belle dangled the beef in front of the dog and he gently took it from her, swallowing it after one loud chew.

She remained at the fire while Jim got up to cut more wood. Though the flames rose high, she covered herself in a blanket to ward off the chill that came from a breeze at her back.

"Go to that lady and don't leave her again tonight," Jim told Ring.

The dog walked over and laid beside Belle, placing his head on her shoulder and then moving it to her lap, keeping his eyes on his master.

"This isn't necessary," Belle said.

"It'll get cold tonight. I checked the thermometer and it's fallen twelve degrees below frost already."

Rodgers tossed another limb on the fire. "We won't freeze up here, will we?"

"Not if you keep the fire going."

Downer laughed. "If we have to depend on him, we'll be ice cubes tomorrow."

"Why don't we all sing a song together," Belle suggested. "Let's begin with a thanks to our great God, who made all this beautiful country and has allowed us one and all to enjoy it. You all know 'I Am Dwelling on the Mountain,' don't you?"

They all nodded.

Belle led:

> *I am dwelling on the mountain,*
> *Where the golden sunlight gleams.*
> *O'er a land whose wondrous beauty*
> *Far exceeds my fondest dreams.*

> *Where the flowers bloom forever,*
> *And the sun is always bright.*
> *Is not this the land of Beula?*
> *Blessed, blessed land of light.*

Downer harmonized and Jim's voice rang loud and clear, pleasing Belle.

"My gracious!" she said. "That was wonderful. Shall we try another?"

Downer broke into "Sweet Spirit, Hear my Prayer" while the others listened. He then sang a song in Latin and followed with a chorus of a Negro spiritual.

When he had finished, Belle asked, "How did you learn such a song?"

"I grew up in Mississippi," he said. "From the time I was

old enough to walk I heard them singing in the fields, every day, dawn to dusk."

"That time has passed," Belle said. "It's my hope that all countries will follow suit."

"The war might be over," Downer said, "but it won't ever be forgotten."

"A few years ago, someone wanted to start slavery here in the fields between Longmont and Fort Collins," Rodgers said. "A marshal from Denver had to step in or there would have been shootings."

"We had those kinds of battles in Britain," Belle said. "I remember how strongly my father protested slavery, as well as all his family. I believe that's why he was run out of one parish."

"Enough of that," Jim said. He led everyone in "The Star-Spangled Banner" and "The Red, White, and Blue," and followed with an original poem:

> Ay, the wind has sang a song of love
> And brought a maiden fair,
> Whose eyes can make the hardest man
> Melt like spring's gentle breath of air.
>
> Oh, the nights that once were cloudy
> And filled with the dreams of woe,
> Now rest so gently on the land
> Where peaceful waters flow.

"You wrote that?" Downer said.

"Yes. Just a few days ago." He looked at Belle.

"Do they come from your past?" Rodgers asked. "I mean, are they inspired by your adventures?"

"Some are. Others come from just sitting in the mountains."

"You have a natural talent," Belle said. "Maybe you should publish some of them."

"Maybe, in time. Let me sing you a song my grandfather taught me."

He began the song, thinking of his grandfather and his friends, the Kirby brothers:

I am a young sailor, my story is sad;
Oh, once I was carefree and a brave sailor lad.
I courted a lassie by night and by day;
Ah, but now she has left me and sailed far away.

If I was a blackbird, could whistle and sing,
I'd follow the vessel my true love sails in.
And in the top riggin' I would there build my nest,
And flutter my wings o'er her lily white breast.

"I've heard that song," Belle said. "You say your grandfather taught it to you."

"Yes. He went to sea when I was young and never returned."

There was silence and Rodgers leaned forward anxiously.

"Maybe you should write down your stories about the life you've led. They say you used to fight Indians and that you guided soldiers."

"I've done both but there wasn't a lot of glory in it, not like you've been led to believe."

"Didn't you help make this area safe for settlers?"

"That doesn't make me a hero, not in my book."

"But the Indians made it hard for the first people here."

"And we made it hard for them. A lot of people died and I could have been one of them. Luck and the Almighty saw me through it."

Everyone sat quiet. At last Belle said to Jim, "No one wants you to talk about those times if you don't want to."

"I need to. These two should know what happens when there's a real fight, not just a schoolyard tangle."

He began a story about how he and another mountain man had been hired by a freight company to guard three wagons headed up the Overland Trail.

"We got past Virginia Dale, up into Wyoming, when a war party of Sioux came at us. There were ten of them, all young and reckless. They came at us so fast we didn't know what hit us.

"My friend, Carter, took an arrow in the leg and another in the shoulder, but he didn't stop shooting. Lucky two of the freighters had Henry repeaters or I wouldn't be telling you this.

"They circled in on us and though we got three of them right away, the rest come in and jumped us from their horses. We started fighting hand to hand and I shot one in the face with my pistol and saw his mouth fill with blood. I cut another one across the middle and he stood there, holding his guts in his hands. I'll never forget, his eyes so big and round, staring at me. He finally slumped down and started singing his death song."

Rodgers and Downer stared. Belle turned away, holding her hand across her mouth.

"I heard Carter yell and I turned around. He had taken an arrow meant for me. It went clean through his stomach and out the other side. One of the freighters had gotten his head sliced nearly off. It was hanging by a strip of skin. Another freighter held him and tried to put his head back on."

Belle got up and walked away, tears filling her eyes. Downer and Rodgers both stared into the fire.

"There was one of those Sioux left," Jim went on. "He was riding away as fast as he could. I got on my horse and rode him down and shot him in the back of the head and then got off and emptied my pistol, point-blank, into his face until you couldn't tell it was a face anymore.

"It took me an hour to clean the blood and flesh out of the barrel and the cylinders, so I could reload and have it ready to fire again. The two freighters buried their partner and left for Denver. I stayed another day with Carter until he died. His stomach was bloated up like a barrel and I couldn't do a thing for him. That, gentleman, is what Indian fighting is like."

Belle stood off at a distance, looking up at Longs Peak,

the moonlight bathing the summit. She turned and looked back toward the fire.

Nugent was standing, rubbing his bad elbow. Memories of bears and Indians, and the effects of the cold, were filling him with pain.

"When you were washing at the creek earlier," Rodgers said, "I thought I saw a scar on your back. Did you get that from the Sioux? Or did somebody shoot you in the back?"

"We don't have time for any more of that tonight," Jim said. "We've got a tough climb ahead of us."

He left to check the horses. Belle made her way to bed, settling in under the arbor with Ring beside her. She lay facing the fire, watching Downer and Rodgers whisper back and forth.

Jim returned with more wood and heaped it on the flames. Belle watched him arrange his bed and crawl in.

Unable to sleep, she turned her thoughts toward the climb, listening to gusts of wind whip the treetops. Wolves howled in the distance and Ring, lying against her back, growled. Belle patted him gently.

"You'd protect me with your life, wouldn't you?"

She looked across the camp to where Nugent lay sleeping, his long locks fanned around his head and shoulders, resting as quiet as a small child. She wondered if there might be something she could do to help his troubled soul. She had, after all, promised her father that she would do good by others and relinquish her own selfish interests. Perhaps she had found a way to fulfill this desire.

She felt better thinking about it, realizing that more than reaching the top of Longs Peak, her goal was to get this man to understand that he was a worthwhile human being.

She closed her eyes, thinking of the words she would write to Henrietta, how exciting it was to lie on a mountain eleven thousand feet high, under twelve degrees of frost, with the stars shining down and the moon bathing the sky and the howls of wolves in the background, with pines for bedposts and a night lamp of flickering campfire flames.

THIRTEEN

Higher, Ever Higher

Serrated ridges, not much lower than that on which
we stood, rose, one beyond another, far as that pure
atmosphere could carry the vision, broken into
awful chasms deep with ice and snow, rising into
pinnacles piercing the heavenly blue with their cold,
barren grey, on and on forever.

ISABELLA BIRD

September

Dawn brought a lemon-colored sky and the deep croak of two ravens as they floated lazily overhead. Jim called Ring to him and took Rodgers and Downer to unhobble and water the horses. Downer hurried back to Belle's arbor.

"Jim says for you to come quick and see the sunrise!"

She and Downer hurried to where Nugent and Rodgers sat along the side of a hill, peering out through an opening in the trees onto an endless sea of plains. Past the yawning craters of rock and forest lay a blue-gray vastness that reached to the far horizon.

The sky, streaked with clouds of pink and scarlet, grew increasingly brighter, illuminating the land until it turned from gray to purple to a soft gold. The sun, appearing first as a streak of light, rose into a dazzling sphere that eased over the horizon. The peaks and ridges and mountainsides erupted into color and the land below continued to grow more brilliant.

" 'The Most High dwelleth not in temples made of hands,' " Belle said.

For the first time since the trip began, Rodgers was speechless. His eyes roamed the expanse of sky and land, his mouth agape.

Downer, equally as impressed, held his hands together as if in prayer.

They watched the sky change for a half hour before going back to camp for breakfast. After eating, the two young men left for a walk.

"I wish now I hadn't told that story last night," Jim said. "It wasn't proper."

"Maybe you should talk about it more, not less."

"You would listen?"

"If it would help you. I see a kind, gentle, caring man in you, Jim. I don't know why you torture yourself so."

"There's a lot about me you don't know."

"I'd like to get to know everything about you."

"No, you wouldn't. You don't even know the half of what I've done."

"Look toward the rest of your life. You can start anew, if you want to."

Downer and Rodgers walked back into camp. Jim began to douse the flames.

"We'd better get started."

They saddled the horses and packed their gear. The ascent began on horseback, along a steep trail that crossed the face of the lower rock slopes. Already Belle could see farther than she had ever been able to see in her life, and the vista made her gasp.

They reached the Lava Beds, which some called the Boulder Field, far different in structure from her Hawaiian experiences. Here the rocks had no live magma among them and the steam and smoke had died out ages ago.

They hobbled the horses and left them behind, as well as coats and extra gear. Belle was thankful she had no cumbersome clothes once they started the steep climb. The boots Evans had lent her proved too large, encumbering her attempts to place her feet among the rocks for sure footing. By a sheer stroke of luck she discovered a small pair of overshoes left along the trail.

"I would say these belonged to the Hayden expedition that passed through here," Jim said. "They were well outfitted."

Belle learned from Jim that Hayden had led surveying parties throughout the West, the first step in establishing legal boundaries within territories.

After she had fitted the overshoes, Belle climbed with the other three and quickly grew tired in the thin air. Even the two young men complained. Shelf after shelf of open rock lay ahead but they worked their way over it, talking about the view that would be waiting at the top.

Rodgers and Downer discussed the upcoming school year and wondered how many of their fellow students would believe the stories they would bring with them to class.

"A world-traveling woman from England and an Indian fighter," Rodgers was saying. "They'll think we're making it all up."

"One never knows who you'll meet in these parts," Downer said.

They climbed ever higher, nearing a landmark known as the Notch. The air grew ever thinner and they stopped often.

Belle noticed Jim coughing badly again.

"Maybe this wasn't such a good idea," she said.

"What kind of talk is that? I'll hear no more of it."

Just ahead lay the Notch, a knifelike ridge of large rock fragments only a few feet wide. The northern side, covered with ice and snow, swept some three thousand feet down at a steep angle. Far below, a lake of green water sparkled in the morning light. Belle spotted more lakes scattered at intervals throughout the wilderness.

She peered across the windswept summits, towering blocks of granite rising into ridges and peaks as far as she could see, breaking off abruptly into deep, shadow-laden chasms and dark green-forested slopes.

She viewed North Park, hazy in the distance, and Middle Park, snowbound and closed to travelers. She saw rivulets of water that broke off both sides of the Continental Divide, seeking their destination in either the Atlantic or the Pacific Ocean.

"Now's when the hard part starts," Jim said.

He tied a rope from himself to Belle, and Rodgers and Downer linked themselves in the same manner. They began the climb along the steep face, inching their way, clawing for handholds in the rock.

Loose fragments fell beneath Belle's feet and Jim often helped her along by dragging her up to him.

"You know," Rodgers remarked, "we'd be up there by now if it weren't for the lady."

Nugent looked down at him. "I wouldn't be up here at all if it weren't for the lady. You want to go ahead without us?"

"No, I didn't mean that."

"Maybe you'd better do less talking and more climbing."

Belle found herself silently agreeing with Rodgers. She had discovered that scaling this incredible peak had become a huge challenge. Though the vision of the vast landscape held her entranced, the sheer effort to attain it had drained her.

She thought about her sister and what she would say to her in the next letter. Never in her wildest dreams had she envisioned such difficulties. Her sore limbs had grown even sorer and her back felt as if it would snap at any time.

As they climbed higher they ran into sheets of sheer ice hanging on the face of the mountain. Jim halted the climb and went by himself to scout the trail ahead. Belle sat and rested with Rodgers and Downer.

"This is a lot harder than I thought it would be," Downer said.

"It's more than any of us bargained for," Belle said. She looked up toward the top of the peak. "We might as well be going to the moon."

Rodgers shivered. "It's about as cold here as on the moon, I'd say."

Nugent returned with disappointing news. "The way is blocked by more ice and snow. We'll have to go down and around, then come back up."

"Is there another route?" Downer asked.

"There are lots of other routes, but this is the easiest one."

"The *easiest* one?" Rodgers said. "I don't want anything to do with the hardest."

For two hours they descended, lowering themselves inch by inch, covering nearly two thousand feet. Pieces of rock came loose and Belle had to catch herself time and again, bruising her arms and legs, tiring herself nearly to exhaustion.

"Hang on!" Jim kept saying. "Keep going. We'll make it."

Their exertion brought on strong thirst. They shared the last of the water as they reached a deep ravine clogged with old snow.

For another two hours they descended one side and hauled themselves up the other, struggling to keep their balance as time and again rocks gave way to the touch. Nearly up the other side, Belle slid partway down while Jim struggled to hold her, skidding down the slope himself.

Downer and Rodgers managed to help and keep both Belle and Jim from sliding to the bottom, also providing refreshment by mixing a cut of ginger they had brought along with melted snow. They all drank and Belle felt invigorated instantly.

Ring seemed undisturbed and loped up and down the steep sides, barking whenever he felt it appropriate.

At the top of the ravine, they squeezed themselves through two huge pinnacles of rock and emerged at the Dog's

Lift. Everyone laughed when Downer pushed Ring up to Jim's waiting arms.

"Now, if only the dog could lift us," Rodgers said.

Belle arranged the rope under her arms and Rodgers offered to let her stand on his shoulders while Jim pulled her up. She squeezed through the rocks and found herself on a trail that twisted around the southwest end of the peak.

The two young men worked their way onto the trail and everyone sat, their lungs heaving. Jim coughed incessantly and Belle worried.

"We can stay here awhile," she said.

"No, let's not waste any time," he said. "We're without water now and the strongest test is in front of us."

The trail followed the curvature of the peak and allowed easier passage except for occasional overhanging rocks that had to be ducked under. Belle realized they had reached the most dangerous part of the climb, though she felt more confident than at any time previous. The rock ledge felt secure and the ascent was not vertical, as it had often been up to this point.

Ring would not test the ledge, however, and remained at the Dog's Lift, whining and finally settling down.

They continued along the ledge and stopped at times to view the scenery. Snowfields lay in every direction together with mountain lakes. Out on the distant plains, glistening watercourses joined to form the Platte River, and far to the south, Pikes Peak rose into the clouds.

"What I'd give to have some water right now," Rodgers said.

"Soon enough," Downer told him. "We'll do what we came up here for and you can drink all you want for the rest of your life."

The last five hundred feet took an hour to complete. Belle thought it more along the lines of scaling than of climbing. Only the slightest of footholds could be found and they spent more time searching for them than moving.

Finally at the top, she stood and waved her arms.

"We made it!" she said through swollen lips.

Jim smiled and hugged her.

She began to sing, the others joining in:

> For the beauty of the earth,
> For the beauty of the skies,
> For the love which from our birth
> Over and around us lies.
> Lord of all to Thee we raise,
> This is our hymn of grateful praise.

"We can all be proud," she said.

Everyone cheered. She walked around the small acre of summit, stepping carefully on the tops of bounders and fragments of rocks, easing herself over the ice and snow.

She viewed the world, triumphant in spirit. She thought of how she would describe it to Henrietta, what it was like to stand upon the top of the Rocky Mountains, tracing the course of the waters that ran to all oceans.

She jotted down a note. "Uplifted above love and hate and storms of passion, calm amidst the eternal silences, fanned by zephyrs and bathed in living blue, peace rested for that one bright day on the Peak."

Overhead, a cloud passed near enough to touch.

Jim stood off by himself, inhaling deeply, coughing. Closer to Belle, Rodgers began to cough blood.

"I've never had this happen," he said when the spasm subsided.

"You'll live," Downer said.

They placed their names with the date of ascent into an empty meat tin and jammed it into a crevice. Cautiously, they descended back down to the ledge, placing their feet into cracks and against rock outcrops. Jim offered Belle his shoulders and she placed her feet against them, allowing him to lower her down safely.

With supreme confidence, Belle worked her way back along the ledge with the others to the Dog's Lift. There Ring barked for joy and tried to jump into his master's arms.

"Downer and I are going down to the Notch this way," Rodgers said, pointing to the most direct route.

"Don't get in a hurry," Jim said. "That's pretty steep."

When Rodgers and Downer had left, Jim led the way across a boulder field, at a descending angle to the mountain.

"No use taking a risk," he said. "We got up safely, so let's get back down the same way."

Below the Notch, they changed course and began a steep climb. Belle slipped and fell, sliding downslope, grabbing for anything she could hold on to.

Her collar caught against a sharp, protruding rock and she came to an abrupt stop.

"I can't get loose," she said, laughing. "I guess I'll just have to hang here."

"If you'll hold still, I'll help you," Jim said.

He reached under her arms and began to lift, then wrapped his arms around her. They stared into each other's eyes and Jim lowered his lips to hers. Their kiss was long and tender.

"Why don't you get me loose?" Belle said.

Jim lifted her and freed her collar from the rock. She lost her balance again, sliding on a patch of ice into a shallow crevice filled with snow.

"Are you hurt?" Jim asked.

Belle was laughing. "No, I'm stuck."

He reached down and took her hand. Still laughing, Belle jerked and he toppled down on top of her.

He brushed snow from his face. "Now we're both stuck."

They kissed again, rolling passionately in the snow. Ring barked at them from the top of the ravine.

"You picked a fine time to bother us," Jim said to Ring.

Jim helped Belle up and over the edge of the crevice.

"It's been quite a day, hasn't it?" she said.

"I hope you haven't given up on me as a gentleman."

"Certainly not, if you will still consider me a lady."

After descending through large boulders and gaining a small drink from a hole filled mostly with ice, they crossed the Lava Beds and found their horses where they had left them.

Rodgers and Downer had already gone ahead. Jim lifted Belle into the saddle.

"I'm so tired," she said. "You must think me weak."

"There are few women I know who could do what you did."

Back in camp, he helped her down and she wrapped herself in blankets while he chopped wood for a fire.

Rodgers and Downer stood with their horses, ready to mount.

"Aren't we going back now?" Rodgers asked.

"Gentlemen, I want a good night's rest," he said. "Hobble your horses."

Neither student argued. Jim started the fire and they drank tea and ate cooked meat.

"You can tell this story for the rest of your lives," he told them all. "It's been a grand day."

Rodgers and Downer finished eating and sat up for a time, talking lowly between them. Jim settled back and began to smoke a pipe.

Belle, barely able to keep her eyes open, retired to her arbor. She forgot her aches and pains, exhalting in the conquest of Longs Peak, and the tender moments that followed. She could still feel the mountain man's embrace and the warm feeling it gave her.

Smiling, she thought of future embraces and fell into a deep sleep.

FOURTEEN

Dark Confessions

This is no region for tourists and women, only for a few elk and bear hunters at times, and its unprofaned freshness gives me new life. All the beauty and glory are but the frame out of which rises—heaven-piercing, pure in its pearly luster, as glorious a mountain as the sun tinges red in either hemisphere—the splintered, pinnacled, lonely, ghastly, imposing, doubled-peaked summit of Longs Peak, the Mont Blanc of Northern Colorado.

ISABELLA BIRD

September

Belle awakened in the dark and rubbed her aching feet. Jim sat near the fire puffing on his pipe, Ring resting beside him. The two students slept soundly.

Overhead, the moon shone brightly, silhouetting Longs Peak against the black sky. The climb now seemed like a dream, something she had yet to truly comprehend. Her whole body ached, though, and she knew for certain she had reached the top of that distant pinnacle.

She grabbed her blankets and made her way to the fire, invigorated by the rest and eager to talk about the experience. She sat down and Ring thumped his big tail against the ground.

"You feel better?" Jim asked.

"I'm stiff, but it was worth it."

"Think what you'll be able to tell your friends and relatives back home."

Belle sat silent for a moment, wondering at her feelings. England seemed so distant. These mountains felt more like home.

"You hungry?" Jim asked.

"No, but I believe I'll fix something hot to drink."

She brewed tea in beef tins and they sipped while watching the heavens—the North Star, the Pleiades, and Orion, all sparkling in the crystal clear air.

"I often think of those twinkles of distant light as my far-off home," she said. "As a little girl I used to dream of visiting there."

He nodded. "There's many a time I wouldn't have made it home without those stars. The North Star in particular saved my life one spring night when three of us were jumped by Utes down in the Garden of the Gods."

He told of how the three of them had been trapping when a war party surprised them.

"Luke and Jean Penrelle and I took a stand and shot four of them but we couldn't get our rifles reloaded before the rest were on us. Luckily I had a cap-and-ball pistol that was primed and got off another shot, dropping the one that came for me. My partners got knifed before I could help them."

"Why weren't you killed with them?"

"I managed to grab one of the Indian ponies. They chased me for what seemed liked hours, but I'd gotten me a sturdy horse and we made it onto the flats before they could catch up.

"Then, for an endless night, I rode watching that North Star."

"Mr. Rodgers told me earlier that he noticed a scar on your back. Did you get that in another fight?"

"I've been in so many fights I can't recall them all, or what wounds I got where."

Belle patted Ring's head. "What a disappointment it would have been to me had you not been here."

He leaned toward her. "And I'm thanking my lucky stars that you came to Estes Park."

A whoofing, grunting sound came from the edge of camp. One of the horses squealed. Ring burst toward them, barking loudly. There came a loud whoof from the shadows.

Jim lurched to his feet. "Bear!" he yelled.

Belle struggled to get out of her blankets. Jim, with his rifle, had started for the horses when he suddenly returned and grabbed her, blankets and all, and pulled her to one side.

Rodgers and Downer were sitting up in their bedrolls, groggy and disoriented, when the horses stampeded into camp, thundering through, kicking up clouds of choking dust.

"After them!" Jim yelled.

The students scrambled from their beds and dressed quickly. They hurried into the darkness as Jim went to his saddle and took an extra revolver from his saddlebag.

"Take this," he told Belle.

"I don't know how to shoot it."

"It's simple." He removed the cartridges and demonstrated.

"That still doesn't mean I can do it."

"If that bear comes around here you had better know how to do it."

"Where are you going?"

"After the horses. If we lose them we've got a very long walk ahead of us."

She huddled in her blankets, the pistol on the ground near her saddle. She watched while he searched the surrounding area thoroughly, his rifle in one hand and his revolver in another. Ring ran in circles, sniffing the ground, whining excitedly.

He returned to her and said, "I don't see anything, but I could sure smell him earlier."

She had noticed the strong, musky odor herself, feeling helpless. Maybe Ring scared him away.

Ring lay beside Belle while Jim melted into the darkness. As big as the dog was, she still worried about the bear. Should it come, she would be learning how to shoot for the first time.

Downer and Rodgers worked their way through a tangle of trees, ducking limbs and stepping over branches.

"I don't like this," Downer said. "If the bear's in here, he could easily jump us."

"Are you saying we should return to camp without the horses?" Rodgers said.

Downer leaned against a tree and caught his breath. "I think I'd rather take my chances with Mountain Jim. At least he wouldn't eat us."

They resumed their search, walking carefully, and came to an open meadow. The moon shone brightly, covering the land in soft white.

Rodgers peered in every direction.

"I don't see any horses."

"They should be out here grazing," Downer said.

"Maybe they ran farther. They were pretty spooked."

The pair continued to look, jumping at noises and shadows. It was too late in the year for crickets and they had only the silence around them.

"I wish Nugent hadn't told that story last night," Downer said, sitting down on a log. "Now I'm seeing Indians everywhere."

"Indians or bears," Rodgers said. "Which would you rather have get you?"

"That's a great attitude."

"Wouldn't you like to know ahead of time? So you knew what to prepare for?"

Rodgers thought a moment. "Do you think Mountain Jim was at Sand Creek, scouting for Chivington?"

He remembered the story of the self-appointed military leader who had led a detachment of cavalry into a peaceful Cheyenne camp on a cold November morning nine years earlier, killing indiscriminately. The news made front-page headlines in Denver after Chivington and his men displayed scalps on a theater stage between acts.

"From what I heard, it was quite a battle," he said.

"It wasn't a battle," Downer said. "Chivington attacked a village of people who had been told the U.S. Army was their friend."

"That's just what the papers said."

"That's a fact."

"So, do you think Nugent was there?"

"Why don't you ask him?"

Rodgers shook his head. "Not me."

"You brought it up."

"I guess I don't care to know, one way or the other." He stood up. "Let's get back to camp. Those horses aren't out here."

❖   ❖   ❖

Belle sat up in her blankets as Jim walked into camp.

"Are Downer and Rodgers back?"

"I haven't seen them," Belle said.

He tied the horses to tree limbs and hobbled them, then began rubbing his mount with a blanket, removing the remains of lathered sweat.

"Where did you find them?"

"They must have run in circles before they got caught up in some timber. They were standing there, shaking. I guess they thought they were bear food."

"Poor things." She patted her pony.

Downer and Rodgers appeared. Jim handed them each a saddle blanket.

"Rub them down good. We don't want them getting chilled."

"Did you see any signs of the bear, Mr. Nugent?" Rodgers asked.

"Nope. I think he's gone."

They continued with the horses, Jim and Belle using gentle strokes and talking softly.

"Sylvester and I were wondering," Rodgers said, "were you at Sand Creek?"

"What made you think of Sand Creek?"

"Well, you being a scout and all . . ."

"No, I wasn't there."

"Did you know anybody who was?"

"Yes, but you won't hear about it from me. Now get to bed."

He turned and walked away. Belle followed him over to the fire.

"You seem awfully touchy."

"Some things I would rather forget."

He cut more wood and they settled in next to the fire. Belle wrapped herself in a large blanket and asked Jim if he wished to share it. They snuggled together while the students climbed into their bedrolls and soon fell asleep.

Jim stared silently into the flames.

"What's bothering you?" Belle said. "Is it something one of the boys said?"

"Just the thought of Sand Creek makes me feel ugly inside."

"Did you lose a friend there?"

"Yes."

"I told you I would listen if you ever wanted to discuss anything."

He lit his pipe. "I knew two people who were there. Silas Morgan and I used to hunt and trap together. He took a Cheyenne wife and was in the camp that day. The other was a scout named Jack Smith, fathered by John Smith, well known in these parts. Jack's mother was a relative of Black Kettle, who led the band that was camped on Sand Creek."

"Were they killed in the fight?"

"Yes, but not by the Indians."

He told how Colonel J. M. Chivington, commander of

the Second Colorado Volunteers, had forced Jack Smith to lead them to the Cheyenne village. Chivington's view was there could be no peace with the Cheyenne, or any other tribe, and that they should all be exterminated.

"Smith, under penalty of death, led Chivington and his soldiers to the camp. At dawn Morgan's wife woke up and said she heard buffalo stampeding nearby. Silas got up and discovered Chivington and his men sitting their horses on a hill above the village.

"Silas told the chief, Black Kettle, to raise the American flag on a pole in the middle of camp while he went to talk to the soldiers. He got out there and saw they meant to attack. He couldn't hold them off and they shot him.

"My other friend, Smith, watched the slaughter. Those soldiers killed everyone they could catch, women and children and old people alike. They shot them down and cut them up to show as war trophies."

Belle said nothing. She had heard of similar atrocities committed by British soldiers in India, where her grandfather had gathered much of his fortune, and South Africa, where other relatives had settled. She had always felt guilty about the treatment of the natives in countries of the British Empire. This frontier was no different.

Nugent's face clouded even darker. "When the soldiers started mutilating the women, Jack protested. So Chivington had him shot."

"I'm sorry," Belle said. "You must hate the military."

"Other commanders condemned the action but I don't think Chivington was ever made to pay for what he did." He relit his pipe. "Let's hear something more pleasant. How about your life?"

Belle told of her childhood in Tattenhall, in northern England, and how her father loved nature and the outdoors.

"It's from him that I received my passion for the land," she said. "He taught me the names of the flowers and the birds, and told me how the sky holds secrets that I could hear if I would just sit still and listen."

"Sounds like he was an unusual man."

"There was none other like him. He would place me in front on him on his horse and we would ride all day through the countryside. It was marvelous."

She went on to tell how her mother had educated them in the arts and in religion, and how she had been given access to her father's extensive library.

"I filled many days reading of far-away lands and peoples, wondering at the differences in their lives and mine. I wanted to visit those places and learn."

She told how, as she grew older, her father bought more books so that she might educate herself, as women weren't allowed to attend college. Then he had taken his family to the Scottish Highlands so that Belle might recover from back surgery.

"It was there I began my writing and traveling. My father gave me three hundred pounds for travel to Nova Scotia. It was after my first visit to this country that he died. He would do anything for me and I always swore I would uphold his standards."

"I'd say you've done quite well."

"I thank you. What about your parents?"

"I come from a good Scots-Irish family," Jim said. "My father was a commander who took my mother from Scotland to Montreal, where he commanded a post for the British army. He didn't think so highly of me."

"Why not?"

"I didn't believe in the things he did and I didn't want to become a soldier. He tried to beat it into me, but I ran off enough times that it worried my mother I'd never come back. So he quit the beatings and just stopped talking to me."

"What did you want to do with your life?"

"I wanted to travel. Like you, I found books that fascinated me and made me curious about the world. But my mother didn't want me reading about other places, for fear I'd run away. My younger brother, Eagen, didn't want me leaving either, and used to tattle on me when he found me secretly reading."

"Where is your brother now?"

Belle saw him blink. "Eagan was the apple of everyone's eye. He did everything right. Though I was the oldest, my father decided to bequeath everything to him. But that never happened.

"I ran away one day and Eagan followed me into the woods. We got farther and farther away and he kept coming, telling me to wait for him. But I led him farther and farther. Come nightfall, I finally lost him. When I got back home, he wasn't there. We never saw him again."

Belle sat silent, looking into the fire. Jim took a deep breath and continued.

"I never admitted that Eagen had followed me. There was talk that Indians had taken him and my father led soldiers to different villages, but never found him."

"How could you have known he'd never return home?"

"I should have told him to go back. Instead I just led him on. I did it on purpose."

He looked at her, his eyes filled with pain, then stood up and walked toward the edge of camp.

Belle realized how much this man cared for her. He had revealed the depths of his soul. She realized also how strong her feelings for him had become.

Taking the blanket, she got up and walked toward him. Ring, ordered to stay with her, followed her every move.

She joined him, knowing he needed comforting but was too proud to allow it.

"I'll never forgive myself," he said.

They stood together in the darkness, looking into the vast wilderness below them. Belle put her arms around him.

"You're a good man, Jim. Don't let yourself believe otherwise."

They held each other tightly, kissing passionately. He led her farther from camp, into a small meadow filled with autumn grass.

As they lay together in the blanket, Belle became overwhelmed with desire. His arms were so strong, yet his manner so tender. She allowed her hands to roam over his body while his lips covered her face and neck. He opened the front buttons on her dress and she felt his warm mouth on her breasts.

She slipped her fingers into his buckskin pants and as the night passed, allowed her passion to blaze as brightly as the stars overhead.

Nearby, Ring lay patiently, wishing they would take him back to the warm fire.

Jim awakened her just before dawn and they hurried back to camp. The fire had dwindled to coals but the students slept soundly.

They built up a good blaze and heated cans of meat. As the eastern horizon grew lighter, he took note of the sky.

"A storm's coming."

The students rose and ate quickly. Belle gathered her bedroll and saddled her horse and Jim's, while he put out the fire.

The ride back offered her a look at wilderness before a major storm. The night had brought heavy frost and the trees were layered with crystals, sparkling in the sunrise. Behind them, above the peaks, heavy gray clouds rolled in, soon obscuring the light.

The birds, normally so active, were silent. Here and there she saw one flit among the branches, seemingly lost. The open skies had vanished under darkening clouds and even the treetops were hidden from view.

They rode in silence, Belle thinking about the night before. Jim seemed very distant, talking only when ordering the students to slow down or when pointing out a deer or an elk beside the trail.

Unable to view the canyons and watch the sunlight play on the hillsides, she fell into melancholy.

Snow began falling in large flakes, twirling in a light breeze. Jim led the way, unerring in his sense of direction. Rodgers and Downer, normally chatty, said nothing for nearly two hours.

They reached Estes Park at noon. At the ranch, Belle thanked Jim for his efforts.

"Glad I could do it," he said, and rode away.

She watched him disappear into the storm and led her horse to the barn. The students met her at the door.

"We're going to the lodge to eat," Downer said.

"I'll rest for a while and be along later," she said.

After rubbing her pony down and feeding him oats, she walked to her cabin, tracking through the light snowfall. Ducks swam on the lake, oblivious to the storm, and a blue jay hopped around in front of the door.

She built a fire, wondering at Jim's somber mood. She decided that she understood, as the climb had been such a marvelous time and having it all end was bound to bring a letdown to everyone.

She curled up in her blankets and fell asleep, not awakening until late afternoon. She sat up and stretched. The storm had passed, and high up, with sunlight shining brightly, Longs Peak rose majestically, covered with white.

FIFTEEN

Waiting in Paradise

This is a glorious region and the air and life are intoxicating. I live mainly out-of-doors and on horseback, wear my half-threadbare Hawaiian dress, sleep sometimes under the stars on a bed of pine boughs, ride on a Mexican saddle, and hear once more the low music of my Mexican spurs.

ISABELLA BIRD

October

Belle decided to stay in Estes Park for a while longer. Though she missed her home in England she knew that should she leave, she would miss Jim Nugent even more.

She had gone to see him the day after returning from the climb, to ask him why he had seemed so distant the day before. He had told her it bothered him to think she was returning to England.

They made love and it had been difficult for her to go back to the ranch.

"When will I see you again?" she asked.

"I'll be going into town to sell some furs," he said. "Then I'll come find you and we'll go riding."

While she waited for him she slept soundly each night and with the dawn looked from her window onto Mirror Lake, wishing she were an artist with a pen or brush, able to capture the purple sheen of the water.

She watched with amazement as the sun rose and the water reflected the surrounding peaks in red and bright orange, followed by the deep green of the pines as the light brightened.

The grass, covered with frost, turned into stalks of sparkling dew, and the dense forest all around became alive with the sounds of nature.

Each morning after breakfast she would return with bread crumbs to feed the chickadees and the pine siskins, and the pink-breasted finches which sang such a sweet chorus.

Blue jays and nutcrackers often spoiled the serenity, flapping among the smaller birds and scaring them away. To ease the problem Belle created two piles of crumbs and guarded one closely. She soon had little birds almost eating from her lap.

As the lake and the peaks provided her with morning magic, the vastness of the sky and plains to the east inspired her by evening. As the sun fell over the mountains, the fading light provided a myriad of colors that splashed across the land and sky.

Wispy clouds, filtered by wind, grew pink and lavender on their bellies, often deepening to red and rich rose, fading to steel gray as the light sank slowly away.

Often the moon hung above the horizon, huge and glowing orange with the impending darkness.

A week passed with no sign of Jim. To occupy her mind she rode every day, trying out various horses and seeing the country in and around Estes Park. Twice she rode to Black Canyon to find him but saw no one. Three times she sought him out at his cabin only to find Ring lying dutifully beside the door. Each time the big dog was glad to see her and leaned against her for affection.

She decided not to continue searching for him and turned her attentions totally toward her surroundings. She rode the trail they had taken to the foot of Longs Peak and watched eagles soar through the vast sky. Along the way she marveled at the magnificent elk, often locked in combat for the affections of the cows. She spent hours watching squirrels and marmots and chipmunks, as well as occasionally catching a glimpse of a marten or a weasel.

She located what vegetation had survived the frosts, including various fern species, hidden under the thick forest mulch.

Though most all the flowers had long since disappeared, she longed for the sight of them, as described by the women at the lodge. "There are larkspurs and harebells and buttercups," Ellie said, "and violets and roses and gentians. There are so many I can't name them all."

Belle had the good fortune to discover that some flowers had survived and sat for a time near a little stream where red monkey flowers grew gracefully from the water's edge.

She noted the variety of evergreens, the abundant ponderosa pines and the spruces and the grand firs, so tall and stately. She awaited the coming of each new day so that she could discover something new and different to tell her sister about.

Despite all there was to see and do, she still missed Jim terribly and wondered why he hadn't returned to see her.

She had already written Henrietta about him, describing his handsome side and his eloquent speech, his poetry and his amazing awareness. "A true child of nature," she had written. He had seemed so pure of heart and mind.

Now she wished he had never confessed his youth to her. She hoped it hadn't ruined their relationship.

Even if she could have forgotten him, she would have been reminded again during each evening meal, when the gossip ran rampant.

"I hear Mountain Jim's on a rampage," someone would say.

"Not again!" another would say.

Lord Dunraven was often discussed and there were many who sided with him. Invariably someone would say that Dunraven had come back and that he intended to fight Mountain Jim himself, or another would argue and say that the rumor was there were men with guns waiting to ambush Mountain Jim very soon.

At last Belle decided to seek the truth and rode to the dairy, where she found Beasley caring for a sick cow.

"I hear you had a good climb," he said.

"It was grand. But now it's over and I feel a bit let down."

"You can't lack for adventure here. It must be something else."

"You hear what's going on in this area," she said. "What can you tell me about Jim Nugent and where he's been this past week?"

Beasley wiped his hands on a towel. "My guess is he's gone into town to drink and gamble."

"Is that his normal routine?"

"It is when something is bothering him."

"But you saw how we got along. Why would he just decide to stay away?"

"Because he's afraid. He cares a lot for you and that scares him."

"I don't understand."

"He doesn't feel worthy of you. Maybe he's trying to forget you and hopes you'll leave before he gets back."

She thought for a moment, recalling her own insecurities. Yet they both seemed happy in his cabin when they had last met. Maybe he had come to some conclusion after that.

"You don't think he feels he's made a mistake in choosing me?" she asked.

"Why would he?"

"I'm too old."

Beasley smiled. "Maybe for Downer and Rodgers but not for some men."

"How do I make him realize he's a good man?"

"*You* can't make him see it. He's got to see it for himself, and it may be too late for that."

"It's never too late for anything," she said. "If you hear any news, don't hesitate to come to my cabin."

"I'm not supposed to mingle with the guests."

"Well, I'm not an ordinary guest. If Mr. Evans has a problem with that, you tell him to talk with me about it."

She rode back to her cabin and sat beside the lake, watching ducks dabble in the shallows. She felt empty inside. The entire effort to climb Longs Peak had drained her physically but Jim had managed to keep her spirits up, even after their return. Now he was gone and she felt weakened in every way.

As another day passed she fell deeper into despair, but by sunset she told herself to stop her fretting and become the woman she was before she met him. The clear water with jumping trout and the purple canyons and the grandeur of the forests and the peaks beckoned to her to see them.

But she could never see that beauty the same again. She could never be the woman she had once been, fully content to travel alone without a thought of anything but that which lay within her hearing and her vision. Jim Nugent had changed her, entirely.

The days passed and each scent and taste of the wilderness reminded her of this man who had, without even trying, captivated her. Now, without him, each night passed with fitful sleep. She couldn't stop worrying and wondering where he might be.

She longed to go after him, even if it meant riding to Denver. She would begin at Fort Collins and check every saloon there and along the way until she found him.

Twice she got three or four miles down the road before realizing that her actions were foolish, that what Beasley had told her carried the clear and awful ring of truth: She could never do for Jim Nugent what he needed to do for himself.

One evening, at her table in the cabin, she wrote her sister:

> Estes Park, Colorado Territory
> October 8, 1873
>
> Dearest Henrietta,
>
> I have held this in for so long that I feel I must burst if it doesn't come forth. I have informed you of "Jim" or Mr. Nugent, who was delighted to help me reach the top of Longs Peak, in all its splendor, something, I feel, no other man could have accomplished. His strength and manner have been most pleasing and I have come to realize that he and I could easily become more than just friends. In fact, I know that to be the case, and he would willingly allow it should I give him any opportunity.

She tore the letter to shreds and threw it in the fireplace. Her sweet sister, who depended on her so, could never accept her love for Jim Nugent. That would be betrayal, fully and without question.

Perhaps she could say it in another way. She tried another letter, less revealing in its contents, but discarded it also. There was nothing she could say to her sister regarding her deepest feelings that wouldn't break Henrietta's heart.

Yet as she peered out the window over the lake, watching the sun fall once again, seeing the colors come and go in the sky and on the land, she realized that her own heart was breaking.

Another week passed and Belle began writing Henrietta again, filling the pages with the depth of beauty she saw all around her and the comings and goings of interesting people.

The Queen Anne Mansion teemed with visitors and new guests. A young man named John Dewey, suffering from the effects of polio, and his wife, Marilee, arrived, along with an Englishman named Ian Cosgriff, whose English mannerisms garnered him the nickname of the Earl.

Among other newcomer arrivals were a miner and a young businessman from Boston, both consumptives who hoped to rid themselves of their infections by becoming hunters, and Evans's niece, Elizabeth, who had been sent to the ranch for reasons no one would discuss.

Travelers, usually hunters, stopped for the evening meal on a daily basis, and asked directions to good hunting grounds. Evans usually replied, "I'm afraid the hunting up here isn't what it used to be. They've gotten all the big bull elk and as for deer, you just don't see that many anymore. If I were you, I'd try another area."

Some of the hunters saw through the ruse and remained in the area, but others looked elsewhere for game. One evening two prospectors arrived asking directions to North Park and Evans told them to stay put.

"You don't want to go over there," he said. "The Indians will give you a bad welcome."

"Maybe you know there's gold to be found over there," one of them said, "and you don't want us finding it."

Not two days later, rumors arrived that the two had been killed, their corpses left in pieces.

Belle again was filled with visions of Jim and his past. She thought of his present situation and wondered if he had been killed or seriously hurt and lay dying in some nameless gulch.

She discarded the thoughts as foolish and wondered if she shouldn't leave and forget him. Each time she began packing she stopped and looked out over the lake, knowing that she had to stay.

From somewhere within she knew he would eventually return to her.

Even without him, she had grown so attached to Estes Park that it felt like her real home. Despite her upbringing and her having become accustomed to servants in her father's house, she grew ever more satisfied with the simple life in her cabin. Mending and dusting and cooking satisfied her and the simple pleasures of the outdoors made her joyous.

Though she could not be too revealing of her inner feelings for Jim, she discussed her love for the park in her letters to Henrietta. So often had she thought of staying that her sentiments couldn't help but appear between the lines.

She felt torn between her own desires and those of her sister. Should she stay in Estes Park, she would likely never see Henrietta again. That would be too hard for both of them.

But Henrietta's traveling to Colorado was not an option; she would never survive the trip. That left Belle with eventually making a decision she would find the most difficult of her life.

Another week began and Belle continued her routine. She rode during the day, occasionally staying out with plenty of warm blankets, viewing the stars overhead. The ladies at the lodge continued to stay on, as the weather remained open. They worried about her but she always told them with a laugh that the Colorado high country had seasoned her and she might never sleep indoors again.

Most often she stayed in the cabin and spent her evenings listening to hunters' stories and writing her sister, describing the scenery as it changed for the season, continuing to discuss the wildlife and their habits, including the fact that the skunk under her cabin had vanished.

Plunk had been ostracized for a time and Belle suspected that the dog and the skunk had met during her absence.

Belle was writing her sister one morning after breakfast when Sam came by on his way to where Plunk had been tied to a tree, out of smelling distance. He carried a leash and a pan for water, and some table scraps, along with a sack filled with tomatoes.

"Mother said to mash the tomatoes in water and that if I could scrub the smell off him, I could bring him back home," he said. "I hope it works."

"I've heard that to be a good remedy," Belle said. "I haven't seen you for a while."

"Father makes me eat alone and stay near the lodge."

"Why is he angry with you?"

"I went to Mountain Jim's cabin looking for him. I don't know where he's at, do you?"

"No. I suppose he's busy."

He toyed nervously with the leash. "There's talk that he's going to shoot somebody."

"Where did you hear that?"

"One of the hunters who came up from Longmont late last night said he heard it there."

"It's probably just a wild story, don't you think?"

"Maybe. The hunters say that he wants them all to get out of the park. They say he already drove Lord Dunraven away, but that he'll be back. Then there'll be real trouble."

"Why do you worry yourself with such stories?" she asked.

"Because I don't want anybody to get hurt."

Tears formed in his eyes and Belle hugged him.

"You shouldn't worry yourself about that, Sam."

He rubbed his eyes. "I wouldn't want to see anything happen to Mountain Jim."

"It's good of you to care about him like you do."

He smiled. "They say you climbed Longs Peak and sang at the top."

"Yes, that's true. It was a wonderful event."

She told Sam about the climb and how exhilarating it had been to see the land from the summit.

"There's so much country that the eye cannot take it all in. It's just magnificent."

"I'm going to climb up there someday. Would you like to go with me?"

"I doubt I'll be here when that day comes."

"Do you really have to go?"

"I won't be going for a while yet."

She looked out the window. The lake was covered with

ducks and geese, and small birds flew to the ground where she had left the bread crumbs.

She noticed the swallows that always swooped across the surface were far fewer in number. Winter was coming and they wanted no part of the ordeal.

A rider approached and Sam hurried to the window."

"It's Mountain Jim!"

The boy rushed outside and Nugent dismounted from his mule.

"Where have you been?" Sam asked.

"I've been busy. I hear your dog squabbled with a skunk."

"Yeah, and he lost."

"Maybe you had better go and care for him," Belle said.

Sam ran down the trail with his pan and leash and scraps, and his sack of tomatoes.

"He's quite a kid," Jim said. "If I was ever to marry I'd want my son to be just like him."

She stared into his eyes. "You're long overdue."

"I've had to take care of some things. It's not that I didn't want to see you."

Belle wanted to hug him.

"I shouldn't be here."

"Yes, I know."

"Gather your things and we'll go for a ride."

Belle caught her mare and tied blankets behind the saddle. Draped in another blanket and her hat, she mounted and followed Jim.

A short distance along the trail to Black Canyon, they stopped to water the horses. Belle dismounted to inspect a small flower blooming beside the creek.

"That's a mountain spring beauty," Jim said. "It doesn't know it's fall."

She laughed. "So dainty and so beautiful."

"It has a root that's good to eat. Want to try it?"

He dismounted and dug up one of the plants with his knife, revealing a small tuber. He washed the soil off in the creek and handed it to Belle.

The taste was sweet and crunchy, unlike anything she had ever eaten.

"This is delicious!"

"You ought to taste them roasted." He handed her another piece. "There are a lot of them out after the snow leaves. You would have to be here in the spring for that."

She mounted. "Even if I were here in the spring, you might not be."

"How so?"

"From what I've heard, you're looking for a fight."

"I've run some people off, but none that didn't need to go."

"Maybe others don't share the same opinion. That could lead to bloodshed."

"I've told you before, I won't let anyone ruin this place."

"You can't stop them alone."

"I've got a good start. But you're right. It's likely only the beginning."

He explained that his friends, the Kirby brothers, had been killed to keep them from going back to Estes Park. It had been made to look as if they had been murdered for their gold claim. Later, after he had paid Lord Dunraven the visit, the land baron had left, but had promised to be back, "after the trouble was settled."

"The 'trouble' is me," Jim said. "I overheard two men talking in a Fort Collins saloon. One of them said two men had shown up wearing guns, asking the way to Estes Park. I know who those two men are."

"Is that why you were gone so long? Did you go off to find them?"

"I couldn't find them. I looked all over."

"Why did you go after them?"

"Because I wanted to get it done away from here. I didn't want you to be anywhere near it."

"Do you think you could get used to living someplace else?"

He studied her. "Are you asking me to go to England with you?"

"Is that such a bad idea?"

"Do I look like I would fit in there?"

"You have the speech and mannerisms. All you need is a change of dress."

They rode farther, crossing into country where beaver dams abounded.

Jim stopped his mule and began coughing violently.

"Your lungs have gotten worse," she said.

"I'll be fine."

"You keep saying that. Isn't there a doctor somewhere you could see?"

"They couldn't help me. Maybe they could give me something for the pain, but nothing else."

"There are cures for what you have, aren't there?"

"Not for what I have."

SIXTEEN

Trouble in Paradise

Grandeur and sublimity, not softness, are the features of Estes Park. The glades which begin so softly are soon lost in the dark primaeval forests, with their peaks piled and poised by nature in some mood of fury. The streams are lost in canyons awful in their blackness. Every valley ends in mystery.

ISABELLA BIRD

October

Belle and Jim sat at the edge of a deep canyon. Sunlight played off the upper walls, bringing out deep red and purple in the rocks.

Though the upper reaches inspired awe, the depths of the canyon were well out of sight. All Belle could see was empty darkness that fell down forever.

Jim stared into the abyss. "I've never taken anyone here before. This is my special hideaway."

She immersed herself in the tranquillity. "It's like no other place I've ever been."

"There are secrets here."

"What did you mean back there by saying there was no cure for your cough?"

"Just an offhand remark."

"It was more than that."

He pointed far down into the canyon. "You see where the light meets the shadows down there. It's never the same on any given day. The light changes angles and the colors turn. You could sit here all day and see something happen all the time. As long as nobody spoils this, I can die a happy man."

"Why do you speak of death so often?"

"You know me well enough, I speak what's on my mind."

"But why death?"

"Everything has its end, Miss Bird. Each day must end; each season must pass into another, and so on. It cannot be helped."

"Why are you being so formal with me? You suddenly act as if you don't know me."

"I'm afraid it's you who doesn't know me."

"I think of you as a perfect gentleman and I always will."

He looked over the canyon. "I'm amazed that you continue to care about me."

"Jim, there's nothing that you've done or could ever do to change my feelings for you. Remember that."

They rode on to a creek where Jim often set his traps.

"When the weather's open I spend a lot of time here," he said. He pointed to where steam rose from the water. "There's a warm spring under the ground. It stays pleasant here most of the year."

"And when its snowbound?"

"I stay with Ring at the cabin. I don't bring him up here often because he won't stop chasing the beaver. He jumps in the water after them."

"You have him so well trained otherwise."

"Yes, but I can't get him to leave the beaver alone."

He had no sooner finished speaking than the dog came bounding up the trail toward them. The beaver slapped their tails against the water and dove under.

"Ring! What are you doing here?" Jim said. "I told you to stay home!"

Ring licked his master's face and lay down next to him, his head on his paws.

Belle smiled. "He's being good and not chasing the beaver."

Jim petted the dog. "Okay, I'll give you a chance."

They sat and talked about Estes Park and Henrietta, and what Belle had planned for the future. She had decided that she should take advantage of her time in the region.

"I want to tour other parts of Colorado," she said. "I'm hoping the winter doesn't set in before I can go."

"What's wrong with just staying here?"

"I must meet some people in Denver, especially Mr. Byers of the *Rocky Mountain News* and former governor A. Cameron Hunt, who has been most generous in offering to help me with my plans."

"You travel in fast circles, don't you?"

"I told you I wanted to have a piece about Longs Peak printed in the paper."

"I remember. I thought you might send it by mail."

"When you intend to do business with someone, it's much preferred to meet him in person."

"Do you intend to travel alone?"

"I could use an escort, if one were available."

"You don't want me along," Jim said. "I would spoil your image."

"Nonsense!"

"Do you think Mr. Byers of the *Rocky Mountain News* would welcome me?"

"You would be front-page news."

"In your circles, you are front-page news, the kind of story society respects. I get the headlines only if they take my picture at the end of a rope."

"So, you won't accompany me?"

"I've got things to get done up here."

"Can't they wait?"

"Not if I want to eat this winter."

"I'll have to go alone then."

"I've noticed you don't keep a pistol, not even a derringer," Jim said.

"I have no need for one."

"Traveling alone you will. I have an extra."

"Why don't you just come with me?"

"I can't, really. I have to get my trapping done and my cattle sold."

The sun began to drop over the peaks and Belle suggested they start back.

"Why don't you spend the night up here with me? I keep warm. Let me show you."

They mounted their horses and he led her to a secluded little canyon leeward from the wind where he had built a small lean-to and equipped it with pine boughs and bedding.

"I stay plenty warm here."

As darkness fell he went into the forest to set a snare and gather wood, leaving Ring to stay with Belle. She noticed that the dog seemed troubled.

When Jim returned, she said, "Is Ring feeling well?"

"He looks fine to me."

He got the fire going and Belle put her hands to the heat. The cheery blaze warmed her all over and she sat against the back of the lean-to, happy and comfortable.

"What more could you ask than this?" he said.

She smiled. Despite her education and background, she had come to find this life more satisfying than anything she had ever known. She had been many places but she had come to realize that her simple life at the foot of Longs Peak was all she had ever sought.

Jim snuggled in next to her. "Hear the wolves?"

She had heard the distant howling for some time. "Are they coming here after us?"

"They never cause any bother. Sometimes they get a bit curious."

"How about me?"

He leaned over and kissed her. The longing she felt for him overwhelmed her and she wrapped her arms around him and pulled him down.

Ring groaned and moved to one side. Jim and Belle began undressing each other. The passion within her rose higher as they kissed long and hard. She held his broad shoulders and ran her fingers down his back. He took his time, bringing her more pleasure than she had ever dreamed possible. Never before had she felt this way and she didn't want it to end.

She had taken one opportunity with a young sea captain during her travels to Australia, which proved to be a mistake. Her upbringing had taught her restraint but at her present age with her renewed love of life, she could see nothing wrong with making love to a man who had captured her heart.

She awakened and dressed in the frosty dawn, Ring by her side. Jim had gone to saddle the horses and as she waited, crimson streaks shot across the horizon.

They breakfasted on a Franklin grouse he had caught in the snare.

"This is far better than rabbit," he said.

She agreed, savoring the tender meat. Though there wasn't much to share, every bite tasted delicious.

They rode back to Estes Park with the sun shining brightly and the forest alive with wildlife. A herd of elk crossed the trail ahead of them. The breeding season had ended and large bulls mixed together with the cows, their huge racks of antlers towering over their heads.

They reached Estes Park at midmorning and Belle learned that Evans was planning on leaving that day. Sam Edwards came into the barn with the news.

"Mr. Evans and his whole family and a lot of others are going to Denver for the winter."

"That's not much notice," Belle said.

"My father and mother are staying, so I don't have to go."

"Please tell Mr. Evans I'll be up to speak with him directly."

The boy hurried out the door. Jim walked out of the barn with Belle.

"Do you have to go?" she asked.

"I don't want to stick around with Evans here."

"Why don't you talk to him?"

Jim climbed on his horse. "He and I have nothing to say to each other."

Evans prepared to leave, loading a wagon that he frequently drove in and out of the park along a narrow road that it seemed only he could negotiate.

He stacked his family's belongings in the front and a lot of horse tack in the rear. When the children complained about where they would ride, he said, "Get up on top, and don't fall off!"

Two days before, Belle had given him a hundred dollar note to purchase a good horse for her trip around the region. As Jim would never leave the area, she was thinking long and hard about returning to England, wondering if perhaps her sister could survive a sea voyage and overland journey.

The air would be good for Henrietta. If she didn't like Estes Park, which she couldn't imagine, there were any number of locations, including Colorado Springs, where people came specifically for their health.

She was making a big assumption believing that Jim would ever move from Estes Park. But if he loved her as much as she thought he did, he just might.

She would take her journey and upon returning, write her sister, then travel over to England and bring her back. Once Henrietta saw this magnificent land she would surely fall in love with it.

Belle could travel back to London on occasion to visit her

publisher. He wouldn't mind that she lived in America, as long as he received her manuscripts on time.

If he did protest, she could find an American publisher. Travel and leisure books were becoming ever more popular.

The guests who were leaving arranged their baggage in another wagon driven by Beasley. He waved to Belle.

"Are you gone for the season?" she asked Evans.

"I'll be back soon," he said. "There are cattle to gather before the cold sets in." He tightened the straps on the harnesses. "And I'll bring the mail."

She was eager for mail as she hadn't gotten a letter from Henrietta for over five weeks.

"Please bring some papers as well," she said. "I haven't read any outside news for a very long time."

Evans laughed. "Don't you get enough news just listening here at the dinner table?"

"I prefer to learn more than just local gossip."

"And there is a lot of that to be had," Evans said with a wink.

Despite Jim's dislike of him, Belle couldn't help but feel fond of Evans. He maintained a jovial nature even though she had demonstrated her distaste for Lord Dunraven's plan.

Genny gave Belle a hug. "We'll miss you. Are you sure you don't want to come along? You could ride on to Colorado Springs from there, and wherever else you want to go. There aren't many left up here to keep you company."

"Thank you for the offer, but I'll be fine."

Evans loaded his family and climbed into the wagon. It sagged with all the weight and the four Belgians strained in harness.

Downer and Rodgers, their horses saddled, shook Belle's hand.

"It was good to meet you," Downer said, "and great to be with you on the climb."

"Are you going to stay up here permanently with Mountain Jim?" Rodgers asked.

Downer frowned at him.

"My plans at this point are like a snowflake in the wind," Belle said. "I don't know where I will be landing."

"Well, the best of luck to you," Rodgers said.

The two climbed on their horses and joined the troop headed down to Denver. Belle watched them for a while and returned to her cabin.

She lay down, feeling the first throbs of a headache. She wished that she had some recent mail from Henrietta, so that she might know what was going on back home. She wondered what her sister would think of moving.

Sam Edwards knocked and came in, followed by Plunk, whose big tail wagged and slapped against the boy's side.

"I was hoping for a story."

"I'm sorry, Sam. Maybe another time."

"Another time, then, when you're feeling better."

He left with Plunk. Within a few minutes she saw Jim Nugent riding toward her, Ring running alongside.

"Somebody's been in my cabin," he said. He dismounted and tied his horse to a tree. "There were two of them."

"So that's what was bothering Ring."

"Yes, that's why he came to Black Canyon."

"A lot of people pass by there, don't they?"

"I mean somebody was waiting for me. They tromped all over the place. They left with one of my saddles and two of my bottles." He began pacing. "I have to find them."

"Maybe they were just passing through."

"There's more to it than that. If they would have cooked something, I might be able to understand. But stealing my saddle and whiskey, that's something else."

"Do you know where to find them?"

"I know where to start."

"Please don't do it."

"I don't have a choice."

"Yes, you do. Stay here with me."

He stopped pacing. "I can't understand why you care so much."

"I don't expect you to right now."

"You're going to take care of me, is that it?"

"Do you know anyone better for the job?"

He smiled and walked into the cabin with her. "No, I can't think of anyone better."

Carlson and Perkins rode to the front of Dunraven Lodge, dismounted, and tethered their horses.

Ever since that night in Idaho Springs they had been thinking of Jim Nugent, waiting for the right time. Their fee for killing him was secondary now.

Carlson, especially, had never allowed a man to outdo him in any fashion, not without making that man pay.

He had come prepared, wearing two revolvers and a bandolier for extra ammunition. Perkins, content to do what he was told, stayed close to Carlson and made certain his pistol was always loaded. He had never seen anyone shoot like Jim Nugent before.

Carlson loosened his red flannel shirt, tight and crimped from the long ride. He carried a bottle of whiskey and drank from it regularly. He told Perkins to loosen the cinches on both saddles while he went inside.

Perkins, like Carlson, had come to the gold fields looking for a strike and had fared poorly. He had paid for starting a drunken brawl with a gunshot wound to the face, which had stripped out the back teeth and part of the bone from his lower jaw. Up to now his life had amounted to nothing, but he believed that by helping get Mountain Jim Nugent, his name would become famous.

Carlson left Perkins to tend to the horses and toured the inside of the lodge, his spurs jingling against the wood floor. He began inspecting lanterns and cooking utensils and looked in the pantry, where he found a loaf of stale bread.

Perkins walked in and looked around. "Big place."

"We've got a kitchen here," Carlson said, "but nothing worth a damn in it. What did Dunraven figure we were supposed to eat?"

Perkins worked his jaw. He was in continuous pain.

"Maybe we were supposed to bring our own vittles."

Carlson pulled the bread from the pantry and sat down at the table. "What would you expect from a high falutin sort like Dunraven?"

"Don't look like anyone's been here for a while," Perkins said.

"Winter's coming on, you fool." He tore a chunk out of the bread and washed it down with whiskey.

Perkins stood near the window. "I wish Nugent had been at his cabin. You said he'd be there."

"That's what Evans told me."

"Do you suppose he was at Evans's place?"

Carlson drank from the bottle. "Evans told me he kicked him off the place and told him never to come back."

"I'll bet he's there, beings that traveling lady is there."

"Maybe we'll go look for him," Carlson said, "but we'll wait until Evans and all the others have left for Denver. That should be today."

Perkins sat down at the table and took the bottle. "How we going to go about getting him?"

"I'll have to think on it."

"Would it be easier to get him at his cabin?"

"I don't know. I'll have to think on it."

"If we go back to that cabin I don't want that dog growling at me no more," Perkins said. "Next time I shoot at him, I'll hit him."

Carlson took the bottle and pulled another chunk of bread from the loaf. He threw pieces of crust on the table. "There's a wagon sitting outside. We'll go up to Evans's place in it and act like hunters," he said.

"Hunters?"

"Nugent won't be able to do nothing to us if Lem Edwards thinks we're hunters. We'll camp by that cabin where the English lady lives. He'll show up there. He's sweet on her."

Perkins reached for the bread but Carlson pulled the loaf away and stood up. He walked to the window.

Perkins chewed on the bread crusts Carlson had left. "I don't think we'd ought to involve the lady," he said.

"We won't shoot her, you fool."

"I mean, if she sees us we could be in for it."

Carlson drank from the bottle. "You listen to me. It'll work if we don't get in a hurry. We'll go down to Longmont for a week or so. Maybe sell that saddle we stole from him. Then we'll come back up here. By then the time ought to be right."

SEVENTEEN

Waiting for the Wagon

You cannot imagine what it is like to be locked in by these mountain walls . . . "Wait for the wagon" has become a nearly maddening joke.

ISABELLA BIRD

October

Belle stood in the kitchen of the Queen Anne Mansion, cutting potatoes. She had already baked a loaf of bread and an apple pie. With Genny Evans gone there was a lot more work to do.

Ellie Edwards stood nearby, staring at the separator. There had been no milk brought in that day and she felt despondent. She helped with the washing and the cooking but whenever she felt upset or depressed, she would turn to the separator.

She sang a hymn to herself while her husband, Lem, told war stories to three new hunters who had arrived the night before.

"That march through Georgia was like something

straight from hell," he was saying. "Sherman told us to burn everything that could be burned. I never saw so much smoke and fire in my life, nor so many bodies blown to pieces. Every night I can see their faces, each one, and the places on the heads where the faces should have been."

"I wish he'd talk about something else," Ellie said. "I don't like it when he says the word *hell.*"

"That's probably the best way he knows to describe it," Belle said.

"He brings it up all the time. You'd think he'd want to forget about it."

"You can't blame him. Some things are impossible to forget."

She had watched Jim ride away toward Black Canyon a short time before. He seemed in one of his somber moods again, but he had promised not to look for or cause any more trouble. Checking his traps is all he had planned.

She wondered what horrible things he had seen in his life. Like Lem Edwards, there was much he would never be able to forget. What had he endured that he might never tell anyone? And why couldn't he see that he was worthy of love?

Her father had told her that the only way to endure was to look upward and turn to God, who forgave all, through his Blessed Son, Jesus, who had also lived on this earth and experienced all the trials and tribulations of human life. But that was difficult to understand for most people, so they spent their lives wondering who Jesus really was.

During their many walks through the city together, Belle had talked with her father for hours regarding the notion that a paradise awaited all those with unshakable faith.

"Paradise is a hard place to find," she had told him. He had laughed and said, "If you look hard enough you can find paradise all around you, even in the middle of chaos."

Her attention was directed to a bird's nest situated in the eaves of a blacksmith shop. The mother bird, so small and delicate, cared for her young, seemingly oblivious to the clanking and pounding all around her.

"Jesus has said that the greatest gift in life is love," her father explained. "With love, anything is possible. That mother bird is not affected by the noise, but goes about her business naturally and methodically.

"You see how delicate she is with those little ones? That was not taught to her. God gave her that gift. Each of us is born with that love and we must learn to hold onto it."

From that time on Belle turned to nature for several lessons throughout her life. She often visited the countryside, with her father and on her own, filled with wonder at the great mystery of life. She learned the names of the flowers and the trees, as well as the birds and other wildlife, always mindful of their place in the natural cycle of creation.

She learned quickly that even though nature was pure and abiding, a strong tempest existed within that holy structure. She witnessed storm destruction and, later on as a traveler, famine and disease.

Since arriving in Estes Park she had only to think of Longs Peak to see the irony.

One day might bring a wind to the peak that could blow a person off into the canyons below or a night filled with bolts of terrifying lightning, yet the day she had climbed to the summit, the calm had inspired her.

"Peace rested for that bright day on the peak," she wrote her sister.

She now realized that Jim Nugent personified Longs Peak. One day he could be bright and cheerful, and without warning become cloudy and ominous.

She had conquered the peak, but not without his help. Had it not been for him, she would certainly have failed.

A week passed and Evans had not returned. Belle rode or walked down the trail a few miles toward Longmont every day, two or three times, in hopes of catching a glimpse of his wagon. Each time she returned frustrated.

Everyone at the lodge waited as well. Whenever Plunk

barked at something, day or night, they all rushed outside, watching for a wagon.

Jim came and went. Her anxiety bothered him and they argued about patience and its true meaning. He spent more time in Black Canyon, harvesting pelts. As the weather grew colder the fur grew richer and soon he would have enough to load his pack mule and ride to Denver.

"The market varies," he told Belle, "but this time of year is the best."

He came by after breakfast one morning to say that he would soon be headed to market.

"Just a few more days of trapping and I'll have a full load."

"What about your cattle?" Belle asked. "Don't you intend to drive them to market?"

"If I get the time," he said. "Maybe you can help me."

"I don't know the first thing about it."

"I'll show you. I'll teach you to rope and tie a good knot."

She rode with him to his cabin, where he had attached a steer's skull with long, twisting horns to a section of log with branches tied on for legs. He gave her a lariat and showed her how to form a noose.

"This is how you lasso a wild cow," he said, throwing the noose over the horns. "Try it."

After many frustrating attempts, she learned the technique.

"It will take me a long while to master this," she said.

"Take your time."

While he watched, Belle practiced throwing the noose over the horns. She tried it from various angles and as the afternoon wore on, realized that with practice she could become competent.

"I'd better get back now," Belle said, "in case Mr. Evans has arrived with the mail."

On the way back they talked about Belle's future. She told him that she intended to write Henrietta immediately, and after a tour of the region, travel to England and bring her sister back.

"Do you mean you've decided to stay?" Jim asked excitedly.

"If I can find a suitable place to care for my sister."

"What's wrong with right here?"

"There's trouble here. I don't want her involved. Perhaps Colorado Springs would be better. I hear there are good facilities for invalids there. You could move down there with us."

"The trouble won't last," he said.

"But it's just beginning. Won't you consider moving?"

"What would I do? There are no streams to trap down there, no ranges for cattle."

"I hear that there are."

"Yes, but the land isn't mine."

"The land up here isn't yours either."

They approached the road and Belle noticed a wagon in the distance.

"Look!" she said. "It must be Mr. Evans! I'll tell the others."

She turned her horse and started toward the lodge at a full gallop. Jim stayed behind and watched as the wagon rolled closer.

Upon seeing Belle coming, Ellie and her family and the lodge patrons gathered in front.

"Is it Mr. Evans?" Ellie asked.

"I believe so," Belle said. "We'll finally have mail and papers to read!"

Little Sam stood nearby with Plunk, jumping with glee.

Jim rode up. "It's not Evans. Two men are coming up in a wagon."

Belle groaned with disappointment.

"It seems late for hunters," Ellie said. "Who could they be?"

As the wagon approached, Jim recognized them. No more brazen pair of killers ever existed.

"What are you two doing here?" he asked Carlson.

"I hear the hunting's good in these parts."

Ring stood in front of the wagon, growling. Sam held Plunk by the scruff and left when his father told him to go inside.

"I don't think you came for elk," Jim told Carlson.

"We did and we've got money," Carlson said. He looked to Lem Edwards. "How about it?"

Edwards introduced himself and said, "There's plenty of room here for boarders. You can hunt or do whatever you please. Eight dollars a week, apiece."

"Sounds fair to me," Carlson said. "We'll set up camp."

"You're welcome to stay in the lodge," Edwards said.

"We prefer to stay in our tent, but thank you just the same."

Jim watched them closely as they turned their wagon and drove to within a short distance of Belle's cabin.

"That's not a good place to camp," he said.

"They can camp wherever they please," Edwards said, "if they pay their rent."

"I'm telling you, they're not hunters."

Edwards stepped forward. "You're not supposed to be on this land, Mr. Nugent. Mind your own business or leave."

Jim walked Belle to her cabin, passing the men along the way. They were erecting their tent, a white army Sibley with two bullet holes through it.

"Wait here a minute," he told Belle. "And keep Ring with you."

"What are you going to do?"

"Just ask a few questions."

"Mr. Edwards is correct, you know. You have no right bothering them."

Belle let him go and he walked toward the men. They stopped their work.

"So you want to do a little hunting, eh?" Jim said.

Perkins talked while he worked. "We want to bag a few elk before the cold sets in permanent."

"You would be well advised to leave."

Carlson turned and smiled. "You'd better back off, or you'll be the one leaving." He pointed toward Lem Edwards, now making his way toward them.

"Why did you decide to camp right here?" Jim asked. "There are a lot better places closer to the lodge."

"This suits us."

"We can settle this someplace else," Jim said.

Carlson smiled again. "We'll settle it here, in due time."

Jim returned to the cabin. Lem Edwards stopped and talked to the men.

"They're not really hunters, are they?" Belle said.

"No. They're two of the three men who killed the Kirby brothers. They're working for Dunraven."

Edwards knocked on the cabin door and entered.

"Time for you to leave, Mr. Nugent."

"Go on home, Jim," Belle said, "I'll be fine."

Jim left the cabin and mounted his mule. He looked down at Edwards.

"Do you know who those two men are?"

"They're hunters, like they said."

"Believe what you want."

"I'll do that. Now go."

"I'll go, like you asked," Jim said. "But if anything happens to Miss Bird, I'll hold you accountable."

That night a violent storm arose. Supper had ended and the guests were telling stories when wind and hail began pounding the lodge, followed by snow that sifted through the chinking and covered the floor.

At eleven Belle decided to make a run for her cabin. Carlson and Perkins, who had eaten in the lodge and had been listening to the stories, offered to assist her.

"I can make it by myself," she said.

"We wouldn't be gentlemen if we didn't give you a hand," Carlson said.

Outside, the wind continued in a fury as they escorted her

to her cabin. At the door, she thanked them and said, "There
is one thing you should know. I feel sorry for you."

The two looked at each other.

"Anyone who must try to stop Mountain Jim Nugent is
in serious trouble. There's no one anywhere who can stand up
to him and win."

They left without responding and Belle lit a fire. She
found she couldn't sleep and got up to write her sister.

She wrote about the two men and how Jim had predicted
that someone would come after him. She included how she
thought they would end up in early graves.

After two full pages she read the text aloud to herself. Realizing that her sister would never consent to living in a lawless land, she tore the pages in half and threw them into the
fire.

When the wind lessened she looked out her window at
Longs Peak. The moon had risen, casting a white sheen on the
newly fallen snow. Everything felt peaceful for the time being.
She wondered how long it would last.

She awakened to a rap at her door. The sun had just risen and
Jim came in.

"You're not supposed to be here," she said.

"I'm going up to Black Canyon. I want you to keep Ring
for me."

She decided not to mention that the two men had helped
her the night before.

"You don't want me along?"

"Not this time. There could be trouble."

"But what if they come after you? There are two of
them."

"I've faced worse odds."

Fifteen minutes later the two men mounted their horses
and started up the trail behind him. Belle knew they were not
after elk.

She did not make her trip along the Longmont trail that

morning to watch for Evans but remained at the cabin, awaiting Jim's return. Ring lay just inside the door, his head on his paws.

She tried to enjoy the morning but couldn't sit still long enough to watch the ducks and geese on the lake or the birds eating bread crumbs near the cabin. She couldn't even concentrate on a letter to Henrietta and finally just paced the floor.

Later, she lay down, hoping to rest. Ring jumped up on the bed and licked her face, so she let him stay and soon fell asleep.

An hour later she was awakened suddenly by Sam Edwards.

"Someone's coming up the trail from Longmont!"

Belle and the boy hurried to the lodge, Ring close behind, running alongside Plunk. A tall young hunter with a lot of red hair, named John Buchanan, rode into the yard, his horse loaded down with mailbags.

He handed out mail and papers, and couldn't stop talking.

"The Indians are burning ranches and killing livestock south of here! A lot of settlers are moving into Colorado Springs."

"What about areas nearby?" Edwards asked. "Denver? Longmont? Fort Collins?"

"It's not the Utes. They say it's Cheyenne and Kiowa and Arapaho out on the plains. There's a big push by whites to hunt buffalo and it's got the Indians riled. They want revenge."

The Indian uprising alarmed Belle, but far more disconcerting was the main headline of one paper:

FINANCIAL PANIC REACHES WESTERN BANKS!

She read that all banking institutions had ceased business indefinitely. No one had any idea when things would get back to normal.

Until the money situation could be resolved, Belle had

no way of exchanging either gold or British currency for American dollars. She worried about her trip around the region and even more about returning to England.

"Where's Griff Evans?" she asked Buchanan.

"He's still down in Denver, trying to decide whether or not to hunt buffalo. There's money in it, they say. But he doesn't want to get scalped, either."

Buchanan distributed the last of the mail. The bags held no letters for Belle and she clenched her fists in frustration.

"Surely there has to be *something* addressed to me."

"That's all the postmaster gave me," he said. "He had more to sort."

"I'll go down after the rest of it," Belle said.

She went looking for a horse but they were all out in the pastures and it took two hours to catch one. She returned to the ranch and discovered that Evans had showed up in the meantime.

She rushed into the lodge, where Evans was passing out even more mail.

"I'm sorry, Belle," he said. "I took your letters out separately so that I could give them to you in a bundle. I'm afraid I left them in Denver."

Belle wanted to scream. She walked outside and looked into the sky. The clouds swirled angrily.

Evans came out with a bundle of letters. "Ellie found your mail in a sack of groceries."

Overjoyed, Belle hurried to her cabin and began reading them. Each began with "Wish you were here," or "When are you coming home?" Other than those sentiments, Henrietta had little news to convey. Life at home was as always, dull and boring.

She packed the letters away, wondering how she would approach her sister about moving. She would think about that during her trip.

She hurried back to the cabin and asked Evans, "Where's the horse you were supposed to buy for me?"

He frowned. "I must confess, I used your money for personal reasons. I ran out of cash."

"I can't get any more cash for myself now. You know that."

"I'm sorry. You can have any horse you choose, and a saddle and bridle, in exchange for the money I used."

Throughout the afternoon Belle tried a number of different horses before settling on a small chestnut mare. She rode toward Black Canyon, with Ring charging up the trail ahead of her. Jim Nugent stepped out from a grove of trees, holding his horse's reins. Ring rushed to greet him.

"Jim!" Belle said dismounting. "What are you doing?"

"Waiting for you," he said. "What about the two men?"

"Their tent is still up."

"I guess they believe they can wait me out. That's a mistake."

She put her arms around his neck and he bent down. Their lips met. She longed to take him back to her cabin, to make him think only of her and forget his violent urges.

"I wish you could stay with me," she said, "but I'm afraid of what would happen. Griff Evans is back."

"I'll go back to my place just as soon as I take care of one thing," he said.

Darkness was falling as they rode to Belle's cabin. He dismounted in front of Carlson and Perkins's tent and after looking around inside, found a kerosene lamp.

Belle got down from her horse. "What are you going to do?"

"Step back," he said.

He poured kerosene everywhere and lit the lamp, resting it inside against the tent wall. Flames rolled up immediately and he hurried back with Belle.

"Those two were careless and left their lamp going," he said.

"You had better leave now," she said. "Mr. Evans will be out here in no time."

He mounted and vanished into the shadows. The tent burned quickly, crimson flames dancing brightly in the last glow of twilight.

EIGHTEEN

Wild Cattle and Gunfire

The great excitement is when one breaks away from the herd and gallops madly up- and down-hill, and you gallop after him anywhere, over and among rocks and trees, doubling when he doubles, and heading him till you get him back again. The bulls were quite easily managed, but the cows with calves, old or young, were most troublesome.

ISABELLA BIRD

October

Belle drove cattle for the next three days, an experience she found exhilarating. She discovered the chestnut mare to be strong and agile, and named her Birdie.

Evans suspected Jim's involvement in the tent fire, but would never be able to prove it. The two men camped near the ashes for one night and, after a talk with Evans, left the ranch.

Despite all the problems, Evans wanted Belle to like him. He continued to laugh in his hearty manner, joking with her at every opportunity. But he knew that her feelings toward him had changed. She avoided him whenever possible and said very little when they were together.

She could not allow herself to dwell on the problems in Estes Park. If she wanted her sister to join her, she must instead concentrate on the surrounding beauty and fill her letters with descriptions of the land and the collection of interesting personalities that made their way to the Queen Ann Mansion.

She began preparing for her trip in earnest, mending all her clothes and washing them thoroughly, including the black silk dress she intended to wear while in audience with former governor Hunt, to whom she had written. His response had been encouraging, with a promise to help her in any way he could.

Evans had plans of his own for the ranch. He had brought a young musician back with him, having decided that music in all forms made the atmosphere livelier and would certainly attract more guests for the following year.

He had also loaded on a supply of whiskey, which livened the songfests considerably. Belle concluded that it was all clean fun, and since none of the men ever grew overly intoxicated, she often joined in the merriment.

The young musician, a Scottish immigrant named Ian McEwan, put on exceptional shows each evening after supper. He switched back and forth from the violin to a beautiful harmonium he had made himself, playing waltzes and reels alike.

His favorite song was a melodic piece called "The Kaimes," which quickly became a popular request. Belle would walk through the forest in the evening, thinking of her times with Jim and the love they shared, while the beautiful strains floated across the stillness. She could often hear the song from her cabin and would watch while the moonlight danced down from Longs Peak and off the face of Mirror Lake.

She often wished that Jim could be there to share the

music with her but knew he had to remain at a distance. He was likely trapping and possibly gathering his cattle for market.

Late one morning, she decided she could wait no longer to begin her journey and rode over to Jim's cabin, but found him gone. Plews lay stacked and tied all over the cabin, to be secured on packhorses.

She left him a note:

October 19

Dearest Jim,

Am planning to leave on my trip at first light tomorrow. Would dearly love to see you before I leave. Don't worry about Mr. Evans. He's forgotten about the two "hunters" and their tent.

Hoping to see you,
I.L.B.

As she left the cabin she noticed dark clouds overhead and rode back to the ranch through wind and swirling snow, which suddenly ended, leaving a sparkling white cover that soon melted.

She waited all afternoon for him and when evening came, went to supper resigned to the fact that she would be leaving without saying good-bye.

That evening after supper Ian McEwan played and Belle checked out the window often for any sign of Jim. She saw nothing but calm shadows and moonlight on the pines. She wondered where the two men had gone and if, no matter what he had told her, Jim had decided to go after them.

Three legitimate hunters had arrived the night before from Black Canyon and now lay on the floor, solemn and silent, dressed in ragged clothes and worn boots. They stared vacantly at her; they hadn't seen a woman or slept under a roof for six months.

Ian played "Rule Britannia" and then "Yankee Doodle" in succession, bringing laughter from the crowd. He then began the Scottish ballad, "If I Were a Blackbird" and Belle sang along while the hunters stared at her intently.

She waited until he began "The Kaimes" before going to her cabin. Still there was no sign of Jim. She walked slowly along the path toward the lake, listening to the music. From somewhere below Longs Peak came the howl of wolves, followed by a strange scream that she had heard before and had been told was the call of a mountain lion.

Dawn had broken when Belle heard a knock at the door. Her luggage sat waiting and she was preparing to catch Birdie to begin her journey.

"Miss Bird, it's Griff Evans."

"Come on in."

He entered, his hat in his hand.

"I need your help. I must get my cattle down from the canyons. I wouldn't ask, but some of my drovers never showed up."

"You're asking me?"

"There's no one among the hunters who can ride anywhere near as well as you. One more day won't matter, will it?"

"I suppose not."

"I would be very obliged to you."

He had already caught and saddled Birdie. He gave Belle the reins and they walked to the Queen Ann Mansion.

"Have you heard from Jim Nugent?" he asked.

"No. Do you have news of him?"

"Only that he's carousing in Denver."

"How would you know that?"

"Hunters come and go here. They hear a lot of things."

"I'll not worry about him," Belle said. "He can take care of himself."

She ate a hearty breakfast and listened to Evans talk to his hands about the roundup.

"We've got nearly two thousand head to find up there,

and it won't be easy. They haven't seen a man all summer."

Three cowhands Evans had hired from Fort Collins finished their meal and checked their gear. Two more from Longmont had not arrived, and there was no time to wait.

They rode from the park toward the canyons, the wind brisk and the skies cloudy. Four dogs came along, which worried Belle. They belonged to the stockmen and were wild and unruly.

"Those dogs are going to be a problem," she told Evans.

"The cowhand that owns them says they can herd cattle. I hope he's right."

They rode all morning, through rock-strewn canyons, fording streams and jumping deadfall timber, climbing to nearly eight thousand feet. Belle found the sun a welcome comfort against the crisp air.

They ate bread and cold roast beef in the saddle and by early afternoon discovered nearly a thousand head of longhorns grazing in a valley below.

Spooked, the herd turned and rumbled toward a canyon across the meadow.

Evans removed his hat and waved. "Head them off, boys!"

Belle fell in with the chase. Her horse plunged down the slope, jumping boulders and fallen timber, keeping pace with the others.

They reached the herd, a bellowing wave of horns and hooves, pounding across the meadow. Belle's bay surged ahead and soon she rode at breakneck speed with the others toward the mouth of the canyon to prevent the herd's escape.

They forged ahead of the herd and took position. She sat her horse with the others as the herd came straight on. At the last instant Evans and the Fort Collins cowhands began yelling and whooping, shooting their pistols in the air.

The herd turned back on itself and, after milling around, calmed down, tightening themselves into a compact herd as Belle and the others began driving them back down to Estes Park.

Evans laughed and said, "Miss Bird, you are quite the cowpuncher. When I saw you riding through the timber, jumping logs and rocks, I forgot you were a lady."

"If more ladies had free rein," Belle said, "we could do just about anything."

"So you could, so you could," he said.

Carlson and Perkins sat in Dunraven Lodge, eating a wild turkey they had shot.

"What are we going to do now?" Perkins said. "We're in a fix. Evans told us to forget the whole thing and leave. Does that mean we won't get paid?"

Carlson drank from a bottle. "We'll get paid, because I don't intend to drop it."

"Evans said Nugent will be impossible to get, now that he's onto us."

"Evans don't know everything."

"So what's your plan now?"

"I'll have to think on it."

One of their horses whinnied out front and Perkins got up to look.

"What the hell?"

"What's the matter?"

"Nugent is here!"

Carlson got up. "What's he doing?"

"He just got off his horse and he's coming toward the door!"

"Shoot him!" Carlson yelled. "Break the window and shoot him!"

Nugent rushed in, his Colt Dragoon drawn. "I asked you both to leave, but you didn't take me seriously."

Perkins pulled his pistol but had no chance to fire. He took two bullets, one in the chest and one in the neck, and dropped to the floor. He gagged and gasped and coughed, staring up wide-eyed at Nugent while his lifeblood poured in red rivulets onto a newly tanned bear rug.

Carlson stared at Nugent's awful face and raised his hands.

"Any reason I shouldn't shoot you, too?" Nugent asked.

"I've got my hands raised."

"You didn't give the Kirby brothers a chance to raise theirs. You shot them in the back."

"It wasn't me. It was Perkins who did it."

Perkins would never again be able to speak in his own defense. His eyes had glassed over and the blood on his neck had turned dark and sticky.

"The law will be after you," Carlson said.

"I shot that man in self-defense, just like your other partner."

"But this time there are no other witnesses but me," Carlson said. "You walked into this lodge and opened up on us. That's not self-defense."

Nugent took a step forward, his pistol leveled.

"You're not very smart, are you?"

Carlson swallowed hard. "Look, I tried to talk Perkins into forgetting the whole thing."

"Sure you did."

"Just don't shoot me."

"No, I have better plans for you."

"What are you talking about?"

"Tell you what," Jim said, putting his pistol back in his sash. "You haul that friend of yours out of here and then we'll talk about what comes next."

Carlson lifted Perkins up by the armpits and dragged him through the door. The bear rug's dark coat was stained and matted where Perkins had died, and Carlson kept his eyes from it. After he had labored to lift the body onto one horse and had tied him securely, he mounted the other.

"I didn't say you could ride away."

"What do you want me to do?"

"Climb down."

Carlson looked to Nugent's horse, where a large rope hung coiled to the saddle. His mind flooded with visions of dangling from a tree limb, kicking and jerking, while the noose tightened around his throat and slowly strangled him.

He had seen any number of hangings and had participated in more than a few. He and Perkins had helped two other men lynch a Chinese railroad worker. They threw him off a bridge, laughing, and watched his head pop off when he hit the end of the rope.

"Just let me ride back to Idaho Springs," Carlson said. "I won't ever come back."

"Get down from your horse."

Carlson's eyes grew wide. He reached for his pistol but Nugent saw it coming and had already drawn his Colt.

His hand froze on the butt of his revolver. He waited for Nugent to pull the trigger. His horse began to dance.

Again he looked at the rope on Nugent's saddle. He would not die in that manner.

As the outlaw spurred his horse, Jim fired. The bullet tore through Carlson's ribs and he yelled, falling sideways to the ground, his pistol flying. He groaned and rolled and tried to sit up, but his insides felt as if they were on fire.

Nugent watched and waited while Carlson started toward his pistol. He cursed and moaned as he crawled over every tormenting inch of ground until finally his hand grasped the butt of the revolver.

As he lifted the pistol, Nugent lowered his. Carlson was facing the other direction, the barrel resting against his temple.

The blast made the horses jump. Carlson flopped over and kicked a few times before lying still.

Jim caught Carlson's horse and draped the body over the saddle. Perkins's horse had run away and his corpse had slid off into a pile on the ground, legs and arms tangled.

After arranging Perkins back on his horse, Jim rode away, leading the two dead men on their skittish horses along a back trail up to Black Canyon. Upon reaching his secluded overlook, Jim untied them and let their corpses fall to the ground.

He took Carlson first, dragged him by the heels, and rolled him off the edge of the canyon. He watched the body flop and bounce until it disappeared over a ledge and into the darkness below.

After Perkins had been disposed of, he took a bottle from his saddlebag and sat down. He pulled the cork, wondering what Dunraven would think of his ruined bear rug.

After a few swallows he began to cough. He became angry and threw the bottle far out into space, watching it disappear into the same darkness where Carlson and Perkins would forever lie in uneasy slumber.

Belle rode through the canyons with Evans, driving lost cattle back toward the main herd. The trip back had proved difficult and groups of longhorns had split off and rushed for freedom into heavy thickets of trees and brush.

"You making it all right?" Evans asked her.

"I'll be fine."

She began to ride easier, hoping the cattle had settled down enough to complete the trip. Then, while going up a canyon, part of the herd broke again, and Belle followed a hundred head over a pass and into an adjacent ravine. One of the dogs followed, yapping and baying, scaring the cattle even more.

In the ravine, she discovered the longhorns bogged down in a swampy spring, plunging through heavy mud. Many of them became stuck and after great effort freed themselves and stood heaving on the other side.

A lone cow with a yearling calf had caught herself fast, struggling in oozy mud up to her shoulders. The dog jumped in, barking, and Belle tried to call it back.

With a quick thrust of one horn, the cow hurtled the dog ten feet away into the trees.

Barking loudly, the hound returned, thwarting Belle's efforts to throw a loop over the cow's horns. Again the dog was tossed into a sprawling heap. Only after the third time, when its leg had been broken, did it leave the cow alone.

Helpless to assist the dog, which sat whimpering, Belle

worked her lariat, tossed it over the horns, took three loops around her saddle horn, and pulled the cow from the mud.

The bawling calf rushed to its mother and the two bolted toward a heavy clump of chokecherry. Belle's horse charged after them and overcame the two before they reached the brush.

She drove the cow and her calf, along with the others, to the banks of the Little Thompson River. The dog, limping behind, whined piteously. She dismounted twice to try to help, but the hound wouldn't allow her close enough to check its broken leg.

At the river, most of the cattle crossed while a few tried to turn back. Belle's pony danced back and forth, forcing two of the cattle into the water. After the rest were chased down, they also forded the river.

In the water, two of the cows attacked the dog. Even with a broken leg it managed to evade them and they gave up. The other two dogs began a persistent harassment of the cattle and a cow became enraged, tearing the ground with her horns.

Belle rode between the cow and her calf. The cow charged and at the last instant her pony reared and turned, evading a swiping horn.

The cow charged repeatedly; each time the pony danced away. Belle's heart pounded in her chest.

The cow chose a nearby calf and hooked it into the air. It fell, twisting and flopping, blood pouring from its mouth. After a second calf was gored, Evans pulled his revolver and shot the cow.

They drove the remainder of the herd on, leaving the dead cow and her bawling calf behind.

Throughout the ordeal Belle thought of Jim and was glad he had taught her the art of throwing a lariat. She wondered where he was and what he was doing, and if she would see him before leaving on her trip.

As they neared Estes Park, the herd calmed. The sun was falling quickly and the air felt damp. Evans said they had been lucky to beat the storm. They drove the herd into a huge corral, built of log posts and rails, standing seven feet high.

Belle was amazed by the skill displayed by Evans and the cowhands from Fort Collins. They herded the cattle into the corral by patience and not by force. When the last longhorn had entered the corral and the gate had been secured, everyone let out a loud whoop.

The Queen Anne Mansion lay another four and a half miles away. They raced their horses across the park and were greated by a host of hunters and the smell of fried beef and fresh bread. Ellie had brewed a large pot of tea for Belle and she drank it eagerly, watching the snow fall heavily outside.

After caring for the horses, they ate and told stories of the drive. The dog with the broken leg lay with the others, resting on its side while one of the hunters set the bone. The hunter had given it warm brandy and milk and the dog lay peacefully.

After the meal, Belle settled back to relax before retiring to her cabin. The snow continued to fall and she wondered if she would be able to start her trip the following day. Storms in the region seemed so unpredictable; it could be snowing heavily one minute and the sun shining the next.

Sam Edwards came over with his dog and sat down on the floor beside her chair.

"Mountain Jim wanted me to tell you that he was sorry he missed you. He's headed to Denver with his pelts and doesn't know when he'll be back."

The boy looked sad and Belle asked him what was bothering him.

"I saw Mountain Jim cough up blood," he said. "He's awfully sick, isn't he?"

"I'm afraid he is," Belle said. "Maybe he went to Denver to see a doctor."

"Is he going to die soon?"

"I don't know. He's a strong man."

"I don't have a good feeling about it."

"There's nothing anyone can do but pray for him," Belle said.

Sam headed to bed and Belle left for her cabin. She walked along the path, tracking through the fresh snow. Already three to four inches had fallen and it showed no signs of letting up.

Inside, she noticed a bundle of blue cloth on her table, a note attached to it, which read:

> Belle—I hope you never have to use this, but take it just the same. The hammer is resting on an empty cylinder. If you shoot, aim a little low.
>
> Jim

She unwrapped the cloth and discovered a Colt Navy .44 caliber, retooled to take metallic cartridges. She built a fire and stared into the flames, wondering if she should carry the pistol. She couldn't wear it outside, but would have to tuck it in a bag or in her coat pocket.

Her thoughts turned to their climb up Longs Peak and she wondered now if he hadn't caused himself considerable harm by taking her. He had said often that the trip was something he could be proud of.

She walked to the door and looked out into the night. The storm clouds had parted and shafts of moonlight gleamed off the new-fallen snow. She wondered if she might see him in Denver, hoping with all her heart that she would, while from the main cabin came the sounds of Ian McEwan's fiddle as he played "The Kaimes."

THREE

❖

THE JOURNEY

NINETEEN

Snowbound!

*How the rafters ring as I write with song and mirth,
while the pitched-pine logs blaze and crackle in the
chimney, and the fine snow dust drives in through
the chinks and forms mimic snow wreaths on the
floor, and the wind raves and howls and plays
among the creaking pine branches and snaps them
short off, and the lightning plays round the blasted
top of Longs Peak.*

ISABELLA BIRD

October

Belle found herself snowbound for three days.
After she walked to her cabin, the storm grew worse
and the wind howled outside, lifting shingles from
the roof. She worried that gaping holes might appear but
none did.

She huddled under six blankets, listening in the dark,
while tree branches snapped and snow hissed through the
cracks and the window rattled incessantly.

She tried to think pleasant thoughts but a whistling tree branch slammed into the side of the cabin and a sudden roar of wind outside brought her back to the present.

Exhausted from the day's work and now the effort to rid herself of fear, Belle finally fell asleep.

She awakened a few hours later to discover frost on the sheet covering her face. Her blankets lay under an inch of fine snow and when she got up to stoke the fire, she discovered that in some parts of the cabin as much as four inches had drifted in.

Her bucket of water had frozen solid.

She lay awake in bed, too cold to sleep. When dawn finally came she noticed her clothes were covered with snow and that her boots were so stiff that she had to hold them in front of the fire and knead them to limber them up.

Buchanan and a hunter arrived and called in to see if she had survived. After shoveling a drift away from her door, they left a bucket of warm water for her use.

She covered herself in coats and blankets and hurried to the lodge, holding her pen and inkwell and writing book close. The front side had been dug free of snow, but the back held a drift that rose over the roof.

The wind had subsided but the clouds were heavy and low, and snowflakes drifted lazily from the sky. Estes Park was snowed in so badly that Belle could not see where the trail led out.

Everyone welcomed her inside.

"We worried that you had perished out there," Ellie said.

Belle found the lodge to be cooler than her cabin. The fireplace, despite its size, could not heat a structure whose logs had never been chinked. The hunters stood or sat, their beards covered with frost.

"I tried to come and check on you sooner," Buchanan said, "but I got lost. I thought I would freeze to death."

"I'm glad you thought of me," Belle said.

"You won't be going back to your cabin anymore, will you?" Sam asked.

"I'll sleep in here," she said. "But I'll go out there from time to time. I don't want the ducks to be lonely."

Sam laughed. "They'd better have some good blankets if they want to make it through this one."

She discovered Evans in bed nursing a hangover, his blanket layered with snow. He said a few words about the Queen Anne Mansion being a poor place for sleep and rolled over. Throughout the previous night everyone had taken turns shoveling the floor, doing their share of fretting over the mud that had formed from the snow mixing with the dirt on the floor.

Despite the mess Belle welcomed the warmth of the cooking stove. She helped make bread and fried beef with potatoes. Everyone ate heartily.

One of the hunters down from Black Canyon stared at her continually. He told her after breakfast that he liked her and that his name was Lamar, adding that he would do anything for her that she asked.

"Thank you," she said, "but I have everything under control."

They all sat in the main room, wearing coats and wrapped in blankets. When Belle sat down to write a letter, she found her ink frozen in the bottle.

Lamar held the bottle before the fire and then cupped it in his hands, breathing into the ink to keep it warm, while Belle wrote her sister.

She spent considerable time discussing the possibilities of having her move to Colorado and suggesting that the change of climate would do her good. She brought Jim up often and told her sister that she could see the possibility of their marriage, even though she had written earlier that such a union could never be possible.

While she wrote, Ian McEwan entertained on the fiddle and everyone took turns choosing a song. Some of the hunters played cards. Others preferred chess—anything to pass the time while the storm continued outside.

In late afternoon Belle decided to try to reach her cabin.

She would need to keep the door free of snow if she meant to get back inside to gather her clothes and other belongings. She certainly couldn't leave on her trip yet, but she wanted to be ready as soon as the snow stopped.

Halfway along the trail a sudden gust of wind blew her off balance. She fell heavily into a snowdrift. Her notebook flew from her arms and papers scattered everywhere.

After she had regained her feet, she covered her mouth with astonishment and concern. Her work appeared to be lost. The snow fell so fast and the wind whipped so strongly that she had no idea even where to start looking.

She began feeling through the snowbanks and gave up only when Buchanan appeared and insisted she come with him back to the lodge. Gravely disappointed, she consented.

"I've lost everything," she said when they got inside.

"I'll find your things when the storm lets up," Buchanan said.

Two hours later the storm lifted and true to his word, Buchanan began a search. Lamar, the hunter, consented to help but soon had to quit. A few years prior he had frozen his fingers and they were very sensitive to cold. They immediately turned blue and he regretfully left Buchanan to the task alone.

Soley by luck, Buchanan discovered the notebook under three feet of snow. The letter to Henrietta could not be found and Belle realized that it and a valuable photograph were lost forever.

She sat down to reconstruct the letter but decided against it. She had said a lot of things during that writing that she might better reserve for after her trip.

She had decided that she wanted to be with Jim for the rest of her life, but realized that his life might end before she could get her sister across the ocean, should Henrietta even consent to move. If he didn't get a doctor's help, his lungs certainly couldn't hold out for much more than another year.

She wondered at the origin of his trouble, something he had never shared with her. She did not believe it to be consumption; he would have already died, or at least be coughing continually by this time.

Perhaps he would never tell her what was killing him. She could only guess that it was an old wound of some kind.

During their lovemaking she had felt the scar on his back and also thought she detected a scar on his chest. The one time she had asked him about it, he had declined to discuss it. Now she felt even more determined to get him to move someplace like Colorado Springs, where the climate and the soothing waters were conducive to healing.

It seemed odd that he hadn't thought of it himself, but he was restricted in his thinking in many ways, something she hoped to help him deal with.

All of that could wait. Instead of the future, she decided to write Henrietta about the present. The storm would enthrall her, and a description of the mountains under a mantle of deep white would make her want to come and see for herself.

She would also talk about the bear tracks that had been discovered behind the lodge. The smell of cooking drifted far out in the chill air, and she would now have to be very careful when walking outside.

The following morning she returned to her cabin and lit a fire. She cleaned until late afternoon and still hadn't finished the job. The snow that had blown in had turned to muddy water with the warmth from the fire.

During the noon meal a hunter arrived from Longmont, announcing that the trail was passable.

"There are no drifts that can't be negotiated," he said. "Anyone on horseback can come and go as they please."

That afternoon she caught Birdie and kept her in the barn, feeding her oats all that evening and throughout the next day.

The night before Belle's departure, Evans said, "You don't have to go on that trip. I'll pay you six dollars a week to cook and clean here."

"I have my plans made," she said. "I'll see you in November."

❖ ❖ ❖

She left at half past nine the following morning. She had hoped for an earlier start but Birdie had gotten out into the pasture and had to be caught. Ian McEwan decided to accompany her down to Longmont. He had tired of the same routine and could play anywhere he wanted.

"Maybe I'll return next fall when there are more guests," he said.

The trail proved passable and the scenery magnificent. Snow lay in drifts under the aspens, their golden leaves not yet shed. The rock walls of the canyons held glitter-frost that turned to sparkling dew in the sunshine.

Ian seemed a pleasant sort, laughing and joking about the guests at the ranch, telling Belle stories of the hunters and how they tried to play the fiddle.

"They were very good at squeaking the strings," he said. "You should have heard the harmonium."

Belle told him she thought him a gentleman and a fine musician who had a bright future, should he choose to take advantage of it.

"I find the big life too much for me," he told her. "Even though I don't want them trying out my instruments, I prefer the little places where the people aren't so proper."

He told her a little of his past, living in the Kaimes region of western Scotland but hearing so much about America that he just had to sail across to see what all the fuss was about. When she told him that she had lived in Edinburgh, the stories began.

The afternoon passed quickly and they left the St. Vrain Canyon, turning south to look for the trail to Longmont in the dusk. After a few wrong turns they found a well-beaten path and finished their journey in late evening.

Ian left her at the hotel, eager to join some friends who lived in a boardinghouse at the edge of town. Belle wished him luck and he returned the tribute.

She took her room. On her way to supper, she was approached by a tall man with thinning dark hair.

"I have been reading much about you," he said, "and

have been wanting to make your acquaintance. My name is Dunraven."

Belle acknowledged him, saying, "I have heard much of you as well."

She studied him, wondering why he had approached her, searching for a clue in his dark eyes. His smile seemed genuine enough, so she decided he must not know of her relationship with Jim Nugent.

He invited her to join him for his evening meal and they chose a private table, Belle feeling a bit guilty. Should Jim ever learn that she visited with Lord Dunraven, she would have to do a lot of explaining.

"This is a country where few ladies and gentlemen can be found," he said. "You are continuing your travels?"

"Yes, I'm interested in seeing more of this country."

"Do you have an escort?"

"I always travel alone."

"A risky proposition in these times."

"I've never met with serious trouble." She sipped her tea. "I understand you have a business arrangement with Mr. Evans, up at his ranch in Estes Park."

Dunraven leaned toward her, as if sharing a secret. "We have a venture in the works, yes. Perhaps he has told you about it."

"No, actually."

"I'm surprised. I believe he told me that you might be interested in investing."

Belle nearly dropped her cup. "I would have thought he might have mentioned that possibility to me before he did to you," she said.

"Yes, you have a point. However, since he didn't, I will."

"It's not something I really need to think about. I'm not interested."

"Oh, but you've been in this part of America long enough to absorb the beauty and rarified air, and know the essential need to preserve it all."

"That's exactly why I'm not interested. I don't believe a private game preserve is the answer."

Belle went on to say that she knew of such developments in India and Africa, owned by English lords, who profited greatly while the wildlife population dropped drastically.

"I see these hunting trips as just a way to close business deals while killing animals—and not for food, but merely for pleasure."

"I do not intend to destroy the wildlife."

"I've never seen a hunting preserve that didn't."

"My preserve would be different."

"How so?"

"I would limit the number of hunters based on the population of game in the area."

"How will you know the game population?"

"By conducting surveys. I will hire competent people to determine how many clients can be brought in without damaging the hunting for the future."

"Right now hunters come and go at Mr. Evans's ranch as they please. Nobody ever speaks about the numbers that are killed. Are you saying you're going to change that?"

"Yes, it will be different when the preserve is set up."

"And how much land will be included in this preserve?"

"As much as I can get."

"Do you realize that settlers coming in will be against this development?"

"We have means by which to administer to those problems."

They were interrupted by a large man with thick graying hair who wore a tailored suit strikingly similar to a Confederate army uniform, complete with a tassled gray hat.

"Miss Bird," Dunraven said, "this is my good friend, Charles Ashberry. He served as a colonel for the Confederate cause."

Belle greeted him, noting that his eyes lingered on her breasts.

"Such a pleasure," he said. "May I join you?"

"By all means," Dunraven said.

Ashberry took a seat and leaned toward Belle. "You have quite a reputation as an adventurer. I'm gaining a wide audience myself."

"Indeed," Belle said.

"Oh, yes," he continued. "I oversaw victories for our cause at Bull Run and Fredericksburg. I only wish I could have risen to a higher ranking. I might have affected the war's outcome."

Belle wondered if this man had even fought in the war, much less commandeered for the winning side.

"I'm only slightly acquainted with the conflict," she said. "I prefer to expend my efforts at travel and discovery."

"She's done quite well at it," Dunraven said.

"Yes, so I understand." Ashberry leaned toward Belle again. "I'm planning an extended trip though the Colorado Springs area, and into environs west."

"Miss Bird, aren't you headed in that direction?" Dunraven asked.

"Yes, actually, I am."

"Really?" Ashberry's eyes again briefly surveyed Belle's breasts. "Perhaps I could escort you."

"As I told Lord Dunraven, I prefer to travel alone."

"A pity," Ashberry said. "You could be wonderful company, I would think."

"If you gentlemen will excuse me," Belle said, "it's getting late and I must retire, for I'll be leaving early tomorrow."

The two men rose from their seats.

"Think about our discussion," Dunraven told her. "You couldn't lose by investing with me."

She smiled politely and left the room. It had become obvious to her why Jim had been so determined to stop Dunraven from executing his plan. She was certain, especially after meeting him, that this English lord would bring to Estes Park the same fate his countrymen had visited on the British colonies.

In her room, Belle continued to think about Dunraven

and Griff Evans, knowing that Jim was bound to clash with them over and over again; and if Jim believed he had nothing to lose, he would push the situation until somebody was killed.

Belle left Longmont the following morning. She rose early enough to avoid meeting either Dunraven or his friend.

A light snow fell and the skies looked blustery in every direction. She feared the storm might grow worse, but by the time she had reached the edge of town the sun began breaking through.

Her intention, upon reaching Denver, was to visit the Evans house before meeting with Mr. Byers of the *Rocky Mountain News* and former governor Hunt the following morning. She wanted to ask Genny if her husband had said anything to Dunraven about investments in the game preserve plan, but decided that Genny likely would have no idea. She had discovered that as heads of the household, the men rarely discussed business with their wives.

The ride began peacefully. A few miles out of town she was met by Charles Ashberry, who rode up beside her.

"You do get up early, don't you?" he said.

"I have a good distance to travel. What brings you out?"

"I've decided that you do need an escort on your tour. I know all the sights to see in Denver and Colorado Springs, as well as points west of there. We'll have a grand time."

"I thought you understood that I didn't want an escort."

"I heard you say that, but I don't believe you mean it."

"I do mean it, Mr. Ashberry, in the strictest sense."

He smiled. "I must say, Miss Bird, you play the game of hard-to-get with authority."

The plains ahead were empty, rolling out to the east farther than the eye could see. In the distance, toward the foothills, riders and wagons appeared like toy figures against the brown landscape.

"Really, Mr. Ashberry," Belle said, "I don't need an escort, but I do appreciate your offer."

"I can't, as a gentleman, allow you to travel alone," he said. "It would be unconscionable."

Belle felt certain that no matter what she said, Ashberry intended to accompany her. She needed to be more forceful in order to change his mind.

"I must confess, Mr. Ashberry, that I'm glad you've decided to accompany me," she said. "No matter what I said, I do believe we can become friends."

He smiled. "I thought so."

"There is one problem, though. There is a ruffian coming up this way from Denver who insists I meet with him. I've tried and tried to tell him I'm not interested, but he insists."

"You let me handle him, Miss Bird."

"I'm glad you offered because nobody else is brave enough to face him. He's killed a lot of men and I understand he's out for more blood."

"Who are you speaking of?"

"His name is Rocky Mountain Jim Nugent."

Ashberry said nothing.

"He knew I would be going to Denver today, as he somehow seems to know all my business. I'm glad you're going to be along."

"Might I suggest something?" Ashberry said. "Why don't we stay here in Longmont a few days? Perhaps he'll give up then."

"I doubt it. He said there was no place I could go that he wouldn't find me."

Ashberry grew more tense. "Have you said anything to Lord Dunraven?"

"Oh, no, I didn't want to bother him. I would hate to see him shot. Since you're trained in war, I believe you can stand up to Mr. Nugent."

He stopped his horse. "Are you suggesting that I shoot a man in your behalf?"

"You could threaten him. If he fails to listen, then perhaps you will have to."

"Threaten Jim Nugent? I've heard he lives to be threatened and that he's as cold-blooded as they come."

"I've heard that myself. So you can understand my situation."

"Have you told him to leave you alone?"

"He's very stubborn. He told me that if he couldn't have me, nobody could."

Ashberry turned his horse around. "I don't believe I should come between two people who are having their differences. After all, it's none of my business."

"You're not going to escort me?"

"As I stated, I firmly believe in staying out of another's affairs."

"That's certainly a gentlemanly attitude. But I don't know what I'll do."

"If I were you, Miss Bird, I'd quit the country."

Ashberry kicked his horse into a trot and rode back toward town. Belle smiled and turned Birdie toward Denver.

TWENTY

Queen City of the Plains

*Denver is no longer the Denver of Hepworth Dixon.
A shooting affray in the street is as rare as in Liverpool, and one no longer sees men dangling from the
lamppost when one looks out in the morning! It is a
busy place, the entrepot and distributing point for an
immense district, with good shops, some factories,
fair hotels, and the usual deformities and refinements
of civilization.*

ISABELLA BIRD

October

The morning passed slowly and a cold wind erupted
from out of the east. Belle turned her face away from
the stinging blasts and longed for the comfort of the
pines, which kept such breezes at bay.

Near noon the wind settled and traveling became much
easier. A wagon train appeared in the distance just ahead of
her, and as she approached, she could see that it sprawled forward for over a mile and included a large herd of mules and
cattle.

She was invited to the midday meal by an immigrant family who rode in what they called a "prairie schooner," a large white wagon with bows that angled out at the top in both the front and the back.

The husband, a man named Trent, paid Belle no mind, but his frail wife, Della, told her they had come from the Illinois farm country and hoped to make a better life for themselves.

"We heard so much about this country out here that we decided to come and try it," she said.

They had been on the trail for three months and the stock they hadn't already lost looked weak and exhausted.

"We've got another month to Wet Mountain Valley," Della added. "I hope we make it before the big snows."

Belle provided tea, for which Della was thankful, and they dined on beef and hominy.

"I'm hoping to find a good place to settle myself," Belle said. "I plan to visit Colorado Springs."

"There's some on the train headed down there," Della said. "They say folks go there to die."

"I heard that soothing waters and a good climate were the area's saving graces."

Della sipped her tea. "Yes, but I'll bet those waters don't cause miracles." She peered into the distance. "I had hoped to make my youngest daughter, Mabel, into a schoolteacher, but she died just this side of Fort Laramie."

Her remaining three children stared and whispered about Belle's unusual dress, inviting their friends from the other wagons to join them. She told them stories of Hawaii and its volcanoes and they laughed, clearly doubting there was such a place.

Della invited Belle to travel with them, but they rolled too slowly. Belle felt sad at leaving them. She soon met a party of young cowhands driving nearly two thousand head of longhorns, their wives and families packed into wagons trailing behind.

She rode the next eleven miles to Denver under newly

formed storm clouds. Just inside the city a sandstorm erupted. The wind blew dust into huge, dense clouds and she couldn't see ten feet in front of her.

Birdie, having traveled the streets many times, carried her unerringly to the Evans house. Genny welcomed her and the children swarmed around the horse, petting her and declaring that they had missed her terribly.

Genny cut pieces of fresh apple pie and brewed dark tea while Belle washed the dust from her face at a porcelain basin painted with red and blue flower designs. The walls were all papered in bright colors and the windows were of thick glass.

"We have a lot of nice things in the city that we can't keep up at the ranch," Genny said. "I like it better here."

They talked over tea and pie, Belle telling of the trip and her experiences along the way, nearly coming to tears discussing grief-stricken Della in her run-down prairie schooner.

"Everybody comes out here thinking it's the Promised Land," Genny said. "There's more shortsighted people in graves around this country than you can shake a stick at."

Belle passed the afternoon inside while the storm continued. She went to bed early that evening and didn't awaken until midmorning.

Outside lay six inches of new snow, topped by heavy frost that sparkled in the sunlight. No one wanted to climb from their blankets to light the stove, but Genny finally wrapped herself tightly and fumbled with newspapers and kindling until she had struck a blaze.

Belle skipped breakfast, as she had a lunch date with William Byers and former governor Hunt. After donning her black satin dress, she rode sidesaddle through Denver to the newspaper office.

The South Platte River ran very shallow and the cottonwoods stood bare of leaves, their twisting branches shrouded in frost. Outside of town, the barren plains stretched to the horizon in a misty white shroud.

She saw little beauty in the city, or anywhere within the nearby foothills and mountains—certainly nothing to compare with Estes Park. The storefronts were jammed with people from every walk of life—miners, teamsters, trappers, and well-dressed sportsmen and travelers—all buying clothing and equipment for settling in the region.

Mixed with these were a vast number of invalids who had come west hoping to improve their health. Many had spent their summer in the mountains and now filled the hotels and boardinghouses, awaiting warm weather.

At the offices of the *Rocky Mountain News,* Belle was greeted cordially by William Byers, a husky man with heavy eyebrows and dark, graying hair. He had been one of the first gold seekers to come to Cherry Creek but had discovered more profit in selling papers than in washing ore from gravel and had become a founding father of the fastest-growing city in the Rocky Mountains.

"I'm delighted to meet you, Miss Bird," he said. "Congratulations on your Longs Peak experience."

Byers had led the first recorded ascension of the peak back in 1868 and knew the rigors of the climb. He took down details of Belle's experience for a feature article. Upon learning about Jim Nugent, he raised his eyebrows.

"He's been a perfect gentleman each and every time we meet," Belle said.

"I can see that you're a fearless woman. Do you plan to tour the area?"

She mentioned her intention to travel to Colorado Springs and then to points west in the mountains, staying to the eastern slopes of the Divide.

"You'll have a challenging trip," Byers said. "For the first part of your journey, I would advise riding horseback as opposed to either rail or stagecoach. You'll see much more country that way."

"I understand there are a number of glorious places to see," she said.

"Yes, the area is beautiful. But first you must tour our fair city. The governor is waiting to meet you."

Byers accompanied Belle to Hunt's mansion where they

were greeted formally and taken to a parlor. The former governor arrived a few minutes later and produced a map he had prepared for her convenience.

"This should help you with your tour, and I have also written a letter of introduction that you can take with you," he said. "It should help you gain entrance to the finer establishments along the way."

The three left the mansion in Hunt's carriage and dined at Sharpio's, the most celebrated eating establishment in the Rockies, featuring every cut of wild game imaginable and many forms of fowl.

After the meal, Byers and the former governor escorted her through town, showing her the many new hotels and businesses that had opened in the last year. She saw the Tremont Hotel and the famous American House, as well as the new Inter-Ocean Hotel across the street.

She saw many and varied travelers, including men draped in gray cloaks—possibly Civil War veterans—and a large number of miners and frontiersmen dressed in every form of garb. They moved along the streets, in and out of the drinking and gambling houses, or loitered on the corners, drinking from bottles and cans.

A large woman in a low-cut evening gown waved at Belle from a balcony. Byers and Hunt shrank with embarrassment, but Belle knew there was no way to tour the city without passing along Blake Street.

There were also a large number of buckskin-clad Indians, the women wrapped in colorful blankets, their hair hanging long and loose. They rode small and sturdy ponies with hide-covered saddles.

"Utes," Hunt said. "Since you'll be traveling through their lands, I want you to meet their chief."

He directed the driver to the south edge of town, where a large village of Indians had camped.

"I think it prudent that you meet Ouray, their most powerful leader," he said.

"Why are there so many of them here?" she asked.

"Ever since the Sand Creek incident, the friendly tribes have gathered close to the city," Byers explained.

Belle said she had learned of the Sand Creek incident and knew how deeply the Indian resentment must flow.

"We're determined not to have any more tragedies occur on either side," Hunt said.

"I understand some of the Plains tribes are raiding to the south," Belle said.

"Yes," Hunt said, "that's another reason the Utes are staying close. They don't want to be associated with the trouble."

Hunt had become friendly with Ouray, who was middle-aged and stout of stature, with hair cut to shoulder length. He stared at Belle with dark, piercing eyes.

"I'm pleased to meet you," she said.

He extended his hand. "Come and eat with us."

Belle took her place in a circle to the left of Ouray, with Byers and Hunt next to her. Other important members of the village seated themselves.

It was unusual to see a female sitting with the men in a council circle and the Indian women of the camp gathered on the fringes to stare and point.

A number of young women passed out bowls of cooked buffalo meat and fried bread.

"We will not be able to serve buffalo to our guests much longer, I'm afraid," Ouray said. "Soon they will all be gone."

"The hunters can't kill them all," Byers said. "There are too many."

"It is said that there are too many," Ouray said, "until suddenly there are no more left."

Belle ate in silence, enjoying the bread and meat.

"I hope your government puts a stop to the hunting soon," she said. "I'm not from this country but I'm still free to have my own opinions."

"I understand that you are a traveler and that you've seen many lands," the chief said.

"I have indeed traveled a lot."

"Have you had some dangerous times?"

"Not with people."

Hunt explained. "She rode through some mountains and encountered a grizzly. The bear ran away."

Ouray laughed. "If you can make a bear run away, you don't have to worry about people."

"He likes to joke," Byers said. "Pay him no mind."

She smiled. "I'm not offended. It's all in good fun."

Ouray studied her. "You can travel alone, since you are protected. You have the bear for a guardian."

"Guardian?"

"Your spirit helper. You don't understand, do you?"

"My guardian angel is a bear?"

"Yes!" He went into his lodge and returned with a bear claw, painted blue on one half and yellow on the other. "My guardian angel, as you call it, is also a bear. Show this to the Indian people along the way and they will know who gave it to you."

He handed Belle the totem and she thanked him. She wondered if her father, looking down from heaven, approved or not.

"Where do you want to go from here, traveling lady?"

"I would like to tour the Colorado Springs area and journey into the mountains west of there."

"That is our traditional homeland. You will like it there."

"I came down from Estes Park, extremely beautiful country."

"Ah, yes," Ouray said, "that is where the outlaw lives. Rocky Mountain Jim."

"I know him well."

Ouray's expression changed. "When you see him again, have him tell you a story."

He up and walked to his lodge and entered without looking back, closing the flap.

Belle noticed the other Utes getting edgy. Byers and Hunt suggested they leave.

She climbed into the carriage feeling very odd. "I certainly said something wrong, didn't I?"

"Think nothing of it," Hunt said. "A lot of people, Indians especially, think of Nugent that way."

All the way back she wondered about Ouray and Jim Nugent. She studied the talisman Ouray had given her, wondering if he would have been so generous had they discussed Jim first.

Their tour complete, Belle parted company with the two men. Both Byers and Hunt wished her a pleasant trip.

"I want details for publication," Byers said. "The Longs Peak story will only whet my readers' appetite."

Belle arrived back at the Evans house worn and dejected. The bustling city had robbed her energy and Ouray's sudden display of anger had discouraged her.

The following morning she shopped for a pair of heavy gloves, finding them in a crowded dry goods store. While she was paying for them, a small child noticed a bulge in her coat pocket and pulled out the pistol Jim had left for her. The child dropped the weapon and it clunked against the floor. Everyone stared.

Belle wondered at her luck: first an irate Ute Indian and now small children searching her pockets. She wondered what lay ahead.

That afternoon she helped Genny with the cooking and made final preparations for her trip. She placed the bear claw in one of her bags, hoping she would never have to use it.

The following morning the stable owner brought Birdie to the house, complaining that she was an ill-mannered "little demon" who had bucked him off.

"You've put a curb on this bit," Belle said, checking the bridle. "It's a wonder she didn't kick you as well."

Belle paid him and he left, grumbling. Yet another small problem that made her wonder.

After thanking Genny and allowing the children to pet Birdie one last time, she rode out of town and, upon consulting her map, headed across the plains toward the foothills to the south and west, following the South Platte River.

When she was past the city, she swung her leg over from sidesaddle, rubbing her aching back as she rode. The rigors of civilization had taken their toll and she looked forward to seeing more wilderness.

The weather remained warm throughout the day and Belle enjoyed her ride, crossing the Denver and Rio Grande Railroad often and meeting many wagons and herds of cattle moving north.

She found a muff lying on the ground containing five hundred dollars in paper. Upon catching up to a lone wagon driven by a older man and his wife, she returned the money to its owners.

"We couldn't have survived the winter if you hadn't found it and given it back," he said.

Belle learned they had recently lost their only daughter, a woman of twenty-five, to consumption and had decided to travel back to New Mexico.

Belle wished them good luck and traveled on, feeling good again about her fortunes. An act of kindness will shoo away any bad luck that might be coming, her father always said.

She reached the foothills and discovered numerous cabins occupied by settlers, none of them equipped to board travelers. They watched her pass, shielding their eyes against the glare off the snow.

That evening she stayed in a large ranch house with carpet and wallpaper, the first of its kind that Belle had seen in the region. Two huge barns stood in the back, holding horses and milk cows, and a large herd of longhorns, crossed with the new shorthorn breed, rummaged for grass along the river bottom.

Two hired women assisted the lady of the house, and the owner had a number of hands working for him.

Hunt had marked the general location of the place on the map and Belle had been lucky enough to find it.

Among the boarders was a tall, strongly built woman introduced as the first white female to settle in the region. Her stories of early Fort Laramie captivated Belle, though much of the history of that outpost was written in blood.

She rose early the next morning and started off again, watching the train go past, wondering if she wouldn't have been smarter to take it and do her traveling faster, as another storm had already begun. She watched the engine smoke drift into the hazy sky and longed for the warmth of the passenger cars.

The snow fell faster and the wind picked up, howling across the flats. She rode four miles farther before she was forced to take shelter where eleven other travelers were packed into a small cabin with a leaky roof. Melting snow dripped through, soaking everyone in the room.

Belle cut potatoes and made scones while the others marveled at her stories of Longs Peak and other lands some had never heard of before.

By early afternoon she was again on her way, riding through light snow and bitter cold. Most of the tracks had become obliterated in the storm and she had to watch closely to stay on the main road.

By late evening the cold had worsened and the trail had all but disappeared. She discovered a cabin nestled under the cottonwoods along a creek and had no choice but to stay for the night.

Had there been any other option she would have moved on, for there among the wayfarers she discovered yet another Etta Chalmers, ranting and raving against Great Britain and the British in general. One man whispered to Belle that they called the woman the Gray Mare and that she never let up.

The woman watched Belle collect snow in an empty can and wash her hands inside the cabin.

"No need for that," she said.

The Gray Mare lit a clay pipe and puffed hard, staring at Belle, all the while deriding people who displayed manners, stating that courtesy was only "so much bosh" when life held no time for such foolishness.

She passed the pipe to her three children, the eldest not over eleven years of age, and they took turns drawing on the stem.

Though famished, Belle ate none of the hard biscuits and beef served with runny, salty gravy prepared by the hard woman with the sharp, unrelenting tongue, who it appeared hadn't washed her hands since sometime in the spring. None of the guests ate much or cared to do anything but huddle together for warmth and try to block out the Gray Mare's voice.

That night the cold settled in deep and the dogs whined and howled so badly they were finally allowed in. The stock moved next to the cabin to gain some heat and Belle made certain Birdie was on the leeward side of the wind, and that she had a good feeding of hay and sheaf oats.

When she returned inside, the raucous woman had fallen asleep over her butter churn. Her children lay like a pile of dogs at her feet.

The guests all settled down and Belle wrapped herself in a rag carpet from the floor and lay near the stove, her head and back both aching, while outside the snow fell softly on a cold and silent land.

TWENTY-ONE

Hard Climbs and Frozen Trails

*The worst, rudest, dismallest, darkest road I have
yet traveled on, nothing but a winding ravine, the
Platte canyon, pine-crowded and pine-darkened,
walled in on both sides for six miles by pine-skirted
mountains 12,000 feet high!*

ISABELLA BIRD

November

The sun rose on a land covered with powdery snow.
Belle had risen before the others and had found a track
to follow left by a passing horseman. She alternately
walked and rode, as the warm sunshine compacted the snow
on her pony's feet, and couldn't be removed.

The divide between the Platte and the Arkansas lay
ahead, beneath a developing storm. She followed her map to
the home of Jameson Perry, a noted millionaire of the region.
Mr. Perry was away but upon seeing her letter from the former governor, his daughter, Julia, welcomed her heartily.

The Perry's had moved to Colorado before the war,

bringing their slaves with them. Five Negro servants covered the table with venison roast and all the trimmings.

After dinner Belle took a tour of the area with Julia's cousin, Nelson Cummings. The young man knew the area well and following a brief snowstorm, led her to an area known as Pleasant Park.

"Though I've never been there, this should compare to Estes Park," he told her.

The pine and red rock, which overlooked deep canyons, was striking but Belle could not place it in the same category as the land where her heart lay.

They toured the area, a huge ranch known as Perry Park, and Belle learned much about the cattle business.

Perry bred and sold shorthorns only, a newer, beefier breed of cattle than the Texas longhorn, and had developed a feud with a neighboring sheepman.

"There's going to be a range war before long," Cummings told her. "The two factions will never come to terms."

That night she slept soundly in a warm bed with warm water at her disposal. The storm settled in and six inches of new snow covered the ground, making her traveling all the next day very difficult.

She rode toward the Arkansas Divide, alone in a pure white land. She saw no travelers and no settlements or even a single lone cabin until she had nearly reached the divide, plodding through thirteen inches of snow.

She approached the cabin, thinking of Jim's little home in Estes Park, wishing in a dreamlike way that he would come bustling out and sweep her into his arms.

Instead an old miner in a topcoat and beaten hat invited her in for biscuits and venison stew, and presented Birdie a canful of whole oats.

"You'll find another cabin on the other side of the divide," he told her. "If I was you I'd get there before sundown."

The sun had fallen and her feet nearly frozen when she reached the second cabin, but was turned away as seventeen snowbound men filled the one room.

"There's a German lives a half mile down," the owner said. "Just stay to the edge of the trees. Don't wander to the left or you'll get lost."

She rode to the third cabin and was invited in by a man named Hanz and his young wife, Gertrud. Her mother lived with them and sat Belle next to the stove with a tub of water to warm her feet.

Though the pain was severe, she discovered they were not frostbitten and said a prayer of thanks.

The following day, after twelve miles of travel, she ate at a cabin filled with boarders and was directed to divert her route through Monument Park, a landscape of rugged rock formations in which she got lost several times.

Guided by the awe-inspiring Pikes Peak, she found her way to the mail trail and down Ute Pass, where she discovered Colorado City, a small cluster of saloons and shanty houses that Belle found particularly ugly. The town had long been a stage stop and now served as a railroad station as well. The streets were crowded with miners and cowhands arguing over a horse. She hurried through, fearing there would be a shooting at any moment.

Turning east, she rode three miles to the edge of Colorado Springs, where she stopped for a time at a cabin and shared pie and tea with a young woman in her late twenties named Clara Westbrook.

Her accent was distinctly British and she welcomed Belle openly.

"There are many from England here," she said. "They've nicknamed the town 'Little London.'"

Just two years old, Colorado Springs was being settled by people already monied and not those who came merely looking to become rich. In addition, the town fathers forbade alcohol of any kind. There was not a saloon or gambling house to be seen, the first such occurrence Belle had experienced since leaving Greeley.

A giant hotel called the Antlers stood as a major landmark, around which shops and stores were springing. With the arrival of the railroad, there would be a lot more settlers coming in a short time.

Clara had recently lost her husband to consumption. They had both liked the area, and even with his passing, she saw no reason to leave.

"I have enough money to live well for a couple of years," she told Belle. "By then I might be ready to remarry."

When Belle stated that she had wanted to bring her invalid sister to town, Clara assured her that many of those who had come were now in much better health.

Belle fixed her hair and donned her black dress. As she changed, she listened as Clara told her the best places to visit if looking for long-term housing and health care. She thought of Henrietta and their future, hoping this location might work for them.

Following Clara's directions, she found a boardinghouse owned by an elderly couple who had as pets a pair of prairie dogs, a cat, and a large hound. She took a room and slept soundly the rest of the day. That evening, while talking with the landlady in the parlor of her home, she noticed a bedroom with the door open.

The landlady, whose name was May Ann, said, "He's not long for this world."

On a bed inside lay a frail young man, fully dressed, in the arms of an older man, while a third, younger, man, who appeared equally as sick, paced in and out of the room, holding his head and leaning against the wall.

There were eight people in the room with Belle, including May Ann, all laughing and talking, playing games and telling stories, paying the men no mind.

Someone in the bedroom yelled for a candle and through the door Belle saw only the feet of the frail young man hanging motionless over the edge of the bed.

The older man came out of the bedroom, followed by the sickly young man, who sobbed uncontrollably, while the eight in the room with Belle continued their games.

Belle stood up, wondering if she could help the sobbing young man.

"That was his only brother," the older man said.

He took the younger one out to console him and May Ann told Belle, "It just turns the house upside down when they come in here to die. We shall be half the night laying him out."

The brother sobbed all night and Belle couldn't sleep. The following morning May Ann, dressed in a fashionable black dress, opened the door for the older man and the brother, whose eyes were red and puffy from grieving. The two men carried a coffin into the bedroom. Children ran in and out of the room while the young man's body lay face-up, uncovered, across three chairs.

The two men struggled to dress the deceased in a new suit, then laid him into the coffin. A wagon waited outside and they pushed the coffin into the back and followed on horseback toward a hill outside of town.

May Ann watched from the doorway, her hands on her hips.

"They all think the springs will cure them," she said. "Soon they'll fill our cemetery."

Belle took all of the next day to outfit herself with warm clothes for the ride west through the mountains, thinking about her decision to bring Henrietta to Colorado Springs. Certainly the area was beautiful enough and the absence of saloons and gambling halls kept the town peaceful. Hopefully there were better facilities to care for the infirm in the area around nearby Manitou Springs.

At breakfast the next morning everyone talked about her heading into the mountains with another storm brewing.

"You are one brave lady," May Ann said as Belle got ready to leave. "I hope they don't find you next spring, lying in some snowdrift."

Belle rode up the Manitou, past pine-covered hills where warm springs flowed into small gulches, sending rising clouds of vapor into the air.

She stopped to eat at a large hotel, where but a few lingering guests shared the meal with her at a long table. Belle discovered that Birdie was limping and walked ten miles up the canyon with her to a cabin where an old man reshod her.

During their travels, Belle and Birdie had grown very close. The little mare would lay her muzzle across Belle's shoulder, begging for sugar lumps, and would follow her everywhere, whether or not she was being led by rein.

No truer horse could ever be found, Belle concluded, and spoiled Birdie even worse, feeding her sugar many times during the day.

The sun grew brighter and Belle rode into one of the region's best-known landmarks, the Garden of the Gods, an area of unusual rock formations. Despite its beauty and tranquillity, the area bothered her, because Jim had mentioned it a number of times. She wondered if this was where his fight with the Utes had occurred.

Farther along she rode into a small canyon named Glenn Eyrie, discovering General Palmer's mansion, a huge structure filled with furs and game heads of all kinds.

William Jackson Palmer, tall and rugged and in his middle thirties, owned the Denver and Rio Grande Railroad, and had visions of extending the line clear to Mexico City. He hailed from Pennsylvania and had been a decorated Union officer during the Civil War.

He and his wife, known locally as Queen, welcomed Belle, and the two were delighted to hear stories of her travels.

After an entertaining time, she rode on, thinking that this country, unusual as it was, was not Estes Park. She wondered if any place existed that could compare. Still, it would do if Henrietta would agree to move. Even if Jim Nugent initially balked at joining them, she believed that he would eventually conceed.

Her last stop before heading toward the deep mountains was a hotel along the Fountain River. During the warm months, some four hundred guests filled the hot-spring pools, hoping to extend their lives.

Belle shared the dining room with but fifteen people, all

frail and in the last stages of consumption. She felt as if she were seated at the table of the doomed and hurried her meal.

The following day, she lingered in bed until noon, knowing she would sleep on nothing so fine for a very long time. By early afternoon she rode Birdie up the slope toward Ute Pass, through the narrow canyon where the Fountain River twisted through walls of red granite. She rode ever higher along the wagon road, crossing and recrossing the current, its roar ever more deafening the higher she climbed.

She ate at a ranch in an open park beyond the pass, where she met a Colonel Kittridge, who insisted his valley to be the most grand of all. Belle followed him twelve miles off her route to Bergens Park, which in her mind could not compare to Estes Park.

Later in the day, she reached another ranch owned by a man named Thompson, where she stayed in rough quarters, and reached Hayden's Divide the following day. Her trip across the top was lonely and uneventful but for discovering a dead mule near the summit.

She viewed the Spanish Peaks and Mount Lincoln, covered in winter splendor. Time and again she thought of Jim and wished for his company as the loneliness of the journey began to detract from the beauty. November had arrived and she wanted to be back with him.

Traveling by herself had given her cause for concern because she had learned that thirty souls had been lost in the area not more than a month before. With that on her mind she welcomed the sight of a cabin at nightfall, where the woman of the house took her in and had her rock a baby's cradle while she prepared the meal.

"We don't find the solitude that bad," she said. "My husband and our two children fare better up here than in a mining camp or a town filled with dying consumptives."

Millie Barns and her husband, George, welcomed guests throughout the summer, rarely seeing anyone after the first of October.

"You're a strong one to be traveling these parts this time of year," she said.

Belle dined on fried rabbit and venison, with rolls and butter, followed by canned raspberries and tea. After the meal she slept for eleven hours in clean sheets and blankets piled on a thick feather bed.

The following morning Millie packed fresh rolls and dried venison for her trip, plus a generous portion of raisins.

"Keep these for energy," she said. "Eat just a few at a time every day."

Belle rode on through snow flurries but nothing threatening and covered forty miles before she arrived at another ranch house, where she boarded for the night, traveling on through the snow the following day. She took Millie's advice and ate sparingly of the raisins, depleting her supply of rolls and venison.

As she passed through the mountains, she realized that she was getting farther and farther away from the main trails that led to Colorado Springs. At one stop a drunken old miner insisted she change her course of direction and head for South Park, advice which she quickly rejected. That would mean crossing the Continental Divide, where the snow lay far deeper than her horse and her together.

Belle spent the remainder of the week riding through the mountains, braving storms, finding cabin after cabin at the edge of nightfall, just in time to save herself from freezing to death. On one occasion she reached shelter after thirty miles of riding through deep snow, eating only Millie's raisins for fourteen hours.

There were times when she wanted to turn back, but realized that in so doing she would be in as much danger as continuing onward. She forged ahead, knowing that mining settlements lay ahead, and, hopefully, better accommodations.

Throughout her journey she never once met or saw any signs of Indians. Jim had told her that they stayed out of the mountains during the winter as there was more game in the foothills and along the rivers of the plains.

During her travels she often studied the bear totem Ouray had given her, wondering at the chief's deep anger toward Jim. She wondered how many dark secrets Jim held within himself.

Having come a good distance through the mountains, Belle realized she must be approaching the Denver wagon road. She rode throughout the day, straining to locate the road. The temperature fluctuated wildly, marked with alternating heat and cold. At twelve thousand feet she became lightheaded and nauseous, fighting the urge to dismount and lie down in the snow.

Discouraged but not defeated, she pushed ahead with her faithful mare and found herself on the divide, looking across a great mountain park filled with cured grass, toward the expanse of South Park.

She viewed wagons and riders on a road in the distance, leaving the mining camps of Fairplay and Alma, rough towns that Belle had heard were so brutal and lawless that even vigilante committees failed to keep order.

The steep, twisting road that lay in the distance now became Belle's destination. But she saw no easy way to reach it and decided that staying to the ridges would be the quickest way to get there.

There was no track of any kind and the way became treacherous. Uneven and often steep, the slopes held pockets of drifted snow where Birdie fell. Belle struggled to keep the horse from turning downhill, taking the easy way out. The Denver road lay to the north and there was no way to reach it but to stick to the higher ground.

Belle forced Birdie on across open, windswept ridges and through stands of weathered timber, always mindful that the road lay just ahead. After riding through an elk burial ground, where skulls and huge antlers protruded through the snow, she discovered a track possibly left by a hunter and followed it until deep drifts ended the trail.

Trapped in over three feet of snow, with no sense of direction, Belle began to get frightened. She frantically urged

Birdie onward but the horse fell often. Belle had to dismount each time and coax the pony forward.

Once, when they fell into a deep drift, Belle wondered if they would escape with their lives. The snow had engulfed them almost completely.

Birdie squealed and panted, trying to free herself, then lay her head sideways in the snow, her eyes rolling wildly. Belle heaved for air and scrambled for footing, holding fast to the reins.

"We can't give up now," she said. "Keep fighting."

Birdie struggled forward time and again, lurching, groaning, gaining ground little by little. Belle sprawled atop the snow, kicking wildly to keep from sinking down.

They reached the edge of the drift and tumbled off and down a slope, rolling and sliding through the snow, and came to a stop on a well-used trail.

Belle smiled, gasping for breath, and patted Birdie.

"We made it," she said.

TWENTY-TWO

Where Shadows Fall Darkly

*The smile she gives me is the same light I knew so
long ago and never dared dream could return. I can't
possibly allow myself to believe it; still, my heart
feels triumph. But would it be wrong to ask an angel
to abide where so many shadows have fallen? Yet
should she remain here surely the forces against me
would retreat.*

ROCKY MOUNTAIN JIM NUGENT

November

He rode his Arab mare, leading his mule behind, into
the streets of Black Hawk, past the Toll Gate Saloon,
and on to the edge of town. The snow had stopped
and though the town echoed with song and music, he paid no
attention to it.

When he reached the undertaker, he dismounted. A large
man dressed in a dark suit stepped outside.

"You've finally come. The stone's been cut for over a
month."

Having sold his furs in Denver, Nugent had decided to make good his promise to the Kirby brothers. He delved into his pocket and pulled out a pouch of coins.

"I'll pay you extra for storage."

The undertaker led Nugent inside and through a room where mourners were standing over the corpse of a young man dressed in a black suit lying on a long wooden table.

The stone rested against a wall in a back room. Cut a foot by eighteen inches, it would lay face up, tilted slightly.

Nugent gave the man a piece of paper on which he had written an epitaph.

The undertaker read:

HERE LIES

THOMAS AND TIMOTHY KIRBY

FINE MEN AND GOOD FRIENDS

1810–1873

"I want the letters etched good and deep," Jim said.

"I'll have it ready this afternoon."

Nugent left the parlor and found Griffith Evans sitting on his horse, waiting for him.

"What are you doing here?" Jim asked.

"I followed you up from Denver. I thought we could have a talk."

Jim climbed on his horse. "What's there to talk about?"

"There's lots to talk about."

"You kicked me off your place. I decided that's the last time I ever cared to talk to the likes of you."

"Maybe we can change things. Let's go to the Toll Gate. The drinks are on me."

They rode to the saloon and found a secluded table inside. Evans brought a bottle and two glasses over.

"What's this going to accomplish?" Nugent asked.

Evans poured the glasses full. "Estes Park is getting to be a dangerous place," he said. "You and I could end that problem today."

"You could end the problem," Jim said, "by sending Dunraven back to England."

"He would have to go of his own accord."

"Then you'd better tell him there'll be no game preserve."

"A man has a right to own property and do with it what he wishes."

"He's not coming by the property in an honorable fashion."

"If the law says he owns it, then who can argue?"

"So why are we arguing?" Nugent asked. "I told you we had nothing to discuss."

"Have another drink, Jim. Calm down."

"I've had enough. I've got some business to attend to."

"The Kirby brothers can wait. I mean, where are they going?"

"You've lost all respect, Evans," Nugent said. "You're no better than Dunraven."

Evans leaned over the table. "If you won't listen to reason, then be fairly warned. You've got to stop the killing. Nobody's seen or heard from Carlson or Perkins in days."

"Maybe they got smart and went back to Idaho Springs."

"They're nowhere in Idaho Springs or Denver, either. I checked. You must know where they are."

Nugent frowned. "And how should I know that?"

"Everyone knows you killed them. What did you do with the bodies?"

"I've got better things to do than this." Jim started to rise and Evans stopped him.

"Wait. Maybe I shouldn't have accused you. Dunraven told me his floor was covered with blood and so was his yard. He said it had to be you. And I know for certain you burned their tent."

"Did you see me do it?"

"Miss Bird told me."

"You're a damned liar!"

Evans saw a look in Nugent's eyes that scared him. "No, I don't mean she told me directly. She just said you told them to leave."

"Everyone heard me say that, and everyone knew they weren't hunters to boot."

Evans leaned back in his chair. "It could be so easy, if you'd just think about things." He pointed to a reddish brown spot on Nugent's coat. "You're coughing more blood, aren't you?"

"That's none of your concern."

"You aren't a well man, Jim. Why don't you settle with Miss Bird in Colorado Springs?"

"What do you know about us?"

"Everyone knows, Jim. Are you trying to hide it?"

"What makes you so certain she won't stay in Estes Park?"

"Her sister can't live up there, so far from a doctor. And, for that matter, neither can you."

Jim got up from the table and tossed his drink on the floor. Before he left, he said, "I'm going up and say a last good-bye to my friends. I won't dishonor them by letting you and Dunraven run me out. That's final."

Belle followed the Denver Road over Breckenridge Pass, passing miners and teamsters who had been in the mountains for weeks or months, possibly years, still waiting for their lucky day. She had ridden nearly fifty miles for the day but had not discovered a suitable place for the night.

Consulting her map, she decided that Hall's Valley, six miles farther, offered the best possibility. It was late afternoon and the canyons had become shadow-ridden and dangerous. The trail, coated with ice, proved so treacherous that Belle had to walk the entire way, often dodging freight wagons and horsemen traveling both up and down the steep road.

She saw sunlight in glimpses. The snow on the trail had alternately thawed and frozen many times, and she wondered if she had made a wise decision trying to make six more miles when she had already survived over three hundred.

As darkness fell completely, she found herself slipping repeatedly on the icy trail, working at the same time to keep

Birdie on her feet. Finally she pulled a pair of men's woolen socks from her pack and fitted them on her pony's front hooves, which worked well until they wore through.

Fitting another pair to Birdie's hooves, she mounted and began the last leg of the trail. It was so dark in the canyon that she could not even see her pony's ears. She prayed they would not slip off the trail and down the steep slope into the rushing water below.

At the mouth of the canyon Belle saw a campfire, where two men sat smoking, and a cluster of buildings. She crossed a partially frozen creek and discovered she had reached her destination.

She was greeted by the proprietor, who swaggered with drink. He led her into a dirty one-room cabin with unchinked logs lit by a kerosene lamp with no chimney.

A miner lay in one corner, groaning with fever, while others lined up at a rough bar smelling of spilled whiskey. One side of the cabin had been torn away and the opening was covered only by a canvas tarp.

The proprietor, a large man who introduced himself as Jed Harkins, leered at Belle and, setting a bottle in front of her, offered her as much free whiskey as she desired.

"Thank you, but no," Belle said.

"What's the matter? Too proper?"

The miners at the bar watched with curiosity. Harkins brought the bottle around and stood over Belle.

"I want you to drink with me."

Belle reached in her coat pocket and felt the butt of the pistol. One of the miners at the bar stepped up to Harkins.

"She's not of a mind to drink. Didn't you hear her?"

"Maybe you should mind your own business," Harkins said.

Three other miners stood up. "He's minding all our business," one of them said. "Didn't you learn yet?"

Harkins threw the bottle against the wall and left. Belle considered looking for other accommodations but learned there was no other shelter for at least five miles, a distance in which she could easily freeze to death.

Harkins had a wife, short and very heavy, with black eyes and a bruised mouth. She went by the name of Candy and wore a patched cotton dress, badly faded and smeared heavily with grease.

"He's a bit difficult at times," she told Belle.

"Why do you stay with him?"

"He provides. You hungry?"

She brought Belle a plate of reheated elk meat and stale bread, swimming in grease. She could stand but a few bites.

The proprietor returned and found another bottle. Candy shrank into a corner and rolled cigarettes while he drank the entire bottle and announced that he intended to run everyone he didn't like out of the gulch. He sat down abruptly on the dirt floor and passed out.

The sick miner continued to groan with fever while the others drank and began a game of cards.

Candy said to Belle, "Would you mind very much sleeping where the wall is gone? The sick man can't be moved."

Belle made her bed on a shakedown and settled in to look at the stars peeking through the gaps in the canvas. Too tired to care about Harkins or hear the men at the bar drinking and laughing, she fell fast asleep, her breath forming clouds in the frosty air above her.

She awakened to sunlight streaming through the canvas and a commotion taking place near by. Two men had served a notice upon Harkins, delivering a letter depicting a hangman's noose dangling from a tree, and a coffin below.

"You'll be just like him if you don't git!" one of the men said to Hawkins, pointing outside.

Belle looked past the canvas to a large cottonwood in the yard, where a man's body swung lazily at the end of a rope, dark-faced and frozen.

She had ridden right past him in the dark and hadn't noticed.

"You hear me?" the man said.

Harkins threw up his hands. "I'll go."

The two men left, stepping over the body of the fevered miner, who had stopped breathing. When they were gone, Harkins hurried out the door and mounted his horse. Candy sat in the corner, rolling cigarettes.

"He'll be back," she said. "They'll hang him, too."

"What did the man they hanged do?"

"He was quarrelsome, like Jed. He tried to knife a card player."

"Do you want to ride out of here with me?"

"I ain't got a horse and no place to go. When they hang Jed I'll take his."

Belle left, passing the hanged man. The road had grown even worse and she met two freighters with the unwelcome news that thirty more miles of treacherous footing lay ahead.

Added to the burden of the icy trail was Birdie's dislike for the miners' pack-jacks. They often tried to bite her and she shied every time they met one, once nearly going over the edge into the river.

Out of the canyon, in a place called Deer Valley, Belle discovered a clean two-story cabin run by a man and his wife and their two daughters, who served hot food with a smile.

For the first time on her trip Belle enjoyed fried chicken with mashed potatoes and gravy. She ate her fill and relaxed near the warm stove. The home had six rooms, each with a door, and numerous oak chairs that gleamed with polish.

She liked the place especially because the husband allowed no drink on the grounds. The freighters who stayed were well mannered and clean, and went to bed early.

She left the following morning in bright sunshine and rode twelve miles before one of Birdie's shoes came loose. After three hours of sitting on a barrel in a blacksmith's shop, waiting while twenty-four oxen were shod, she watched while her pony's shoe was repaired and refitted.

She rode another twenty-three miles and slept in a grocery store, sharing the floor with a large family and three teamsters. She left at 4 A.M. after leaving her money on the table.

Denver lay eighteen miles away, down Turkey Creek Canyon. She passed a small Ute village near the bottom. The people payed her no mind, sitting huddled next to fires in threadbare blankets, their pots devoid of meat.

The scene disturbed her. Had this been ten years earlier, she had learned, she would surely have ridden past camps filled with laughing children. Since the gold strikes, the displacement of the tribes had become nearly complete.

During her travels she had overheard many conversations about Indian people by whites who regarded them as a dangerous nuisance. She could see now that there was no need to send armies into their villages in the dead of winter. Starvation was easier and a far surer way of eradicating them.

On approaching Denver, she looked north to see Longs Peak and Mount Meeker, side by side, glistening with snow, and her urge to get back up to Estes Park became overwhelming.

Before that she needed to tend to financial affairs. She hoped the banks had opened again during her absence in the mountains.

But first she needed rest and rode to the Evans house, where Genny rushed out the door.

"Oh, how good to see you! We feared you might never return."

"I've seen what I wanted to," Belle said. "I know where the best country lies."

Genny laughed heartily at the stories Belle told, and the children took turns riding Birdie around the yard. Genny had to scold them often for their arguing.

Belle learned that numerous letters from her sister had been bagged up and sent to Estes Park.

"I would have kept them here," she said, "but Griff thought you might go back to the park from the west side."

Griff Evans rolled up in his wagon, filled with the carasses of three elk, a grizzly bear, and a bighorn sheep.

"We've got meat and hides aplenty," he said. "Everyone has left the Queen Anne Mansion but the Edwards family."

Turning to Belle, he said, "They're looking forward to your return."

"Do you know anything about the banking situation?" she asked.

"I'm afraid they're still closed. You should have stopped in one of those gulches you visited and panned for gold."

Disheartened, Belle considered what she would do. As it was Sunday, she sought out an Episcopal church and attended services, hoping to get some answers in prayer.

The air proved significantly warmer than in the mountains and she nearly suffocated, while the woman majority in the congregation fanned themselves and stole glances at her.

From the church, Belle rode the outskirts of the city, uninterested in the rowdy activity downtown. With the coming of winter the streets were packed with miners down from the high country.

She visited with the Evans family the rest of the day, enjoying their company, but eager for the following morning to arrive so that she could return to Estes Park.

Evans said, "Don't miss visiting Green Lake on the way back, in the canyon behind Boulder. You can't finish your trip properly without going up there."

He suggested she pass through Golden City and possibly stay a night, as the town was prospering and there were interesting sights to be seen.

"You might catch up with your letters there," he said, "or maybe in Boulder."

Belle went to bed with many things on her mind. She wondered how Henrietta was faring and what she had to say in her letters. She wondered if the financial panic would ever subside, knowing she couldn't make any decisions regarding the future without money.

TWENTY-THREE

There Is No God West of the Missouri

Agriculture restores and beautifies, mining destroys and devastates, turning the earth inside out, making it hideous, and blighting every green thing, as it usually blights man's heart and soul.

ISABELLA BIRD

November

Golden City was an assortment of brick, frame, and log houses huddled along an uneven street, devoid of boardwalks except for those in front of the finest saloons and dance halls.

Upon arriving in town, Belle visited the post office. The postmaster smiled and asked for her autograph, then told her he had sent her packet of letters out to Estes Park the day before.

"You'll catch up with them in Boulder," he said. "They get a lot of mail through there and it takes time to sort."

Belle was able to get a stable for Birdie and accommodations for herself. The landlady apologized to her for the room.

"I've never had a woman stay here before and I don't wash the sheets regular."

After getting clean linen, Belle slept for two hours. She found the room to her liking but not the town. She decided to cut short her stay and headed into the mountains the following morning via Toughcuss, the miners' name for Clear Creek Canyon, eager to visit the fabled Green Lake, high atop the Rockies.

She made a visit to Birdie at the stable, giving her a pat and an assurance that she would return, and left for the depot. Though she had purchased a first-class ticket, she was placed in coach.

"It's the end of the sight-seeing season," the conductor said. "You'll have to make do."

The tracks followed the narrow canyon bottom, often coursing directly through the stream bed, on their way to Idaho Springs and Georgetown. High rock blocked Belle's view of the surrounding mountains and she saw little but the great chasm itself.

At the end of the tracks she boarded a Concord coach, built for only twenty passengers. Overloaded, the coach swayed from side to side, greatly disturbing the driver, who cursed continually at the horses.

They arrived at Idaho Springs and discovered the town completely deserted. Belle learned that a new gold strike nearby had lured the townspeople away. The shops and saloons appeared as if they had been suddenly abandoned, leaving dresses on the racks and glasses on the tables.

Many of the passengers were men looking for gold. She listened to them, comparing them to Jim Nugent. Their crudeness made the mountain man stand out as a gentleman even more and she wished they had met earlier in their lives.

Georgetown, at just under ten thousand feet up, had just been dusted lightly with snow. Perched among the rocks, the town reminded her of a Swiss village, its gabled houses resting tightly together, water flowing between them.

She noted that the smaller houses were shored up on the

leeward side with pine logs to keep the raging gales from toppling them off the mountain.

At three o'clock in the afternoon the sun had already faded behind the mountains, but Belle still inquired at a hotel about tours.

"No one's been up there for five weeks," the landlord said. "But I'll inquire at a stable."

He returned shortly, saying, "The livery owner says that if it's the traveling English lady who's inquiring, she can have a horse, but that he'll send no one with her."

She started up the trail to Green Lake, some two thousand feet higher in the mountains. She rode through the mountain shadows, hoping to come out into afternoon sunlight and see the lake before nightfall.

Above Clear Creek she entered a narrow valley, passing frozen waterfalls and silver mines whose values she had seen quoted in the *New York Times*.

The mines were active night and day, and she witnessed the workings of stamping and crushing mills, and miners commuting in and out of the mountain on small rail cars.

She remembered Jim's telling her about how they burned the trees from the hillsides to be able to dig, and how the piles of tailings left behind scarred the landscape forever. As she passed the larger diggings, she saw individual miners standing in the freezing waters, ice forming on their pant legs.

"There aren't but a handful who ever make more than a slim day's pay at it," Jim had said. "The rest go to an early grave."

She stopped to ask directions to Green Lake and a miner politely replied, "Keep to your right along the mountain. You can't miss it."

After leaving the mining area she struck a foot of powdery snow, wandered through a dark, dense forest, and came out on a steep slope at twelve thousand feet.

Just below, surrounded by evergreens and bathed in the sunset, lay Green Lake, now covered with ice two feet thick.

As she gazed upon the jagged mountaintops, the sun fell

below the peaks, bringing twilight and then various shades of blue and gray. The cold intensified and she started back down the steep trail, passing miners still working in the darkness, their small diggings lit by coal oil or kerosene lamps.

She allowed the horse to move slowly on the treacherous footing, reaching Georgetown long after dark and leaving on the stage the next morning at nine. It was still dark, as the sun wouldn't top the mountains until after ten.

The coach took her back down to the train, and the conductor, who remembered her, said, "I understand that you're traveling just to see the country. You can sit on the platform in my chair if you'd like."

Belle thanked him and enjoyed the view all the way back to Golden City, where she dined and then mounted Birdie for the trip to Boulder.

It took her nearly all night to find a place to stay. She wandered across the empty, snow-covered plains, looking for lights until finally discovering a house only eleven miles from Denver. The rancher and his wife welcomed her and she ate beef and potatoes and drank strong tea.

The following morning she started north toward a deep cleft in the mountains. "Head for Bear Gulch and you'll find Boulder," the rancher told her.

Belle rode across ground so overgrazed by livestock that only cactus and a few shrubs could be found. Oppressed by unusually warm temperatures, she rode with a headache and nausea.

Upon reaching Boulder, she checked at the post office and learned her mail was en route to Estes Park.

"If you're going that way soon," he said, "I have another bag filled with letters."

Belle agreed to take the mail and told him it would be a few days yet.

"Take your time," he said. "There's lots of things here for a traveling lady to see."

Frustrated and bone tired, she located a hotel and talked briefly with the landlady, who wanted to know all about her.

"I'm afraid I must take to bed," Belle told her. "The climate is far different down here than in the mountains and I haven't adjusted yet."

She rose early the next morning, and after paying her bill was left with twenty-six cents. She thought of going back to Denver and checking the banks again but after reading a newspaper article that discussed the continued panic, decided against it; she would have to wait for them to notify her in Estes Park when they could honor her notes.

She looked forward to returning to her little cabin, living beside the lake in the pure mountain air. She could stay there for nothing and work for Evans, riding after his longhorns that strayed into the canyon.

At Longmont, she stayed at a newly built hotel, where the landlady insisted she stay for free if she would tell stories to her friends. Ian McEwan had remained in town with his friends and they played tunes in a small community hall where the townspeople had gathered for a potluck supper.

She walked over with the landlady, who had brought many of her friends in to meet Belle. During a break in the music, Ian came over to greet her.

"It's good to see you again," he said. "I thought you'd be traveling back across the sea."

"I will in due time," Belle said.

He laughed. "Word has it you want to stay here."

She blushed. "I'm not certain of that yet."

"Bring Jim down to one of the dances," he said. "I'll play a special tune for the both of you."

That night she told the landlady and her friends stories of her winter horseback ride. Later, she walked in the crisp air, listening to Ian's violin, thinking about Estes Park. There was no place she would rather be. Should she be able to convince Henrietta to move, Colorado Springs would do, but her heart was set on the little cabin in the hollow below Longs Peak.

She left the next morning, loaded with her own luggage and a second mailbag. The foothills were overcast, as a storm was expected, but the sun greeted her as she reached the canyon of the St. Vrain. She rode slowly as the heavy load caused the mare to work very hard.

After fifteen miles she stopped at a ranch that usually fed and boarded travelers. The buildings stood vacant. She had no better luck at the next place. Finally, at a cabin inhabited by two young hunters, she was given hot tea and a meal.

After dinner she moved the mail bags inside and dropped one on the floor. Letters spilled everywhere, including one from from Henrietta. It read:

> Edinburgh
> November 10, 1873
>
> Dearest Isabella,
>   I've taken very ill and have been forced to take to bed at the hospital. I do hope you receive this with Godspeed, as I miss you so and do want you beside me. I cannot say how long I will be here but I trust you will come at the earliest possibility.
>   Much love,
>   Henrietta

She took the letter outside and looked into the sky, remembering her promise to her father that she live her life for others and not for her own selfish gain. Certainly her sister needed care that only she could give her, but couldn't she have some true happiness for herself?

The answer was clear. As soon as the banks reopened, she would have to return home.

She rode from the cabin, tears streaming down her face. Darkness caught her in a densely wooded gulch, filled with ice and snow. Wolves filled the night with long howls and she reached Jim Nugent's cabin well after midnight.

She found it dark and it appeared that he hadn't been there in some time. Perhaps he hadn't yet returned from Denver.

She urged the horse forward, in the direction of the cabin. Soon, she heard a dog barking.

"Ring?" she called out. "Is that you?"

The big dog bounded to the side of her horse and put his paws up on her saddle, whining and licking her hand.

Jim appeared, holding a torch made of pitch pine. A man with him led a horse laden with furs, and tipped his hat when Jim introduced him to Belle.

"Take the furs and hole up at my cabin," Jim told him. "I'll be along directly."

The man rode away, becoming a shadow in the darkness.

"I hired him to help me do more trapping," Jim said. "We've got my cabin filled with hides." He rode closer to her. "Will you accompany Ring and me to the Evans Ranch?"

"Why would you be going there?"

"There's a lady who needs an escort that direction. She's had a long, hard ride and is in need of comfort."

They rode together, quiet at first. Belle could not bring herself to break the news about her sister.

"You'll be the lone lady at the ranch," Jim said. "Yesterday morning the Edwards family left for the winter. John Buchanan and a friend of his named Nate Kavanagh are the only ones left. They're watching the stock until Evans gets back."

The cold had settled in even deeper. Birdie was slumped with fatigue, so they dismounted and walked the rest of the way to the ranch, she telling him of her journey and how, after seeing all that new, beautiful country, Estes Park still held the top position in her heart.

"Maybe now you can see why I'm fighting to keep this place safe from outsiders," he said.

Belle stopped and pulled out the bear totem. "This was given to me by a Ute chief I met at Denver."

Jim studied the bear claw.

"His name is Ouray. He said you would know who he was."

"He gave this to you?"

"For protection on my journey."

"I do know him," Jim said, handing the totem back to her. "But you don't want to know about it."

"Does it have to do with the scar on your back, and the one on your chest?"

"In a roundabout way."

"Tell me about it."

Jim tore off his coat and angrily stripped his shirt open.

"If you've got to know every damned thing, he shot me with an arrow. It went through my back and out my front. See for yourself."

"Why didn't you tell me?" she asked.

"I didn't see it as that important."

"No wonder you've been sick and coughing all the time. You should never have taken me up on Longs Peak."

"Why not? If I can't do something good before I die, what's the use in hanging around?"

They walked in silence, the frosted grass crunching under their feet. In the distance wolves lifted their noses to the dark sky and howled.

A biting wind arose and they jogged the last half mile, entering the Queen Anne Mansion and surprising the two young men. Nate Kavanagh wasn't as tall as John Buchanan, but his hair was just as red. The cabin looked a mess, unswept for many days and cluttered with clothes and dirty dishes.

Buchanan greeted Belle, saying he was glad to see her.

"We've got beef and potatoes, and some milk," he said. "Mr. Nugent, you can stay and eat, if you'd like."

"Thank you," Jim said.

During the meal, the young men discussed the possible reasons why Evans hadn't made it back from Denver. Up to the point of Belle's arrival, they had blamed it on the weather. But if a woman had made it through, they wondered, then why couldn't he?

Their anger was fueled by the fact that they had gone nearly a month and a half without any pay. Evans had hired them to watch his herd while he was gone, which had been far longer than he had told them.

Belle searched the mailbag thoroughly but found nothing addressed to either of them.

"You know that because of the panic the banks are closed," she told them. "He can't get to his money."

Buchanan frowned. "He can't get to his money?"

"No. Otherwise he would have paid you," she said. "He's honorable enough for that."

She realized immediately that Jim would be insulted that she had spoken on behalf of Griff Evans. His face clouded over and he stood up.

"I'd better be going. That storm's getting worse."

Jim hurried through the door, Ring behind him. By the time Belle got outside he had mounted and was but a blur galloping away through the storm.

She called after him, but he kept on riding. She stood in the snow, staring into the darkness where he had disappeared. She thought about mounting her horse and trying to catch him, or even riding on to his cabin, but knew Birdie could not stand the exertion, especially in the cold. She had worked so very hard already and shouldn't be pressed to go any farther.

Belle finished dinner in silence, listening to the wind outside. Kavanagh and Buchanan argued hotly between themselves about the chores they should already have completed.

"You were supposed to chop wood this afternoon," Kavanagh said. "Now look at the fix we're in."

"We've got plenty for tonight," Buchanan said.

"I'm talking about tomorrow. There should have been more cut and put in the shed. Now everything will be too wet to burn."

Belle spoke up. "I suggest we all three decide on how to get things done. Like it or not, we're here together for a while and we have to make the best of it."

"I can help with the cooking," Kavanagh said, "and do some hunting."

"I'll hunt as well," Buchanan said.

Belle smiled. "Good. I'll take care of the cleaning and other indoor responsibilities, and along with the game, you two make certain there's plenty of wood and water."

"You'll have little to work with in here," Kavanagh said.

"They've taken all the sheets, towels, and tablecloths with them."

"I can sleep in blankets," Belle said, "and I can eat on a plain wooden table. But we're going to have to find something to use for towels. I will not go without washing."

"There are a few worn cotton shirts they left behind," Buchanan said. "I think they belonged to little Sam."

"They'll do," Belle said.

She cleared the table and washed the dishes while the two young men picked their strewn clothes up and swept the floor. Kavanagh brought her three little shirts that belonged to Sam, and Belle held them, feeling the soft cloth in her hands.

What she wouldn't give to see the boy right now, along with Plunk.

Her difficulty in relating to children had always plagued her and she wished she had forced herself to spend more time with Sam. Somehow he had understood and had never held it against her.

She could still hear him saying, "It's all right, Miss Bird. Maybe another time, when you feel better."

She blinked and set the shirts aside. The dishwater was getting cold so she took a pot of water from the stove and added more to the basin.

Thinking of the boy Sam made her think of Jim, and of their similarities. When he was in good humor, he was as carefree as any boy who had ever run through the tall grass with his dog. She wished he could maintain that humor.

When the dishes were done, she made herself a bed on the floor near the fire, arranging blankets so that her feet were toward the flames. Buchanan and Kavanagh offered her their beds but she declined. She had discovered an old spring mattress and planned to fill a bag with hay to spread over it.

With the other two retired, Belle lay listening to the wind, a horrendous gale that sounded as if it would rip the cabin from its foundation. The storm grew more intense, moaning and groaning, spewing snow through the unchinked logs.

She wondered if she would be forced to spend the winter

in Estes Park. At first the thought gladdened her, but she worried about Henrietta, who needed her now more than ever. Should her sister die, Belle would be heartbroken and would never forgive herself for not being there.

And what about Jim? She had told her sister that he was a man any woman could love, but one whom no one should marry.

Still, she felt he could change and they could be happy together—if Henrietta recovered and wished to move from the British Isles.

No matter what she wished for, she lay at the mercy of finances and the weather. Knowing this to be true, she wrapped herself tighter in her blankets and fell asleep.

TWENTY-FOUR

Terrible Secrets

*He made me promise to keep one or two things se-
cret whether he were living or dead, and I promised,
for I had no choice; but they come between me and
the sunshine sometimes, and I wake at night to think
of them.*

ISABELLA BIRD

November

"Mr. Kavanagh, you bake the best bread I've ever
eaten!"

He blushed and took a second loaf from the oven.
It was late Sunday and the storm continued to rage outside.
Belle likened it to a hurricane. All they could do was stay in-
side and wait it out.

She had awakened to blankets covered with ashes and
soot. A downdraft had emptied the chimney into the living
room. In addition, a number of shingles had blown off and on
the parlor floor lay two inches of mud, which she shoveled out
the door.

AFTERWORD

Isabella Bird never returned to Estes Park. On June 10, 1874, six months after her departure, Jim Nugent was severely wounded by a shotgun blast. Griffith Evans had burst from his cabin and ambushed him while he watered his horse at the creek. The first blast killed the horse and toppled Jim to the ground. The second round tore into his face and shoulders, his neck, and the back of his head.

A doctor hunting in the area was called in and Nugent was taken to Fort Collins for treatment. He lingered there until his passing on September 7, 1874. A postmortem established the cause of death as acute inflammation of the brain resulting from shotgun pellets imbedded in the anterior lobe.

On August 12, 1874, during his fight to recover, Jim Nugent published a letter in the *Larimer County Express*. It read in part:

> It would seem that an all-wise providence has spared my life; that a hell-born plot to deprive a man of his life might be exposed. Justice is sometimes tardy, and the red-handed assassin and highway murderer ofttimes escapes the gallows and the prison cell. Sometimes by successful escape; sometimes by resort to gold. . . . Great God! is this your boasted Colorado?

That I, an American citizen who has tred upon Colorado's soil since 1854, must have my life attempted
and deprived of liberty when the deep-laid scheme to
take my life has failed, and all for British Gold?

Though Griffith Evans was arrested, he was never
brought to trial. He defended his actions by stating that he
had been protecting the virtue of his teenage daughter, though
there had never been any indication that Nugent had ever
showed any interest in her. Many say that Evans and a man
named Haigh, who was with him at the time, had been drinking heavily and that Haigh goaded Evans into shooting Nugent.

An uprising followed. Settlers defied Lord Dunraven and
defeated his attempts to secure Estes Park for a game preserve. Though Dunraven built a hotel named after himself in
1878, he left the area in the early 1880s.

Jim Nugent was buried unceremoniously. Today no one
is certain of his grave site.

After learning of Jim Nugent's death in a letter from Genny
Evans, Isabella Bird gave up all plans of returning to Col-
orado. Her sister succumbed to typhoid fever in 1880. A year
later, after long hours of soul-searching, Miss Bird married
Dr. John Bishop, Henrietta's physician, ten years her junior.
He died five years later.

Though she found him "very gentle, tender, and kind,"
their marriage was a lonely one. "Sadness underlies even my
best moments," she confided to a friend.

After his death she never married again, and though she
continued to travel extensively—including Japan, Malaya,
Sinai, Tibet, Persia, Korea, and China—there are those who
say she never got over leaving Jim Nugent and her little cabin
in Estes Park. She died in Edinburgh on October 7, 1904, at
the age of seventy-two.

Today Estes Park, Colorado, is a busy mountain community, alive with history and culture. Nearby Rocky Mountain National Park is a mecca for tourists and adventurers, many of whom attempt to conquer the heights of Longs Peak.

In the blue hollow, Belle's little cabin is long since gone, as is the lake she loved so dearly, which has been lost to forest growth and changes in stream course. Jim Nugent's cabin in Muggins Gulch has suffered a similar fate.

But their story will never die. Each night when the shadows slide down from Longs Peak and the moon rises overhead, there is a faint melody carried on the wind. Those who listen carefully can hear a distant violin playing a soft and haunting Scots-Irish waltz.

She found the horses and drove them back, locking them securely in the corral. Kavanagh had killed an elk and was carving meat for the evening meal.

"Where is Mr. Buchanan?" she asked.

"He went after Mountain Jim."

"Whatever for?"

"He said he was doing it for you, that you're a lively sort when Jim is around and quite depressed when he isn't."

"It isn't up to Mr. Buchanan to care for my moods."

Buchanan arrived an hour later and put up his horse. Inside the lodge Belle helped Kavanagh with supper.

"Any luck?" she asked.

Buchanan shrugged. "I saw no trace. He shouldn't be up in those mountains now."

They ate dinner in silence and Belle retired early. Breakfast was late the next morning and after the two men left, she spent the morning cleaning the lodge and taking stock of her situation. With no way to cash her notes, she had gotten down to but a few items of clothing. She had but a pair of snow boots and a pair of slippers for wearing inside the lodge, and only her Hawaiian riding outfit and her black silk dress were fit to wear at all.

She sat patching her Hawaiian dress, wondering how many more times she could sew it together before it fell completely apart. She had to wear it during the day, no matter the work, and there were many things that needed doing each morning and evening.

There was a cow to milk and geese and ducks to care for, as well as the horses, who needed oats and watering at the lake twice a day. The longhorns generally stayed in the vicinity but had to be watched closely and herded into the park when bad storms developed.

As the days passed Belle worked as much outdoors as in. She helped chop wood and carry water, and assisted in nursing the sick cows. One died and the three of them tugged the carcass out of the barn. That night a pack of wolves devoured everything but the bones.

Belle sat near the window, watching them arrive in the

twilight, their dark shadows a blur of movement as they growled and fed.

"They seem to have an order, don't they?" she said.

"The lead male eats first," Kavanagh said. "Then they all get their share in order of their rank."

"It sounds like a constant challenge," she said. "It's good that we three have enough of Mr. Kavanagh's bread to go around."

The next morning Belle rose early and built a fire. The mercury read seventeen below. She thawed her ink near the fire and began a letter to Henrietta.

Kavanagh knocked at the door and stuck his head in.

"Mr. Evans has just arrived. The banks are open again. He says that yesterday was Thanksgiving."

She went back to her letter, including the news that the banks had reopened and that she would be leaving for England immediately.

She heard another knock, followed by heavy coughing.

"Can I come in?" Jim said.

Belle opened the door. He looked pale and gaunt, his cheeks white from frostbite.

"You should have come back way sooner," she said.

He took her hand. "I've found something you have to see. Come with me."

He pulled her up behind him on the Arab mare and they rode to the beaver dam. A short ways beyond, he helped her down.

"Why did you bring me here?" she asked.

He led her into a little clearing in the trees where a large collection of duff and pine needles had accumulated, blown into a pile by the wind.

He parted the debris and had her peer inside.

There, safe from the weather, was a small flower, a delicate spring beauty, whose dainty white petals were spread wide open.

"I found it by accident," he said. "I know you won't get to see them in England."

Belle touched the small flower, saying good-bye to a part of her life she realized she would never forget.

"You can take it with you in your heart," he said.

She stood up and held him tightly, tears streaming down her cheeks. She never wanted to let go of him but she realized she must. The time had come for her to leave.

TWENTY-FIVE

Where Love Has Gone

A veil of blue spiritualized without dimming the outlines of that most glorious range, making it look like the dreamed-of mountains of "the land which is very far off," till at sunset it stood out sharp in glories of violet and opal, and the whole horizon up to a great height was suffused with the deep rose and pure orange of the afterglow.

ISABELLA BIRD

December

Belle awakened before dawn and sat at the window to watch the sunrise. The sky turned crimson and then gold, lighting up the peaks as the sun topped the horizon. Then a bank of clouds rolled in and it began to snow softly.

She breakfasted on bread and beef, with little said by anyone.

While she washed the dishes, Evans said to her, "I cannot say what things will be like soon after you're gone from here, but I'm glad you got to see it now."

"You mean before it all changes? Before the common man has no more access to the beauty here?"

"That's hardly fair."

"You are making your own choices, Mr. Evans."

"Let me say this. If I had three or four hands half as good as you, I wouldn't hesitate to keep this as a cattle venture."

"I'm sure you could find adequate help if you paid them justly."

"It's not the pay, it's the isolation."

"No one is isolated in this kind of beauty."

"Perhaps if you were in my shoes, you would understand."

"You're right," Belle said. "I have no right to judge you."

"It's an unhappy situation," Evans said, and walked away.

After cleaning the Queen Anne Mansion one last time, dusting with the buffalo tail and mopping the last traces of mud from the parlor, Belle walked to her cabin. She packed and set her luggage by the door, then paid a last visit to the lake.

The ice had crept far out from shore. A small flock of ducks flew by, headed to the lowlands. Chickadees sang in the trees nearby. They always seemed happy, no concerns of any kind.

It was the swallows, now gone far south, that she longed to see, circling and dipping across the water's surface. Many months would pass before they would return.

She walked toward the lodge, taking one last look at the little cabin she had called home.

"Are you ready?" Evans said. He stood loading her luggage on Birdie's saddle.

She mounted and followed Evans along the trail that led out from the ranch, stopping to view Estes Park one last time.

They rode toward Jim Nugent's cabin, as Evans had decided he couldn't take her down to meet the stage, but needed to gather cattle before the impending storm.

"It's good that Jim agreed to take you," he said. "He'll care for you like no one else. But you know that already."

At Jim's cabin she dismounted and, with his help, loosened her luggage.

"You can use my Arab mare," he said.

She thanked him. The mare was a good horse and would be comfortable for the ride down. But much as she admired the mare, she would never forget Birdie, who nuzzled her for sugar.

Belle slipped her last sugar cube between Birdie's lips.

"I can't tell you how much I appreciated riding this little horse," she told Evans.

"You are more than welcome." He handed her an envelope filled with cash. "I appreciate the loan."

She took the envelope and stuffed it in a bag, then rubbed Birdie's nose and patted her gently, thinking of the seven hundred miles they had traveled together.

"I shall miss you, gentle little horse," she whispered.

With Jim's help, Belle tied her luggage on the Arab mare's saddle while Ring stood beside her, his tail wagging, leaning heavily against her side.

"I'll pet you soon enough, you big spoiled dog," she said.

Evans leaned over the saddle, down toward Jim. "You'll watch out for her, won't you?"

"You know I will."

Evans turned and rode back along the trail, and was soon lost in the distance.

Jim stood at the cabin door.

"Come in. I want you to see something."

The inside had been cleaned and rearranged, everything neatly tucked away, not even a loose sock out of place.

"I did the housekeeping myself."

Belle smiled. "You'll make someone a fine wife."

"And I'll bet you will, too," he said.

Outside, snow began to fall, heavier than before.

"We'd better get on the trail," he said. "We don't want to get snowed in. But before we go, I've got something for you."

He rummaged through a pile of beaver pelts on the floor and found a small, mouse-colored fur. Belle remembered his telling her that a fur of that particular color was rare and valuable.

"Take this to remember me by."

Belle held it tightly. "Thank you very much."

She mounted the mare and he his white mule. The snow fell in thick, heavy flakes, floating on a soft breeze that felt like a whisper.

He led the way down from the gulch, taking a shortcut off the main trails. As they rode, the storm eased and blue sky appeared overhead.

They rode farther down through the timber and looked out through an opening in the foothills over the sprawling, snow-covered plains below. Recent warm weather, followed by a quick freeze, had rendered the surface mirrorlike.

"While here I have seen more treasures to the eye than anyone is allowed in any one lifetime," she said.

Jim led the way onward, down through timber laden with snow, while Ring bounded ahead. As they rode, he spoke of the many times he had ridden alone through these woods, wishing he had someone along who could understand what he was feeling.

Listening to him, she realized that it was his lust for the land that was in itself driving him mad. He truly believed that such terrible change was on the horizon that even the mountains themselves could not survive it.

"If Evans and Dunraven have their way, this whole paradise will be no more!" he had said so many times.

Together with his failing health, Jim's passion to keep Estes Park free from ruin had driven him to the brink of madness. Often he ranted nearly out of control, yet today he talked with complete reason, never once losing control.

Upon looking over a vista, Belle said, "This has been as charming a day as I can remember."

As evening waned and twilight approached, they rode down into the canyon of the St. Vrain. With the darkness came the stunning color of the aurora, the northern lights—

waves of misty white laced with crimson, blue, and orange
streaking through the blackness overhead.

Near the foot of the canyon Jim worried about crossing
on the ice in the poor light, but they reached the opposite
bank with no difficulty.

"You act as though I'm too fragile to take any chances,"
Belle said.

"If I'm to remember you the way I want to, then I want
our last hours to be spent in comfort."

They reached a cabin that took in boarders and a young
man named Silas Miller greeted them and offered fresh biscuits.

Jim stoked the fire and the young man heated a stone for
Belle's feet. The mercury had already hit eleven below zero
and would fall further.

Ring lay beside Belle with his head on her lap, his large
eyes staring up at her.

"He knows you're leaving," Jim said. "He'll miss you."

"I shall miss him," Belle said. "I never realized how wonderful an animal like this can be for the disposition. I trust he
will get over my absence."

"As well as can be expected," Jim said.

She looked at him and he studied her a brief moment and
turned away.

Belle lay in her blankets, Ring beside her, listening to the logs
pop in the fireplace. With the dawn she would be leaving the
mountains. Her stay had been the dream of a lifetime. Nothing could compare to the adventure of climbing Longs Peak
and the wonderful nights listening to stories beside the fire.

Her world had changed so very much and would never be
the same. She had been drawn to this land like no other and
she would be leaving a piece of her soul behind.

She struggled to sleep, trying in vain to get Jim Nugent
out of her mind. His laugh and his poetry warmed her heart;
his soft eyes enveloped her. She could feel his strong arms

helping her up Longs Peak and back down again, encircling her, drawing her to him.

Reaching over, she felt Ring. The big dog licked her hand and she pulled him closer.

At sunrise they made a hard crossing of the St. Vrain. The river had frozen solid but for a gap of two feet near the middle, where the water ran frigid. Belle inched herself across on a log. Jim had trouble getting the frightened animals across the ice, but brought them safely to the other side.

The snow had passed and the skies were clear. Past the foothills a cold wind blasted the plains, making a stop at a local ranch house necessary.

From there Belle gazed out at the frozen mountains, Longs Peak standing rigid in the winter air.

"The land sleeps as if to sleep forever," she said.

"You got out at the last possible moment," Jim said. "Another couple of days and the snow would have been too deep."

The day passed without their meeting anyone. The wind swept across the open and they had to turn their faces away. Ring bounded ahead of them and back throughout the afternoon, never tiring of keeping watch.

In late evening they reached Namaqua, a cluster of houses outside of the settlement of St. Louis. A woman dressed in a heavy overcoat, with a shawl wrapped around her head and face, beckoned them into her home. After a bowl of stew, they felt warmed and refreshed.

"I assume you plan to stay in St. Louis," she said. "There's a dance at the hotel tonight."

Belle, who desired only a good night's sleep, said, "I suppose there are no other hotels in the area."

"None," she said. "But why would you want to miss the dance?"

"I have an early stagecoach to catch."

The twilight settled in cold and crisp. The hotel in St.

Louis had already filled with revelers, leaving Belle with no option but to accept a small cot in a room occupied by a pair of sisters, one a widow and one with a huge bun of hair piled atop her head. The two ran the kitchen and were in charge of cooking for ten men.

"You can sit by the stove while we work," the widow told Belle, "and tell us all about your climb up Longs Peak."

The landlady, a bustling woman named Dot, came in and, in a booming voice, asked all kinds of questions, including whether or not the man with her was Rocky Mountain Jim.

"The men are all saying that it's him. I don't believe it."

"Well, he is one and the same," Belle said.

Dot covered her mouth. "Do tell! That quiet, kind gentleman?"

"There are many who misjudge him," Belle said.

The landlady laughed. "I used to tell my children that if they didn't behave, Rocky Mountain Jim would get them. 'He comes down from the mountains and takes a child back to eat,' I would say."

The widow asked Belle again about her climb up Longs Peak. They all listened intently while she told her story, interrupted only by the widow's two young sons who cried and scuffled incessantly, slamming doors and chasing each other throughout the kitchen.

Nugent walked in and the children stopped and stared. He sat down and they hurried over to him.

"Did you know that I wrestle grizzly bears?" he told them. "One of them chewed my eye out, but I made him pay dearly."

They sat, one on each knee, while he told them stories of the mountains and his Indian fighting days. They remained calm, playing with his long curls while he talked.

Supper was served, and after the ten boarding men had finished, all of them staring at Jim the entire time, Belle took her place with the women.

After the meal, to escape the noise, they walked to the post office and were invited to see the postmistress's living quarters. A charming woman near Belle's age, she showed them her living room, finished nicely to Belle's taste.

Jim stood outside smoking and the postmistress said to Belle, "Is that truly Mountain Jim?"

"It is."

"He is such a gentleman. He could not be guilty of the misdeeds attributed to him."

Belle thanked her for the tour, then she and Jim returned to the hotel, where the dance had just begun.

The attendees were young settlers, out for a good time with no drinking. To Belle's astonishment, the band consisted of Ian McEwan and his friends.

"I see you've taken me up on my offer," he said to Belle. "What's your request?"

"You know my favorite," she said. "Maybe later in the evening."

He smiled. "Your wish is granted."

They started the evening with a rousing Gaelic fiddle tune. Dot stood by, watching the dancers, clapping her hands and shouting.

"Why don't you join them?" she asked, and jigged away.

Belle and Jim walked into the kitchen. A few young, unmarried women were talking and pointing at a group of young men standing near the door.

Belle settled at one of the tables and began writing while Jim removed a book of poetry from his coat. After flipping through the pages a short time, he set the book down.

"I can't read," he said. "How can you concentrate on that letter?"

"I must admit, it is difficult."

She followed him through the crowd of dancers and out the front door, past horses and carriages and a few sled wagons loaded with hay.

They stood by themselves on the riverbank while music and laughter from inside echoed out.

"Are you going to miss these nights?" he asked her.

"Terribly."

"You've heard more about me than I've ever told anyone."

"And you've made me a different person as well."

He took her hands in his. "You came into my life too late."

"I'll always think of you the way I truly know you," she said. "A true gentleman."

From inside came the sound of a guitar playing a soft introduction to Belle's favorite tune: "The Kaimes." Ian McEwan played his violin and Jim drew her close.

They waltzed slowly, holding each other tenderly, wishing the song would never end. Overhead, the moon shone brightly and in the far distance, Longs Peak rose into the night sky.

The mercury rested at minus twenty as Belle watched the stage arrive. Frost sparkled on the snow and clung to the tree branches, glistening in the clear air.

The driver pulled the horses to a stop and jumped down, his breath a heavy cloud.

"It's a chilly day for a ride, ma'am."

Belle drew her coat tighter. "I enjoy a crisp morning."

The driver went inside the hotel to check for more passengers. He came back out and threw Belle's luggage atop the coach.

"Have a safe trip," Jim said.

They held each other again for the last time, tighter than they had ever held anyone before.

Belle gave Ring a rub on his head and took a seat facing the mountains. She watched Jim climb on his mule and lead the Arab mare out from the hotel, Ring following close behind. A distance out, he sat the mule and looked back.

The driver snapped the reins, calling to the horses, and the stage began to move. Belle strained to see Jim as he turned and rode slowly away, his long hair windblown and gleaming in the sunlight.

She rested her head against the back of her seat and

thought of Mirror Lake and the little cabin. Soon the ice would be completely solid and the ducks and geese would all have left.

She wondered if the swallows were happy wherever they had flown for the winter, or if, as she did, they missed their wonderful home in the blue hollow below Longs Peak.

inside her. She shouldn't have let Jim ride off into the storm.

Once he was gone the park would never be the same. There would be no one to stand up to Lord Dunraven and those like him. She told herself to stop thinking about his death and believe that she could bring Henrietta back, but it didn't seem feasible.

She lay in bed, her eyes brimming with tears. Nothing she tried to think of took her mind off Jim.

She fell asleep and the room stayed warm for a few hours, until the logs burned down. She awakened in the darkness with her eyelids frozen shut. Warming her hands with her breath, she gently rubbed her eyes until they came open.

She got up to rebuild the fire and heard a knock at her door. Kavanagh and Buchanan entered.

"We thought you'd died in the storm," Buchanan said. "Where's Mountain Jim?"

"He went off to check his traps."

"He's just as crazy as they say he is," Kavanagh said. "I suppose you noticed the horses are gone."

"Where are they?"

"The corral gate came open and they got out. We'll go after them in the morning."

"I'll help you," Belle said. "I need something to occupy my mind."

"Are you hungry?" Buchanan asked.

"I'll wait until morning."

"Will you be all right out here?" Kavanagh said.

"I'll be just fine. Please have breakfast ready by seven. And Mr. Kavanagh, be certain you have two loaves of that bread of yours baked."

After breakfast, Belle rode into Black Canyon looking for the lost horses while Buchanan and Kavanagh looked elsewhere. While she rode she again wondered why her life wasn't meant to be lived out among the tall peaks that rose so high and gleamed so white after the winter storms. She had never known such feelings and realized she never would again.

He took her in his arms and they held each other a long time. She reached into her coat and took out Henrietta's letter.

"I have to go back home," she said. "I'll return with my sister."

Jim read the letter and gave it back. "She'll be too sick to travel."

"Perhaps not. I need to be with her, though."

"I know you do."

The snow began to fall heavily. Jim got up and told Belle to start back, that he had to check his traps.

"I'll be fine," she said. "I've ridden through many storms."

"This is going to be a bad one. I'll take you to a trail that will lead you straight down into the park."

She mounted Birdie and followed him to the trail.

"You'll promise not to discuss the nature of my confession with anyone?" he said.

"I promise. But why check your traps in this weather? Do you want to die?"

"I've got a lot to think about," he said, and turned his horse into the storm.

Belle thought there could never be another man so complicated. She watched him become a blur in the swirling snow and started down the trail.

She reached the lodge well after dark having had to stop in the shelter of some trees until the wind died down. Kavanagh and Buchanan were gone. They had left a note saying that if she got back before either of them to stay put, for they had gone looking for her.

She rubbed Birdie down and fed her sheaf oats in the barn. The other horses were missing and she wondered if they had gotten out again. She would ask Kavanagh and Buchanan about it.

Too tired to eat, she walked to her cabin and built a fire and crawled under her blankets, hoping to escape the feelings

She got up and he caught her.

"Why must you tell me this?" she asked.

"Because you are the only one in all of my life that I have ever loved so deeply."

They caught their horses and rode to the beaver dams, where a family of beaver was hard at work. They sat down on the edge of the stream to watch.

"Another storm's coming," Jim said. He pointed to the sky. "It will be here soon."

"Maybe we should go back," Belle suggested.

"I need to finish my story first," he said. "When I left Hudson's Bay, I scouted for the army and used that as an excuse to kill Indians whenever I could. I had a bitter hatred for them. One of those I killed was Ouray's brother, in the Garden of the Gods."

Jim described how he had tried to forget his past by moving to Missouri, where he took up a homestead and a wife. A disaster he felt he could have prevented took place while he was away.

"Her name was Charlene and we had a baby boy, Eagan, just past six months. One night, while I was off drinking, they were killed. Indians—I don't even know which tribe—bashed his head against the cabin and raped and beat her to death. They did so many things to her I can't begin to describe them all. I took it out on Indians and whites, blacks and Chinese, it didn't matter. I didn't care what color they were, I killed them.

"I came out here and picked fights in the mining camps. Nobody dared challenge me. They all knew me, with my red sash and my revolver and knife, riding with my long hair hanging down my back. But I never bothered women so I never got lynched."

"You can put that all behind you, if you want to."

"I've done too many things for that." He tore open his coat and pulled up his buckskin shirt, pointing to the massive scar on his back. "I'll die from this arrow wound before another year."

"I want to be with you as long as I can. I love you, Jim."

"You need to know more about my wounds."

"Is there more to tell?"

"Much more. If you want to know how a man can become nearly a devil, I'll tell you now."

They rode to his favorite place, the canyon overlook. The sun shone brightly overhead, bringing out the red and purple in the rocks. They dismounted and Belle sat beside him as an eagle sailed past into the blue distance.

"When my brother Eagan died, everything changed for the worse," he said. "I knew then that nothing would ever be good in my life. I guess I had it coming, as in many ways I was glad I killed him."

"You didn't kill him."

"The same as. If I hadn't kept going he wouldn't have gotten lost."

"He didn't have to follow you."

"But he *did.*"

"I believe you wanted a way to get back at your mother and father, and it went too far. But you didn't kill him."

"Yes, but even though I missed him terribly, I delighted in his death. I used to watch my mother weep and then I'd go off and laugh, God have mercy. She thought so much more of him than of me. I knew she wished it had been me who died."

"That's all in the past."

"I'm not finished. At seventeen I met a young girl in church and decided to see her. We got real close and both of us wanted to marry. Naturally my parents opposed our union. They even went as far as to tell the girl's parents that I wished not to see her.

"The girl went crying out into a storm and got lost. The next day she became ill and by the end of the week had died of fever. I took to drink and ran away from home. I signed on with the Hudson's Bay Company and trapped for some years in the Saskatchewan before leaving their service. They were a lawless bunch and I was the worst of the lot. We had free rein to kill anyone who stood in our way and pillage American trappers as we saw fit."

"I don't care to hear about it."

Dear Miss Bird,

    I didn't want to go down to town for the wenter but pa said I had to. I wanted to stay and see you. I told him you would come back. You like it up here so well. I think of you a lot. So does Plunk.

    Some day when I get growed up maybe I will see you again. I think you would be a good grandma for some boy.

Yor frind,
Sam

She sat down at the table with the letter and gazed out across the lake, its surface rippling in the light wind. She wished it were autumn again and little Sam and Plunk were playing along the shore, as they had been so many times before.

She heard a horseman outside. Jim rode up and dismounted, Ring by his side.

He walked in the door, looking somber.

"I'm going up to Black Canyon. Would you like to ride along?"

"What's wrong?"

"I'll tell you on the way."

She caught Birdie and saddled her and they rode across Estes Park toward the canyon. He grew increasingly more sullen and silent as they rode on.

"I don't understand you. You ask me to go with you, yet you ignore me as if I weren't along," she said.

"I guess I don't understand why you would want to ride with a man like me."

"I've told you often enough, I see you as a gentleman."

"You're one of only a few people who have ever treated me like a human being."

"You know that's not so. There are any number who think well of you."

"They don't know me, really, and neither do you."

"I know you as I wish to know you. Isn't that good enough?"

She would be using the shovel a lot if the weather stayed bad, and even if it cleared she would have trouble, for all she had to dust with was a buffalo tail.

At least she wouldn't be doing all the kitchen work. Buchanan and Kavanagh had agreed to wash the evening dishes every night if she would agree to do all the house-cleaning.

Monday arrived and the storm continued. Belle shoveled more mud out of the parlor and she discovered an old shawl that she made do for a tablecloth.

But she had already tired of the menu: salt pork, a small amount of milk, and an occasional egg. None of the hens would lay in the cold and of the thirty milk cows only one could be found, and she was drying up. All that comforted them was tea that Belle had found in her bags.

On Tuesday the skies cleared and the wind diminished. In one of the sheds Belle discovered a leg of beef hanging from a rafter, but it proved to be green and inedible. They would have to dine on elk and deer meat.

After bringing in wood and water, Buchanan and Kavanagh went hunting. Though the day was brilliant, Belle could do nothing but sit and watch it go by. Birdie had been turned out and neither of the two horses in the corral were fit to ride, having loose shoes and sore feet.

She brought a chair from the kitchen outside and, wrapped tightly in blankets, watched a long string of geese honking loudly as they winged their way overhead. When they had passed she sat in the cool stillness for a time and decided to visit her old cabin.

The snow had blown off the trail and any remaining was beginning to thaw. She opened the door and saw that everything was as she had left it, except where the storm had dampened parts of the interior.

Looking closely, she noticed a small envelope on the table partly covered with snow. Inside she found a short letter from little Sam Evans: